AGED FOR DEATH

D0711105

BOOKS BY FIONA GRACE

LACEY DOYLE COZY MYSTERY
MURDER IN THE MANOR (Book#1)
DEATH AND A DOG (Book #2)
CRIME IN THE CAFE (Book #3)
VEXED ON A VISIT (Book #4)
KILLED WITH A KISS (Book #5)
PERISHED BY A PAINTING (Book #6)
SILENCED BY A SPELL (Book #7)
FRAMED BY A FORGERY (Book #8)
CATASTROPHE IN A CLOISTER (Book #9)

TUSCAN VINEYARD COZY MYSTERY
AGED FOR MURDER (Book #1)
AGED FOR DEATH (Book #2)
AGED FOR MAYHEM (Book #3)

DUBIOUS WITCH COZY MYSTERY
SKEPTIC IN SALEM: AN EPISODE OF MURDER (Book #1)
SKEPTIC IN SALEM: AN EPISODE OF CRIME (Book #2)
SKEPTIC IN SALEM: AN EPISODE OF DEATH (Book #3)

BEACHFRONT BAKERY COZY MYSTERY
BEACHFRONT BAKERY: A KILLER CUPCAKE (Book #1)
BEACHFRONT BAKERY: A MURDEROUS MACARON (Book #2)
BEACHFRONT BAKERY: A PERILOUS CAKE POP (Book #3)

AGED FOR DEATH

(A Tuscan Vineyard Cozy Mystery-Book 2)

FIONA GRACE

Copyright © 2020 by Fiona Grace. All rights reserved. Except as permitted under the U.S. Copyright Act of 1976, no part of this publication may be reproduced, distributed or transmitted in any form or by any means, or stored in a database or retrieval system, without the prior permission of the author. This ebook is licensed for your personal enjoyment only. This ebook may not be re-sold or given away to other people. If you would like to share this book with another person, please purchase an additional copy for each recipient. If you're reading this book and did not purchase it, or it was not purchased for your use only, then please return it and purchase your own copy. Thank you for respecting the hard work of this author. This is a work of fiction. Names, characters, businesses, organizations, places, events, and incidents either are the product of the author's imagination or are used fictionally. Any resemblance to actual persons, living or dead, is entirely coincidental. Jacket image Copyright Kishivan, used under license from Shutterstock.com.

FIONA GRACE

Debut author Fiona Grace is author of the LACEY DOYLE COZY MYSTERY series, comprising nine books (and counting); of the TUSCAN VINEYARD COZY MYSTERY series, comprising three books (and counting); of the DUBIOUS WITCH COZY MYSTERY series, comprising three books (and counting); and of the BEACHFRONT BAKERY COZY MYSTERY series, comprising three books (and counting).

MURDER IN THE MANOR (A Lacey Doyle Cozy Mystery—Book 1) is available as a free download on Amazon!

Fiona would love to hear from you, so please visit www.fionagrace-author.com to receive free ebooks, hear the latest news, and stay in touch.

TABLE OF CONTENTS

Chapter One

"Mine!" Olivia Glass said. "All mine!"

She could hear the mingled excitement and disbelief in her own voice, as she approached the simple, double-story farmhouse.

As of yesterday, it was signed, sealed, paid for, and hers. This dilapidated yet beautiful home, set in the hills of Tuscany, was where she was going to start her new life. She'd impulsively bought the farm—all twenty acres of it—after falling in love with it. Olivia supposed that one day, the romance would wear off, but for now, she felt tingly all over as she walked up to the house and, after a struggle with the rusty handle, pushed open the front door.

Goosebumps prickled her spine as she stepped inside her new home.

Her feet kicked up plumes of dust as she walked through the hallway, where builders had been working the day before doing urgent repairs, and into the kitchen. This was a large space with a view of the hills beyond, equipped with broken counters and cupboards with no doors, and rusty taps that worked sporadically. Probably, fixing the water supply would be a very minor challenge.

She felt her heart constrict with excitement and fear. The house had so much potential, but was so badly neglected. A mountain of work lay ahead of her. Olivia wasn't scared of hard labor, but she did wonder how long it would take her to restore this echoing, peeling, cobwebbed shell into the comfortable and functional home that she'd imagined it had been in the past, and could be again.

Olivia sneezed. The kitchen was very dusty, and as yet, she couldn't open the windows, which were jammed shut by dirt and rust. She decided it would be better to wait outside where her best friend, Charlotte, was going to join her for a walk around the farm.

As Olivia headed back into the sun-filled hallway, she stopped in her tracks, staring in horror at the new arrival that had suddenly appeared.

Between her and the door, in the middle of the peach-colored stucco flooring, crouched a huge, hairy spider.

Olivia backed away as he crawled into the center of the sunbeam. She began breathing rapidly. She was petrified of spiders.

Her apartment in Chicago, where she'd lived for the past six years, had been newly built and she'd been on the eighth floor. The spiders hadn't worked their way up that high during her stay there, so she'd all but forgotten how scary she found them.

Now, she was remembering.

She found them terrifying!

Suddenly, Olivia found herself starting to doubt the wisdom of selling her safe, cozy apartment and plunging all her life savings into a place filled with threatening wildlife. The farmhouse was draped in cobwebs. Probably, she realized now, this meant hundreds of arachnids had made it their home.

"Out?" Olivia tried, in a quivering voice. Even she could tell it didn't contain the necessary authority. The spider ignored her, seemingly quite happy in his patch of sun.

Unable to take her eyes off the monster, Olivia groped behind her. Her clutching fingers closed around a piece of board that had been left by the builders yesterday.

She could nudge him with the board and that would encourage him to move out of her path. Then she would be able to walk calmly outside.

More likely, sprint in a panic, she admitted to herself.

Olivia couldn't kill the spider. That was not even an option, no matter how scared she was. She couldn't possibly kill an innocent, if terrifying, being who'd believed this home was his own. He played a valuable role in the ecosystem. Olivia's knowledge of the role was sketchy, but she knew it was important.

He just needed to be encouraged to move. Outside, preferably at least a mile or two away.

"Go!" she said, shaking a blond lock of hair out of her eyes as she pushed the board toward the spider.

The spider scuttled onto the board and Olivia shrieked and dropped it, leaping back.

"That's not what you were supposed to do!" she yelped.

Her shoulder bumped against something. It was the scaffolding that the builders had left there the previous day, because the hallway's high ceiling had also needed fixing up.

The eight-legged apparition on the floor had so hypnotized Olivia that she'd forgotten about the scaffolding above her head.

The builders had been standing on a plank that ran the length of the hallway.

If Olivia climbed up the scaffolding, she could crawl along the plank and then climb down again by the front door.

This daring aerial maneuver would allow her to bypass the spider completely.

Olivia glanced up at the scaffolding and the plank.

It looked farther up than she remembered. She wasn't that good with heights.

She glanced back at the spider.

Heights won the day.

Olivia grasped the metal scaffolding, noting how it clanged and rattled as she clambered up carefully. It couldn't be that dangerous, she told herself. After all, the builders had worked there the whole day, humming opera tunes to themselves as they balanced on the board while hammering and drilling into the ceiling.

Now that she was up here, Olivia wasn't sure how they had done it.

Teetering on all fours, she placed a tentative hand on the board.

It wobbled alarmingly and Olivia let out a squeak of terror.

She was thirty-four now. She wanted to live to be thirty-five! Was this idea too reckless?

"There's no going back," she urged herself, and put another hand on the unsteady board. The scaffolding on the far side seemed a long way away.

From her vantage point, she could see light filtering in through the stained glass panels set above the wooden front door. They were caked in dust, but from here, she could see how pretty the design looked, and visualize how charming the panes of blue, yellow, red, and green would be once they were dust-free, polished, and letting the morning sun stream through them.

Encouraged by this positive thought, she set out along the plank.

"Eeek," she whispered. It was so narrow that it was difficult to balance, and it wobbled as she crawled forward, making her stomach seesaw in response.

Imagine if she lost her balance and fell onto the spider.

Although it was a long way down, she could still see it there.

Waiting for her.

Olivia snorted in alarm at the thought, clinging to the plank as she edged another few inches forward. Who would have thought that buying a farmhouse would have necessitated such risky behavior? She'd expected hours of cleaning and scrubbing, renovating the dusty and derelict kitchen—which, though run-down, was spacious, with countertops on two sides and glorious views of the hills through the biggest window. She was sure this would become the heart of her new home. She visualized a wooden table and chairs installed in the center, and a big, new, shiny stove, and the ragged, broken counters replaced with light, bright slabs of granite, and pots of herbs lining the windowsill.

She'd had visions of refurbishing the upstairs master bedroom, which had a panoramic view over the valley as well as a large bathroom with a huge bathtub but no shower—yet. She'd imagined its walls repainted in warm cream, yellow curtains installed on either side of the window, her bed against the opposite wall with a feature painting above it.

She hadn't expected to be on all fours, creeping along a narrow and unstable plank that was dizzyingly high off the ground, to avoid one of the largest and most unpredictable spiders she'd ever seen in her life.

Her home renovations were not proceeding in the way she'd hoped.

Olivia was starting to worry that she was running out of time. The villa that Charlotte had originally rented, and which Olivia was now sharing, was booked until the end of summer. She didn't know if a couple of short months would be enough time to transform this beautiful but neglected place into anywhere near habitable, especially if she had to vacate the area every time a spider appeared. That was going to put a serious wrench in the works.

Then Olivia looked up—causing the plank to teeter yet again—as she heard quick footsteps outside.

"Sorry I'm late," Charlotte called. "I got delayed at the villa. The maintenance people came to fix up the outside fountain. I was thinking you should install one here."

"Hello!" Olivia called down nervously. "Don't come in! It's dangerous! Wait by the door!"

Charlotte peeked inside the doorway and stared up at Olivia in astonishment.

Olivia stared down—far down, as Charlotte was quite short—at her friend's round face, framed by long, red-streaked hair, and her wide, surprised eyes.

"What on earth are you doing up there?" Charlotte asked incredulously.

"There's a huge spider," Olivia explained, her voice shaking from fear.

"I don't see anything." Charlotte peered into the hallway.

"There!" Risking life and limb, Olivia removed one hand from the plank to point at it.

"Oh, there. That little thing?" Charlotte sounded surprised. "You want me to shoo it out for you?"

She marched into the hall as Olivia's heart accelerated.

"Be careful," she squeaked.

Charlotte walked fearlessly up to the spider.

"Out!" she ordered in a firm voice. "You're scaring my friend."

She clapped her hands and the spider scuttled obediently outside.

As it passed the front doorway, Olivia saw to her astonishment that it seemed to have shrunk. It was only about half the size that it had been before Charlotte had arrived.

Perhaps more like a quarter as big as she remembered it.

Feeling ashamed of herself, she clambered down the clanging metal framework, sighing with relief when her feet touched down onto solid ground again.

Charlotte shook her head, laughing.

"Olivia, you're the only person I know who'd defy death on sky-high scaffolding rather than walk past a spider. I remember how scared you were of them in school, but I thought you'd outgrown your fear."

Olivia rubbed dust out of her blue eyes.

"I think it's only gotten worse," she admitted.

Charlotte checked outside.

"He's disappeared," she reassured Olivia. "Probably gone to find a new home somewhere quieter. Perhaps he'll set up his house in that pretty creeper climbing over the side wall. So, this morning is Exploration Day. Are we ready to start?"

"We are!"

Olivia stepped out of the warm, dusty house, inhaling the fresh air gratefully. She picked up a whiff of adventure in the breeze. Today was the day she was going to explore every yard of her new property, and see what secrets and surprises it revealed.

To Olivia's surprise, the old farm's background remained shrouded in mystery and she had been able to find out very little about who had lived here, or for what purpose the previous owners had used the hilly twenty acres.

Today, she had the morning off from the tasting room of La Leggenda, the winery where she worked as a sommelier. She and Charlotte had decided to use the time combing every yard of the wild and overgrown property, looking for clues and evidence about the former owners.

Olivia couldn't wait to find out what secrets they might uncover.

Chapter Two

A s she and Charlotte walked away from the farmhouse, Olivia turned to look back at it, feeling happiness fill her. In dire need of fixing up it might be, but this modest two-story building, with its arched windows and solid stone walls that glowed bronze in the morning sun, was as elegant as it was sturdy. It must be at least a hundred years old, she guessed, wishing she knew its detailed history.

Who had built it and who had lived here? What had their lives been like? What romance and heartbreak, hopes and dreams, had played out under the ocher-tiled roof, and in the shade of the surrounding cork and olive trees?

Turning away, she stared out over the hills.

Was she lucky or what, to have the most dizzyingly beautiful view in Tuscany from this high-lying property? The dramatic vista changed every hour as the sun and shadows moved. Now, morning light was spilling over the faraway hills, highlighting the patchwork quilt of vineyards, wheat fields, forests, and grasslands in shades of deep gold and green. She felt a sense of disbelief that this was her home now, the view she would see every day when she was living here.

Of course, the disadvantage of having a high-lying property in a hilly, arid area of Tuscany was the stony ground. It probably wasn't the best place she could have chosen to buy, when her ambition was to grow grapevines and start her own wine label.

That was Olivia's crazy life goal, which had started as nothing more than a wild dream. After a hostile break-up with her boyfriend Matt back in Chicago, Olivia had quit her advertising job and accepted Charlotte's invitation to join her for the summer in Tuscany. She'd been hired by La

Leggenda, and discovered the farm for sale, and on impulse, had decided to sell her comfortable apartment in Chicago and plunge all her money into a brand new life.

She had no idea whether she was cut out to be a wine farmer, or even if this land was going to be viable.

Arid ground produced the best quality grapes. That fact gave her hope.

However, you had to grow the vines first, and that was a daunting prospect.

Olivia made a mental note to scout out some good places for planting vines during their walk.

"I hereby announce Exploration Day open," she said. "Let's follow the fence first."

They set off, slipping and sliding down the steep, stony hill until they reached the farm's boundary. There was a low fence demarcating it—a flimsy, double-strand wire barrier that anyone could easily step over. It wasn't enough to keep in a goat. That could be a problem, as Olivia had adopted a goat.

Well, to be more precise, a goat had adopted her.

Erba, a white goat with orange spots, was owned by the winery where Olivia worked, but had taken a liking to her, and had had gotten into the habit of following her home every evening.

Erba also followed her out and about, and as she reached the fence line, Olivia wasn't surprised to see the small goat caper energetically toward her, abandoning the geranium plant she'd been snacking on.

"Come along, Erba, let's see if there are any wild herbs for you on our travels," Olivia encouraged her, rubbing the top of her furry head. Erba was the Italian word for "herb," and Olivia had to admit, the winery had named her well.

"Have you been able to find out anything about the farm?" Charlotte asked, as they headed toward the next structure—a large, well-built barn within shouting distance of the house.

"I haven't," Olivia admitted. "It's a mystery. I was hoping that Gina, the retired lady who sold it to me, would know, but she had no idea."

Olivia had been surprised by the conversation she'd had when the color-ful, elderly woman had arrived in her tiny Fiat to hand over the keys. She'd expected a full account of the farm's history, but Gina had told her that she'd inherited the property after the death of a distant cousin, who had bought it from a friend a few years before, and she had no idea of its background.

Gina and her husband had only visited the farm a few times, as his handbag manufacturing factory had kept him very busy. They had discussed retiring there, but in the end, they chose to remain in their home in Florence, close to their friends and family.

"Perhaps we will find some hints on our walk," Olivia said.

She hoped the barn would provide her first clue.

The first time she'd glanced inside its high, stone walls she had thought it would be a perfect winemaking headquarters. Although the floor was cracked and the doors had long since disappeared, she imagined it spruced up and returned to its former glory, with gleaming steel vats and oaken barrels lining the inside walls.

With the sunlight streaming through the large gap where the doors had been, it had clearly been empty and abandoned for many years. There was a large pile of rubble at the back. Olivia would have to clear that out at some stage, or else get someone to do it for her, as there looked to be a few heavy rocks.

She was disappointed that the barn offered no further information.

"Do you think they farmed livestock here?" Charlotte wondered, sounding perplexed.

If they had, why were there no signs of their presence? There was certainly no visible fencing on the farm, and precious little good land for grazing either.

Erba leaped over the low wire fence, heading purposefully to a wild rose bush growing on the other side.

"Maybe chickens?" Olivia hazarded. Chickens were a possibility. Would this barn have provided a safe overnight shelter?

Leaving the barn behind them, they followed the fence line along a grassy ridge, and then up into the hills again. It seemed as if every twist and turn of the boundary brought another discovery. Olivia was entranced by the hidden grove of juniper bushes in a curve of the hills, the trees ripe with their distinctive purple berries, and the tall, striking downy oak that provided a focal point at the top of the slope.

At the very back of the farm, they discovered a crumbling structure that looked to be very old, its walls little more than head high, and no sign of a roof. Olivia wondered if this had been the original farmhouse, abandoned when it fell into disrepair, and a new one built on the sunnier side of the slopes. She didn't investigate it too closely as she worried that all the evacuated spiders might be making a new life in these cozy ruins.

Behind the farmhouse were a few hazel trees, with a crop of nuts ripening along their slender branches. Olivia loved hazel nuts. How amazing to think that she could take a brisk walk to this side of her farm and pick some for breakfast when they ripened.

They followed the fence line to where it bordered the quiet sand road, and then headed back toward the farmhouse. Although it had been a great day for tree spotting, Olivia had to admit that the walk had provided very few clues.

And then Charlotte shouted in excitement, pointing to a building half-hidden in a cluster of white-blossomed hawthorn bushes.

"There's another building up there. Look!"

A glance at the color of the stone walls told Olivia that this must have been constructed in the same timeframe as the ruined farmhouse.

They headed eagerly up the steep hillside. Olivia had a strong feeling about this small, square stone structure, camouflaged by trees. She'd never dreamed it had existed, and was certain there would be an exciting find here.

She picked her way across the sandy ground, breathing in the fragrance of the wild lavender bushes that were brushing her legs. As she neared the building she saw a small window, more of an air vent, set high in the stone wall.

Olivia placed a hand on the cool stone. Nestled in the curve of the hillside, and without any big windows, meant that this place had functioned as a secure storeroom. If so, there might still be something inside.

Holding her breath in anticipation, she walked around.

There it was. Her heart beat faster as she looked at the wooden door.

Although the outside was chipped and weathered, the door looked solid and thick, and it was firmly shut.

She couldn't wait to see what was inside.

"We've got a find here!" she announced.

"Oh, I'm so glad we're getting results." Charlotte crowded in beside her, staring up at the solid door.

Olivia took a deep breath.

"This is it. We'll solve our mystery now."

She turned the handle, her heart beating faster as she wondered what she would discover inside.

Then she let out a groan of disappointment.

The door was securely locked.

As she walked to work at midday, Olivia found her thoughts returning again and again to that mysterious room. What was inside, and how could she access it when even the windows were too small to climb through?

She wished she'd had more time to search for a way in.

Breaking the door was an option, but Olivia was reluctant to smash something in such perfect condition, especially since there was a visible keyhole. She would rather leave it undamaged and remain hopeful that she could find the key.

Perhaps it was hidden in the old ruins, in the middle of a giant spider web.

Or else, seeing the storeroom was in such perfect condition, Olivia needed to revise her ideas about the ancient farmhouse. Perhaps it had suffered from a fire, or had a tree fall on it, or there had been some other catastrophe that had partly destroyed it. In that case, the farmers might have continued to use it after moving to the new place.

She resolved to search the surrounding area, and also keep an eye out for a key as she cleaned and cleared the farmhouse. Surely, it would turn up at some stage.

Olivia put her thoughts aside. She couldn't dwell on the puzzle of her new home when there was a busy day ahead at the famous winery, La Leggenda.

As she made her way down the quiet, cypress-lined road, Olivia acknowledged that her current job title of sommelier was still far above her skill set.

She'd applied at the winery several weeks ago on impulse, and had been hired as an assistant for the summer season. Then, after a bizarre turn of events in which the sommelier had been murdered and Olivia had helped to solve the crime, she'd found herself accepting the job in his place.

She had all the enthusiasm required for the post. She was just scarily short on knowledge. Since taking on her new role, Olivia felt as if she needed to catch up on ten years' worth of experience, in as many days, in order to justify the generous salary that she was receiving.

She knew that at present, her role was more of a tasting room ambassador, since she was in charge of welcoming guests, managing the wine tasting, and sales—which were substantially higher than last year, proving that she was excelling in this sphere. But she was working as fast as she could to acquire the knowledge she needed to become a full-fledged sommelier, even studying at night. Well, some nights. After all, Charlotte was on holiday, so they ended up visiting local restaurants two or three times a week. But on other nights, she was trying her best.

Her heart lifted as she saw La Leggenda ahead. What a gorgeous workplace she had. Built from honeyed stone, the winery's elegant buildings seemed a living part of the green and gold landscape in which it all sat. As she walked up the winding driveway, she felt a surge of pride that she was a small part of this historic destination.

"Good morning, Olivia."

Her heart lifted even higher as she saw the winery owner, Marcello, at the doorway. La Leggenda was a second-generation family business, which today was owned and run by forty-year-old Marcello, his younger sister, Nadia, and his younger brother, Antonio.

"*Buon giorno*, Marcello," she greeted him in turn.

He was signing a delivery note, but he put the paper aside and walked over to her with a smile that lit up his eyes, as he kissed her cheeks in greeting.

Olivia felt herself blush. She'd given up trying to stop this automatic response to Marcello's presence. Not only was he tall, dark-haired, and stunningly handsome, with a strong jaw and blue eyes that were deep enough to drown in, but she had a sense that there was a spark between them.

Marcello was charming to everyone, but Olivia sensed that he was particularly attentive toward her. She wasn't imagining it. She wasn't! Other people had also noticed and remarked on it.

Plus, her intuition confirmed it was real.

She'd intended to go straight through to the tasting room and start setting up, ready for the busy day ahead, but to her surprise, Marcello placed a warm hand on her shoulder.

"Olivia, will you wait a moment, please? I want to ask you something."

"Of course! Sure!"

Scenarios spun through her mind, starting with a coffee date. It wouldn't be a coffee date, though, Olivia told herself firmly. She sensed that Marcello had imposed personal boundaries on himself regarding the dating of winery staff. Probably, he just wanted to discuss changes to the tasting menu.

She'd better have a new wine in mind. Olivia thought frantically. There was the unwooded chardonnay that the winery had just released, which was being touted as a probable medal winner. That might be a good addition.

But then Marcello's phone rang.

"You had better go," he told her. "I will talk to you later."

Pleased that her day would include a second encounter with Marcello, Olivia headed through the high archway into the tasting room.

This spacious area was the heart of the winery. From the wide, gleaming wooden counter, to the dramatic backdrop of wine barrels with the La Leggenda logo in gold above, it oozed atmosphere.

After opening time, the large room was always thronged with guests, admiring the winery's awards and certificates, and reading the history of La Leggenda which was displayed on huge posters around the walls—a recent, tourist-friendly addition to a place that was already a tourist magnet. Seeing it was the height of summer, Olivia knew she would be busy today and would have to ask Paolo, one of the waiters from the winery's famous restaurant, for help.

Olivia unlocked the side door and walked behind the counter. This was her domain, lined with fridges and shelves and cupboards where glasses were stored. Behind the dramatic backdrop was an even bigger area—the spacious storage room, lined with ranks of shelves stocking thousands of wines.

The babble of voices announced that guests had arrived. A group of three couples headed toward her.

Eagerly, Olivia stepped forward. She recognized their accents, and it always gave her a special thrill to serve people from her own country. After all, she knew how many hours she'd spent back in the States, poring over travel sites and imagining the day when she would be able to set off on her dream vacation.

She wanted all her compatriots to have the experience of a lifetime at La Leggenda.

"We've booked for lunch here," the dark-haired woman at the back of the group announced to the others. "There's time for a quick wine tasting first."

Olivia's smile disappeared. She stared at the group in consternation.

The woman sounded familiar.

In fact, Olivia was sure she knew her.'

If her memory was correct, this woman's name was Leanne Johnson. In her previous career, Olivia had known her well, but she was somebody that she had never expected, or wanted, to meet again.

If Leanne recognized her, Olivia knew that her past would immediately catch up with her, in the worst and most embarrassing way.

CHAPTER THREE

P anic surged inside Olivia as the group approached.

If Leanne figured out who she was, it would be humiliating at best and disastrous at worst.

In her previous career as an advertising account manager, Olivia had headed up a campaign for a brand called Valley Wines.

She'd poured her energies into this campaign. She'd worked into the small hours for weeks at a time on the tagline and branding, the images and wording, and the overall strategy.

The campaign had been astonishingly successful and the brand had guzzled market share, wiping out several competitors along the way.

Halfway through the campaign, Olivia had realized that the wines weren't just ordinary, they were appalling. In fact, they weren't really wines at all. They were grape juice mixed with flavorants and low-grade alcohol. Valley Wines had cut every corner there was in the manufacturing process. They'd cut corners in places no corners had existed before.

While this trash wine was riding on the success of Olivia's efforts, earning her a massive bonus and obliterating its more deserving competitors, the FDA had raided the premises and exposed the illegal ingredients and unhygienic processes, even finding a dead rat in one of the storage tanks.

The raid had sunk Valley Wines—and Olivia's reputation in the advertising world—for good.

Her biggest fear was that her current employers would find out about her association with this notorious brand. Everybody knew what had happened after the FDA raid. The news had traveled worldwide and every winemaker, wine merchant, and wine drinker had avidly discussed Valley Wines.

Rats in the vats! Was there anything that could be worse? The team at La Leggenda, and Marcello in particular, would be shocked. They'd believe she'd falsely represented herself as a passionate wine lover. They might fire her immediately.

Now here she was, staring with a frozen expression, as Leanne Johnson approached.

Leanne headed up a PR company that Olivia had used throughout the Valley Wines campaign. Leanne's company had coordinated many of the launches and events that had taken place countrywide.

Leanne was a loudmouth of note, with a piercing voice. If she recognized Olivia, the whole winery would soon know how they were connected, and the role Olivia had played in tirelessly promoting this trash wine. By the time their lunch was over, most of Tuscany would have found out what Olivia had done.

Olivia glanced nervously into the restaurant, her heart plummeting as she saw the well-groomed manager, Gabriella, standing at the reception desk.

Gabriella was Marcello's ex-girlfriend and she'd taken an immediate dislike to Olivia, instinctively sensing that Marcello favored her. If she heard about Olivia's association with Valley Wines, she'd use the information to sabotage Olivia in any way she could.

Olivia had spoken to Leanne almost every single day. They'd joked they needed a hotline to each other.

But—and this was the only thing that might possibly save Olivia— she and Leanne had seldom seen each other. They'd had only one meeting at the start of the campaign, because Leanne was based in New York and had handled the out-of-state events that Olivia couldn't attend.

It came to Olivia in a flash.

She would have to pretend to be Italian.

If she adopted a strong Italian accent, it would conceal the American drawl that would be an instant giveaway.

Olivia plastered her smile back in place as Leanne leaned her elbows expectantly on the counter. She hoped she'd be able to get away with this. It was her only chance.

"*Buon giorno,*" she announced.

Her voice was higher than usual. Okay, that was because she was terrified about being recognized, but even so, it worked in her favor.

"I welcome you so warmly to La Leggenda," she squeaked, trying her best to sound exactly like Nadia, the head vintner, did when she spoke English. "Allow me to introduce you to our tasting menu."

Nobody seemed suspicious of her strong, fake accent, and luckily, Leanne was staring at the tasting sheet in fascination, entranced by the descriptions of the wines.

One of the other couples in the group started speaking rapidly together in a different language and for a horrifying moment, Olivia's heart stopped. If they were Italian, she was so busted. Her pathetic attempts at subterfuge would have failed.

She gasped in relief as she realized they were speaking Spanish. Thank goodness, she was saved.

She didn't dare look at Leanne as she began introducing the first wine.

"This is the magnifico vermentino," she announced, displaying the bottle. "It is a—er—magnifico wine, made from local grapes which thrive in regions close to the sea. It is known for its floral and fruity flavors, and is particularly renowned for its citrus and salty overtones. Magnifico!" she finished with an extravagant arm gesture, feeling proud of the Italian authenticity she'd brought to her delivery.

The guests reached eagerly for their fine crystal glasses and swirled their tasting portions. She loved watching the concentration on their faces as they tried to pick up the flavors and aromas she had described, and their expressions of delight as they finally sipped the perfectly made wine.

Except for Leanne. She was staring at Olivia curiously, and Olivia felt her stomach start to churn.

"Do I know you from somewhere?" she asked. "It might sound like a weird question, but your face looks familiar. Have you ever been to New York? Are you involved in event management at all?"

Olivia goggled at her, feeling breathless. What could she say that wasn't an actual lie? She didn't want to lie, even though a few scenarios spun through her head—she could say she had a sister who had appeared on reality TV, or a cousin who was a model in Manhattan. But those would end up getting her into worse trouble. She couldn't risk it.

"I am in many photos of the winery, many! We have a website and everybody photographs us on Instagram. All the *turistas* love to do selfies of this *magnifico* place!"

She waited, the bottle clasped tightly in her hand, to see whether Leanne would believe this perfectly true, although also entirely wrong, explanation.

"Yes, that's it!" Leanne snapped her fingers. "I checked your venue out on Instagram when I was planning our wine tour. It certainly is a photogenic setting." She turned to her partner. "That reminds me, I must show you the shots I took on my walk this morning. The sunrise over the hills was spectacular. I'll find them for you right now."

"Enjoy the vermentino." Olivia smiled. "I will be back in uno momento to pour the next white blend, which is a blend of local friulano, pinot bianco, and sauvignon blanc grapes."

She walked away on legs wobbly with relief, heading straight for the back room to consult the Italian phrase book she kept in her purse. It occurred to her she might have been too free with the use of the word *magnifico*. She urgently needed to look for alternatives.

After the lunchtime rush of tourists, Olivia realized she was down to only one bottle of the famous Miracolo red blend in the storage room. There had been a nonstop flood of guests over the past week, and Marcello's brother, Antonio, who kept the shelves stocked, had been planting a new field. That had kept him too busy to bring stock inside.

Olivia decided to take advantage of the lull in the crowds to find Antonio.

Quickly, she detoured to the restaurant, where the main lunch service was finishing. Paolo was clearing tables in the outdoor courtyard. To reach him, though, Olivia would have to run the gauntlet of the restaurant manager's dagger-like stare.

Walking into this restaurant felt like walking into a minefield, Olivia acknowledged, as she saw the well-coiffed Gabriella turn and glare at her.

"*Buon giorno*," Olivia called out, trying to take the high ground and be friendly regardless.

It wasn't her fault that Gabriella had taken a dislike to her. As Marcello's ex-girlfriend who'd kept her job after the breakup, Gabriella, Olivia had learned, hated on anyone Marcello seemed to like. It wasn't personal—or maybe it was.

"What are you doing here?" Gabriella called, sounding suspicious.

"I need to ask Paolo to stand in for me while I fetch more wine," Olivia explained. "I should only be twenty minutes."

"We are busy. Very busy. I cannot spare him," Gabriella argued, making a sweeping gesture around the nearly empty restaurant.

Olivia knew that her protests were futile, because Marcello himself had said she was allowed to request help.

"Just twenty minutes," she repeated, smiling again, aware that Gabriella was seething with resentment.

Paolo abandoned his table-clearing immediately and followed her eagerly to the tasting room.

"I am feeling more capable to describe the wines every time," he confided. "It is fun to watch people appreciate them. More fun than watching people eat, which in any case they do not like you to do. Perhaps one day I can become your full-time assistant."

"I hope so. I'm thankful for your help, and you are doing great," Olivia encouraged him. She wasn't sure whether Paolo really loved the winery work or whether he was simply glad to be away from Gabriella's domineering control.

With the tasting room manned, she hurried out of the cool interior, taking a moment to stop and enjoy the glorious afternoon sunshine. It was a perfect day, warm and still, without so much as a cloud in the azure sky. She breathed in the sweet, floral scent from the Tuscan jasmine that climbed over the front of the building, before heading toward the upper levels of La Leggenda, where Antonio was planting on one of the highest-lying slopes.

During the brisk uphill walk, Olivia resolved to learn as much as she could about what he was doing and why. These higher reaches of the winery looked very similar to the terrain on her new farm. There must be secrets to success in planting vines in this arid, stony soil.

A small tractor, two of the winery's SUVs, and a white-paneled van told her where Antonio and his team were working.

"Hello, Olivia," Antonio called when he saw her. "I have forgotten to bring you new wines! What are you in need of?"

"The Miracolo is down to one bottle, and we're also short on the sangiovese," Olivia said.

"I will provide them this afternoon," Antonio promised.

He stretched his arms above his head and then patted his pockets for cigarettes, clearly relieved to take a break from the arduous work.

"Is this land newly planted?" Olivia asked.

"Yes, it is brand new. We decided to rest the previous terrain as it did not yield well last year."

"What variety are you planting?" she inquired.

"Nebbiolo. It is a thin-skinned red grape that produces a high acidity wine with the most incredible bouquet. These are tricky vines to grow, and you have to choose the sites carefully. They love sunshine and sandy soil, and this varietal prefers the high-lying southwest slopes, but soil acidity can be a problem in the wider area, including here."

"Really?" Olivia pricked up her ears. She would have to test the soil on her farm before planting.

"We add an organic fertilizer and a layer of compost mixed with lime. The compost also helps to keep water in. These high-lying soils drain very fast, too fast for the healthy growth of grapes, especially when they are young."

This was a lot of information. Olivia repeated it to herself, aware that Antonio was staring at her curiously.

She was tempted to tell him all about her crazy venture, but decided it would be better not to mention it. Even speaking the words out loud might jinx the endeavor at this early stage. She felt nervous at the thought of planting her first vines, because it would mean the possibility of failure.

For now, she would keep quiet about it and try to pick up whatever knowledge she could.

Thanking Antonio again, Olivia headed back to the winery.

As she walked in, she saw Marcello coming out of his office, located at the back of the tasting room.

"Olivia. Let me speak to you now if you have time?"

"Of course," Olivia said, glancing at the counter where Paolo was serving a group of young Danish women with great enthusiasm. Looking at the smiles all around, Olivia could see he had the situation perfectly in hand as he rolled up his sleeves to expose his muscular arms before presenting a bottle of vermentino white wine with a flourish.

"I definitely have time," she confirmed.

"Tomorrow morning, I have to go to Pisa," Marcello explained. "It is a business trip, and I would like you to come with me, as I feel it will be a good learning experience for you. We will need to leave here at seven a.m., and we will be gone for the whole day."

Olivia felt breathless with excitement. The chance to spend an entire day learning more about wine was an opportunity in itself, but to do so in Marcello's company? That was the cherry on top.

"I'd love to accompany you," she agreed.

Was it her imagination, or did Marcello look thrilled by her enthusiastic agreement?

"I am looking forward to it," he said. "I think it will be a productive day for both of us."

Olivia was fizzing with excitement. This learning experience was exactly what she'd hoped would come her way while she was working at La Leggenda. It would be an adventure to see how other wine farms in the area worked, and what their wines were like.

"I saw you were speaking to Antonio," Marcello observed. "Does he owe you some wine?"

"He does," Olivia said. "He promised to bring the bottles later today."

Marcello nodded. "We ran late planting this field. We are hoping for a mid-season crop of grapes next year, but it may already be too late for the vines to mature in time. We decided today is the last possible day for planting. No matter how late we work, the seeds have to be in the ground by the time the sun goes down."

At that moment, someone called Marcello and with a quick apology, he ran outside to attend to them.

Olivia stared after him in concern.

She'd thought she still had days—weeks, in fact—to plant her first vines, and that she'd be able to think and plan and gain information before taking this important step. Now, the bombshell Marcello had delivered had changed that timeline.

She didn't even have the luxury of another evening if she, too, wanted a mid-season crop next year.

Straight after work, she was going to have to buy and plant her first seeds.

Chapter Four

Breathless and eager, Olivia and Charlotte hurried into the hardware store in the nearby village of Collina, just five minutes before it was due to close.

Olivia was still in her work clothes. She hadn't even taken the time to change. She'd arrived back at the villa, and in a mini-hurricane of activity, had whirled herself and Charlotte into the Fiat and headed to the village at a speed that would have made the local Italians proud.

Olivia hadn't even taken the time to slow down as she passed the scenic ruined castle which stood at the town's entrance. Gazing at it had become a ritual for her, and she knew she'd caused traffic jams in the past as she craned her neck to admire it. She never got tired of looking at its crumbling walls and gray stone battlements and wondering what it had looked like hundreds of years ago, in its full glory.

This time, focused on her urgent task, she didn't even glance in its direction.

Calling out a friendly *buon giorno* to the motherly store attendant, Olivia made a beeline for the section that stocked winemaking equipment.

The hardware store was like the village of Collina, Olivia thought. It was surprisingly small and cramped, and yet it contained everything a person could need.

What to get? She stared at the closely packed shelves in confusion. She'd hoped to approach this in a far more systematic way. She hadn't even had the time to make a list.

"We're going to need a cart, aren't we? I'll get us a cart," Charlotte said.

She hurried back to the entrance as Olivia paced the aisles, fretting over which type of fertilizer she should choose, and whether her farm's soil would also need added lime. It was too late to even consider compost.

Then there was the question about what grapes to grow. That was something else she hadn't considered. Olivia thought frantically back to the conversation she'd had with Antonio, as well as the knowledge she'd picked up from her work behind the tasting counter.

Her farm was a higher-lying area, without a doubt, and it had hilly slopes.

Vermentino should grow well then, and if it did, perhaps chardonnay would too.

Antonio had been planting nebbiolo, but from what he had said, they were fussy customers to cultivate, and as a beginner, she needed tough, hardy grapes. The local sangiovese red grapes would be better, she decided. They were adapted to the area and would hopefully grow more easily.

She added a watering can to the cart, as well as a rake and a spade.

A small plastic watering can seemed insufficient when Olivia thought about the vast, hilly tracts of land she'd have to plant, but the alternative was to install irrigation, and that would be an expensive and time-consuming exercise. For now, the can would have to do.

"I'm a can-do girl," she told herself optimistically.

"I'll be able to help you water," Charlotte said. She was also looking at the lime green can with doubt in her eyes. "I can help you do everything you need. After all, the farm is such a fun project."

"Really?" Olivia asked. To her, it felt more daunting than fun.

"Absolutely. I've always loved the idea of farming. I feel I've got potential as a daughter of the soil."

Olivia glanced at Charlotte gratefully, but found herself looking into the sparkling brown eyes of the man standing behind her friend. Olivia wondered how long he'd been patiently waiting as she'd rummaged through the shelves, absorbed in her panic buying.

"Sorry, we've been holding you up." Olivia did her best to push aside the cart to give him room to pass.

"Not at all. I am in no hurry." He paused, looking at her more closely.

Olivia stared back at him. Preoccupied as she was by her shopping, she couldn't help noticing that he appeared to be about her age, fit and strong-looking, with a roguish smile and exceptionally well-groomed hair. His dark head was cut in a perfect fade, with a zigzag detail along his parting, and the top gelled in perfect spikes. Even his stubble was precision-trimmed.

"Forgive me my curiosity, *signora*," he said. "I know of only one old farm for sale near here. Is this the property on the hillside, above the *strada regionale*?"

He was referring to the narrow tar road that led from Collina to the next village, three miles away, Olivia guessed.

"Yes, that's the one."

"Seriously? You bought it?" His smile widened into an incredulous grin. "That old place?"

"Yes," Olivia said, feeling defensive.

Was he laughing at her? Clearly, he was a local who was familiar with the area. Did he know something she didn't?

Had this investment been a drastic mistake? Olivia wondered with a chill.

"It's a lovely farm," she insisted. "The views are beautiful."

He raised one eyebrow quizzically.

"Indeed, yes, it is ideally situated for a holiday home."

Now he was staring into their cart.

"But you are not making a holiday on this farm. You are planting vines there? Vines? Now? On that hillside terrain?"

"Yes, I'm going to plant them this evening. I'm hoping for a mid-season crop next summer," Olivia said.

The man shook his head, laughing merrily.

"*Americanos!* What a people! I love how you are so mad, so optimistic. No challenge is too great! Pretty lady, I wish you well—you will need more than my wishes, though." Still chuckling to himself, he weaved his way past the cart and headed to the till.

Charlotte stared after him, frowning.

"Was he warning you about something?" she asked.

Olivia shrugged. "I think he was just teasing us," she said. At any rate, she hoped so.

Looking at the contents of her cart, she realized that this last-minute buying spree was turning out to be an expensive exercise. She hoped it wouldn't turn out to be a disastrous decision.

After cramming their shopping into the Fiat's tiny trunk, they headed back to the farmhouse. It was midsummer, so there were approximately three and a half hours of daylight left, but even so Olivia knew they would have their work cut out for them. Once the planting was complete, they could reward themselves with pizza and wine at the restaurant down the road.

She was relieved that she'd left a spare pair of sweatpants in the dusty upstairs bedroom, knowing that she would need scruffy clothes to change into when she worked on-site.

Hurrying up the stairs, she wriggled out of her work skirt and pulled on the faded pants. She'd worn them for all her jobs around the farmhouse, as well as for some gardening. Not only were they stained and dirty, but there was a large hole in the seat of the pants where a rose thorn had ripped them open.

Olivia folded her smart skirt and jacket and placed them on the window frame, which she'd wiped the previous day and was thus one of the only non-dusty surfaces in the house.

She paused for a moment, staring out the window.

One day this empty, echoing room would be her bedroom. She would sleep here, with the room warmed by the evening rays, and wake to look over the brightening hills. The high ceiling and spacious area would be perfect for a double bed and a comfortable armchair, as well as a wooden desk and perhaps a huge, old-fashioned wardrobe.

Or would built-in cupboards be easier?

Olivia was still agonizing over that choice, which she knew she would have to make soon. But that was a fun decision, because she knew she couldn't go too far wrong and either one would work. It was like the bedroom walls. Should she refresh them in their golden cream shade, or go for a lighter, brighter off-white? Again, no wrong answer.

Choosing where to plant the seeds she'd just bought was a difficult decision, because there was every chance she might mess it up.

From below, she heard Charlotte squeal with excitement.

Olivia hurried downstairs to see what had happened.

"Look, he's back! Remember that cat we saw a few days ago? He's here again. Perhaps the people fixing the ceiling scared him away for a while."

"Oh, I'm so glad to see him."

Olivia bent forward, twiddling her fingers and cooing at the small, nervous black-and-white cat that seemed to have made the abandoned farm his home. Scared as he was, he was not as flighty as he had been. He must be hoping for food. Charlotte rummaged in her purse for a packet.

"I have one left."

Triumphantly, she tipped the contents into the plastic bowl that they'd bought and left on the porch.

Standing side by side with Charlotte, Olivia realized they had identical fond smiles as they watched the cat hungrily devour his supper. No matter how urgent her planting job was, Olivia was unable to tear herself away from the rewarding sight, until the cat had licked the last morsel of food out of the bowl and began to wash his face contentedly.

"To work," she announced.

Rummaging in the trunk, she lifted out a bag of fertilizer and, at random, a packet of seeds.

"Vermentino it is," she announced. "You will be the frontrunner crop on Glass Farm."

She surveyed the terrain.

"Thinking logically, I guess we should plant them out of the way. Because there's going to be a lot of work getting done on the house, and we don't want to plant them where vehicles would need to drive, or materials be delivered."

"How about we plant this lot all the way over at the back of the farm, near that storeroom you can't unlock?" Charlotte suggested.

"There's no water supply on that side," Olivia remembered, and Charlotte nodded.

"Don't they prefer arid ground? We can water them now. A couple of trips with the watering can might do it."

"Good idea," Olivia decided.

"I'll be the water carrier today," Charlotte volunteered.

Grabbing the spade, Olivia headed up the hill.

A short, brisk walk later, she arrived at the outbuilding.

How far apart should she plant them? Olivia hastily thought back to the vines she'd seen at La Leggenda. Probably two wide steps between each plant would be enough.

Using the tip of the spade, she traced a large rectangle, dragging the outline through the sandy ground with its profusion of wild herbs and plants. Then she set about creating small beds for the seeds, sprinkling a handful of fertilizer into each one. She dug each bed vigorously, feeling a pang of worry that the tip of the spade often seemed to be hitting solid rock. Surely that wasn't possible? More likely, the ground was just baked hard.

After half an hour of vigorous digging, her first site was ready for planting.

As Charlotte crested the hill yet again, wiping a trickle of sweat from her forehead as she made her third trip with the watering can, Olivia began planting the seeds in the freshly dug and watered beds she'd created.

This was exciting, exhausting, and terrifying all at the same time, she decided, trying to subdue her fears and be filled with positive energy as she knelt on the damp ground and patted the soil into place. Didn't they say plants picked up on your thoughts and feelings? She needed to shower these seeds with hope and happiness.

"Grow, dear ones!" Olivia cried, causing Charlotte to look at her curiously.

She climbed to her feet, brushing soil off the now-muddy knees of her sweatpants.

"How about we work our way back, doing a small Chardonnay planting near the ruined building, and then we plant the sangiovese below the big shed?"

"That sounds—well, to be honest, it sounds exhausting," Charlotte laughed. "But let's get to it. The sooner these babies are in the ground, the sooner they can start making wine!"

Heading back, Olivia was surprised that every muscle in her body was burning. This wine farming was hard work! She was starting to understand why Antonio looked so lean and fit.

She picked up the packet of sangiovese seeds. She was excited about these. No matter how the other types fared, a local varietal must surely have an innate advantage.

She headed down the hill and marked out the bed with the edge of her spade.

After marking out the bed, Olivia took a break from her digging, leaning on the spade handle while she rubbed her aching buttocks.

Seeing an approaching shadow behind her, she called, "The ones on the left are ready for watering, Charlotte."

"Are they, *signora*?"

Olivia dropped her spade in shock.

The voice from behind her was warm, deep, and unmistakably masculine.

Spinning around, she found herself staring into the amused eyes of the man from the hardware store.

CHAPTER FIVE

"What are you doing here?" Olivia screeched.

Her outrage was eclipsing her embarrassment—but only just. She'd been bent over, massaging her backside when he had walked up behind her.

Worse still, she had a giant hole in the seat of her sweatpants. Olivia felt her face flood with mortification as she remembered that.

This was not an auspicious moment for an unannounced visit.

"Sorry for the surprise," the man said, giving her a conspiratorial wink. "I was passing by. I thought I would arrive here and perhaps offer my help."

He bent and picked up the spade. Hastily, Olivia pivoted to keep facing him. She wanted to keep that gash in her pant seat out of sight, although he must already have seen it.

What underwear had she put on?

She thought she'd chosen gray that morning. And the sweatpants were gray, so hopefully the wide rip had been camouflaged.

"You have been hard at work," the man said, staring down at the two rows of seed beds she'd dug so far. "However, I can immediately notice that you are doing certain things wrong. You have not planted vines before, yes?"

Doing it wrong? What a rude thing to say! Olivia felt outraged by the insulting tone of his comment. How could you dig wrong? It was just putting the spade into the soil and loosening it up. Olivia didn't think there could be a right and a wrong way, and besides, she was very proud of the neat beds she'd created.

"I have planted them before," she said defiantly. Which was true. She'd just planted about a hundred seeds in other areas of the property. After nearly three hot, tiring hours of work, she was a seasoned expert.

"I don't think so." Laughingly, this spiky-haired man called her bluff. "I can already see what you are doing wrong. You are a beginner, who knows nothing and needs to learn correctly. Shall I show you where you have made the big mistake? Before you waste all the money you have spent?"

He was still holding the spade, in a way that told her he wasn't eager to hand it back, and she didn't like his smile. It seemed as if he were laughing at her, as did his tone of voice. In fact, he'd probably driven here so that he could impose his chauvinistic attitude on the proceedings and try to show her up.

He walked quickly to the other side of her mini vineyard and Olivia whirled around, conscious of the need to keep facing him.

Had she put on gray panties that morning? Now that she was thinking back, the gray ones had been all the way at the back of the drawer, and she'd been in a hurry to get dressed.

She wished she could recall. Not being able to remember, combined with the shock of this unwanted visit, was making her face flame. She was sure he'd noticed that, too. Olivia got the impression that this unlikeable man, who sported a hairstyle far too good for his personality, didn't miss a trick.

"Give me the spade back," she demanded, suddenly unable to cope with the complexities of the situation for as much as another minute.

"You are ready for me to show you?" he asked, seemingly pleased that she was coming around to his way of thinking.

Olivia didn't want that either. In fact, she wanted it even less. Watching would involve him standing behind her when she bent over. She could practically feel the evening breeze gusting through the massive rip in the seat of her pants.

She decided suddenly that she didn't want this man here at all. He hadn't made an appointment, or even asked permission to arrive at her brand new vineyard. He was being insulting and demeaning to her, implying she was a hopeless winemaker. Worst of all, he might have seen her panties!

"I would like you to leave," she demanded, stepping forward and grabbing the spade from him. "I don't need your help at this point, or in fact at any other point in the process. I work for a winery and know what I'm doing. We are managing just fine on our own. You're annoying me, and you're wasting my time. I have to finish this planting before it gets dark, because my friend and I are both starving and we need to go for pizza and wine."

To her surprise, she thought the man looked momentarily wounded, as if he hadn't expected such an unequivocal dismissal.

Then he shrugged.

"My name is Danilo," he said. "I would like to know your name, too, but I can see now is not the time to make these introductions. Here is my business card. Call me if you need any help." He winked at her again and Olivia wondered if she'd imagined the brief flash of hurt in his eyes. "I am sure we'll see each other again soon!"

She felt herself bristle all over again. The nerve! He simply couldn't stop himself from insinuating that she was incompetent.

Reluctantly, Olivia took the proffered card. The man turned to go, and as he did, Charlotte walked around the house carrying her watering can.

She saw Danilo's eyebrows shoot up at the sight, and sensed that he was trying to conceal a laugh as he watched her friend toting the small green container down the hill.

"Good evening, ladies. *Buona sera*. Enjoy your pizza and wine."

He strolled jauntily out of the gate and climbed into a white truck parked on the side of the road.

A moment later, he'd roared out of sight.

Olivia couldn't help it. She had to know.

Pulling down the waistband of the sweatpants, she took a look at the color of her underwear.

She scrunched her face up and closed her eyes, wishing that the past ten minutes had played out differently. She'd chosen the bright orange panties that morning, so vivid they seemed luminous.

They must have looked like a dazzling sunset peeking through a gray cloud. There was absolutely no way that Danilo could not have noticed them. No wonder he'd been smiling so widely.

"Ugh!" Olivia said aloud.

She shook herself, trying to banish the feel of his gaze.

"What was that all about?" Charlotte asked. "Was that man from the hardware store trying to micromanage our planting process?"

Olivia nodded grimly.

"I had no idea pushy locals would be part of the landscape here. As if I need any unsolicited help!"

Charlotte looked astounded.

"Planting is basic gardening, isn't it? He was clearly trying to interfere."

"Exactly," Olivia agreed.

Privately, she found herself flooded with doubt. As much as she tried to push the thoughts aside, she wondered what would happen if her first crop proved to be a disaster.

"Please grow," she begged the seeds, conscious that they might be picking up vibes of anxiety and even desperation from her now.

These beds were visible from the road. At any time, Danilo could cruise past in his dusty white truck and take a look at their progress, or the lack of it.

Olivia couldn't bear to think how embarrassing it would be to have to call him back and beg him for the advice he'd so confidently offered.

She hoped the seeds would sprout quickly, so that Danilo would be astounded by how they were thriving, and realize how rude and unnecessary his criticism had been.

At that moment, Olivia's phone rang.

She rummaged in her pocket. This late in the evening, it was probably someone calling from the States, where they were a few hours behind.

It was her mother on the line.

Olivia sighed.

They hadn't spoken in more than a week. She hoped this conversation wouldn't cut into her pizza time. Since her mother wasn't known for having short discussions, Olivia decided to run upstairs and change back into her smart clothes while they spoke.

"Hello, Mom," she said, heading for the farmhouse.

"Olivia!" Her mother sounded anxious. "You tried to call me on the weekend."

Olivia could imagine her slim, nervous mother, perched on her floral armchair in their sunny living room, with Olivia's father reading on the seat opposite. Olivia knew that only when her mother's voice hit a certain pitch, would her father raise his eyes from his book.

"Yes, I did call. You said you were driving and I should call back another time."

"I must urgently tell you that your email has been hacked."

"It has?" As Olivia scampered up the stairs, she felt her heart quicken in alarm. That was the last thing she needed.

"Yes. You must report it immediately."

Olivia put the phone onto speaker as she wriggled out of her pants. Really, she should throw them away. Or at least, mend the rip. Perhaps there was a repair shop in town, although she felt embarrassed to take such shabby pants in for darning.

It would be easiest just to keep them here, torn and comfortable as they were.

"How do you know there's a problem?" she asked.

Her mother announced the bombshell dramatically.

"The hackers emailed me, using your name, and stating the most ludicrous thing. They claimed you had bought a farm in Italy."

Olivia blinked.

"Uh, Mom—"

But Mrs. Glass continued, ignoring Olivia and steamrolling smoothly ahead.

"They didn't ask for money directly, but it was easy for someone as worldly-wise as me to see that they were laying the foundations for it in their next mail. It's called phishing, honey."

Olivia heard her father mutter something in the background.

"Oh. It's not phishing, angel, it's a 419 scam. That's what the hackers have done. Is that more serious, Andrew?"

She paused as Olivia's father spoke again.

"It's the same, only different, apparently. But anyway, honey, you have been phished. I mean, 419ed, and you should notify your contacts right away. They have probably sent this out to your entire database! It wasn't a well-written mail, and clearly penned by a non-English speaker, but even so, one of your naïve friends could easily believe it."

Olivia rolled her eyes as she scrambled into her skirt and slipped on her dusty sandals again.

"Mom, it was me. I wrote the mail, and it's true. I have bought a farm in Italy. You were busy and couldn't talk when I called, so I decided to write you with all the details."

Olivia found herself prattling on to fill the sudden, shocked silence that resounded down the line.

"It's really lovely. In fact, I'm standing in the bedroom now. And now I'm walking down the stairs. The house is a little neglected but the structure is very strong, and it's on twenty acres, like I said in my mail. I'm going to grow wine! I plan to launch my own wine label next year."

"You what?" her mother replied faintly.

Olivia was certain that she was sufficiently briefed on all the facts, and the cell signal was crystal clear. She was just having difficulty taking it all in.

"My own wine label," she repeated, just in case.

"I don't believe this," her mother whispered. "Olivia, this is unthinkable." She continued, sounding suspicious. "Have you fallen in with the wrong crowd? Have you been brainwashed, or kidnapped by a cult, who are using your money to further their ends? If you need help, angel, I want you to say the word—the word—let me think what could be included innocently in conversation. The word 'water' will do! Use it very clearly in your reply to me and I will alert the authorities."

Olivia reached the bottom of the stairs.

"Are we ready to go?" Charlotte asked, scrambling up from her cross-legged position on the porch.

"Yes," Olivia told her friend hurriedly. She needed to wrap up this annoying conversation and tell her mother goodbye. Dinner was calling, and right now, after the day she'd had, wine was calling louder still.

Olivia looked down at the newly planted vineyard.

"Oh, we should put the watering can away," she added quickly, noticing the flash of bright green in the sandy bed.

Olivia's mother uttered a shriek.

"The code word! I knew it! Andrew, Olivia has been brainwashed by a cult, who have used her to purchase a farm in Tuscany as their headquarters! We need to track this call urgently and get help to her! Does the FBI operate in Italy?"

"Mom, I'm fine!" Olivia protested. "I have to go. I don't need help, and I'm not involved in a cult. Right now, I'm on my way to a restaurant. I'll call you tomorrow. Love you! Love to Dad! Everything's good! Promise!"

She disconnected, hoping her reassurances had been convincing enough.

She wouldn't put it past her mother to organize the entire FBI to descend on Tuscany in order to rescue Olivia from the imaginary cult.

CHAPTER SIX

The following morning, Olivia's alarm woke her at five-thirty a.m.
She bounced excitedly out of bed, glancing out of the villa's large window at the rising sun. What a glorious morning it was! The air was fresh and cool, and the shadows of the trees stretched across the deep green lawn. Beyond it, hills and fields led to the faraway horizon in the misty morning light.

Since the tasting room didn't open its doors until mid-morning, she'd gotten into the habit of sleeping in until eight. It felt like an adventure being awake at the start of the day.

Today was her outing with Marcello to Pisa. Business trip, Olivia hastily corrected herself. Not an outing, she must be very clear about that. Business trip.

It was likely to be a long and demanding day, she told herself sternly. She would need to remain professional, alert to learn whatever she could, even if the discussions with his colleagues and clients took place in Italian.

Even though this was a business trip, she couldn't help hoping that they would have a chance to pass by the Leaning Tower of Pisa, even if it were only to glimpse it from the road. It was one of the sights she'd always wanted to see. Imagine viewing it in Marcello's company.

Olivia told herself firmly to stop getting excited. This was a work outing and she must take it in her stride.

Heading out of the airy bedroom and into the luxurious en suite bathroom, she showered, spent some time styling her shoulder-length blond hair, and made a few last-minute changes to the outfit she'd gotten ready the night before. She switched out the high-heeled dress shoes that had been her first choice, for low-heeled summer sandals that would be easier to walk in. The turquoise knee-length dress was perfect, but she was going to take along her beige leather jacket, which showed more Italian stylishness than the white cotton jacket she'd picked out yesterday.

In her purse, she packed a notebook and pen, as well as her phone charger. And, of course, lipstick and lip gloss and perfume, in case she needed to freshen up during the day.

For instance, after she and Marcello had lunch together.

Stop it, Olivia told herself. More than likely, lunch would be a quick sandwich eaten in the car.

She glanced out the window, noticing Erba making her way purposefully to the house from the villa's fruit trees, where she'd been scavenging fallen pomegranates. Usually, she took the morning sun on Olivia's windowsill, and Olivia had gotten used to pulling her curtains back and viewing the unusual sight of a basking goat.

"We're heading into work early," she warned Erba.

After one final check she had everything she needed, Olivia hurried into the kitchen. Of all the rooms in the villa, she loved this one the most. A big, bold frieze of grapes covered one tiled wall, and the clay pots of herbs on the windowsill were fragrant with the scent of rosemary, basil, and thyme. Of course, her favorite part of this warm-hued kitchen had to be the large red and chrome coffee machine that dominated the counter.

Quickly, Olivia fixed herself a double-strength cappuccino and sipped it while staring out the window at the tiled courtyard, with more herbs and shrubs planted along its stone walls. She wanted a courtyard just like this outside the farmhouse kitchen. Perhaps she could lay the tiles herself. She loved how they looked, each block interspersed by thyme and catmint.

Enough dreaming, Olivia told herself, draining her coffee and grabbing her purse.

"Come, Erba," she called, heading down the corridor and closing the imposing wooden door carefully behind her. "Walkies!"

She arrived at La Leggenda at ten to seven. Marcello was already outside, loading bottles into a cooler in the back of the SUV. He looked especially handsome this morning. His dark hair was freshly trimmed, the tousled fringe falling just above his brows. He was wearing a charcoal dress shirt and a smart pair of jeans.

"We are taking a gift," he explained with a smile. "You look lovely this morning. I am excited for our day ahead."

"Me, too," Olivia said, feeling herself glow at the compliment.

He kissed her on both cheeks and she felt her knees momentarily buckle at his closeness, and the spicy hint of aftershave she picked up on his strong, defined jaw.

Luckily, she was getting used to the effect that Marcello had on her, and it took her racing heart only a few moments to return to normal speed.

Heading into the tasting room, she grasped the remaining two bottles on the counter and slotted them into the custom-made padded cooler.

A minute later, they were driving out of the winery's elegant gateway.

"Our journey will be scenic, as we are taking the quieter roads," Marcello explained, turning the music up so that the subtle sounds of opera—which gave Olivia a shiver of romantic excitement—provided a melodious accompaniment. "We are heading to a wine farm, and I would like your opinion on it."

Her opinion? On a wine farm? Olivia felt simultaneously flattered and panicked. From what perspective? What could she hope to offer in terms of expertise?

She was glad she'd had that strong cappuccino before leaving home. At least she was wide awake, and thinking at full speed, as the car traveled down the narrow, cedar-lined tar road, heading for the *strada principale*—the main road which led to Pisa.

But before he reached it, Marcello turned right, accelerating onto a ribbon of tar that zigzagged its way through the hills, each curve of the road revealing another exquisite view. Olivia spotted a dark, mysterious forest, hidden away in a deep, shadowed valley. There was a huge stone castle set on a green hill with a winding river forming a makeshift moat around it, and flags flying from its battlements.

Olivia had thought she'd struggle to make self-consciously polite conversation during the drive, but in fact, the opera music filled the car and her heart, and she was able to breathlessly admire the scenery without feeling at all awkward.

Before she knew it, Marcello was slowing the car. He turned down a sandy road, and a mile later, eased the SUV through a narrow gap in the wire fence.

There was a sign by the right-hand wooden post. What did it say? Olivia craned her neck to look, but the paint was too faded for her to make out.

This didn't look anything like the wine farms she'd visited so far. Were they stopping somewhere else first, or what was happening? she wondered, mystified.

The driveway was bushy and overgrown, although bright with wildflowers and butterflies. At the end of it was a clearing just large enough for two cars. One, a modest, elderly truck in faded blue, was already parked there.

Beyond the clearing was a small stone house.

"*Salve*, Franco!" Marcello called, climbing out of the car.

"*Salve!*"

A lean, gray-haired man appeared at the front door.

"Welcome, welcome," he greeted them, spreading his arms wide.

He and Marcello enfolded each other in a hug.

He then took Olivia's hand and, to her surprise and delight, bent to kiss it.

"Welcome, *signorina*," he enthused, his dark eyes sparkling in his lined, tanned face.

Marcello lifted the cooler full of wine out of the car and they headed to the weathered front door.

Olivia followed Franco inside and gasped in amazement.

The interior of the house looked nothing like she'd expected it to. She felt as if she'd stepped into another world.

It wasn't a house at all. Inside, you could see that the building, which had looked so small, was somewhat larger than she'd expected—high-roofed and airy.

It was a rustic, yet productive, winemaking facility.

The interior was humming with activity, as two workers moved a long pipe into one of the oak barrels that lined the far wall. There were three large vats on the other side of the room. They weren't gleaming, brand-new ones like at La Leggenda. These looked older and worn, but well cared for and serviceable.

Olivia breathed in the aroma that had become familiar to her, the evocative scent of well-matured wood and fermenting wine. It never failed to give her a thrill of excitement.

"Come, come," Franco invited them. "Follow me this way."

The floor was plain, well-worn stucco with an occasional uneven ripple, as if it had been poured in stages and smoothed out by hand. Olivia wondered if this entire facility had originally been Franco's labor of love.

There were no dramatically large doorways or wide, bright windows as there were at La Leggenda, but peeking through one of the modest, narrow windows, Olivia caught sight of rows of vines outside, stretching down the hillside and into the valley.

"Our tasting room is not your standard," Franco apologized as they followed him into a small annex off the main building. Here stood a large oak table with four chairs around it, an old-fashioned sideboard, and a cabinet with well-polished glasses.

"So, let me introduce you to our children!" Franco announced.

Olivia wasn't too surprised when he opened the sideboard and reverently took out a number of wine bottles. She'd already guessed that this man's farm was his passion and his world.

"Our Daily Chianti," he announced, removing the stopper from the bottle and reaching for three glasses. "It needs a better name, I know."

It had been a while since Olivia had been on the receiving end of a wine tasting. She'd grown used to pouring, not holding the glass and swirling the wine, breathing in the bouquet before sipping.

What a treat!

"It's wonderful," she exclaimed, hoping as she spoke that she wasn't being forward. Should she have waited for the elderly man to explain the wine, or for Marcello to offer his opinion?

But Marcello was smiling, nodding in approval, as the elderly man clapped his hands in delight.

"Go on?" Marcello said.

"It's smooth, it has a very well-balanced flavor, it's the kind of wine that—"Olivia struggled to find the right words. "That is easy to relate to. You don't have to be an expert to enjoy it. I could pour this for all of my friends and they'd love it, even if they weren't usually wine drinkers."

"Exactly!" Franco beamed. "That was our intention with this wine. And now, our Daily Blend."

Olivia sipped on this red wine, enjoying it just as much as the other. She was almost sure of the flavors she could discern, and felt proud of her progress since she'd started work at La Leggenda, but she was nervous about making a mistake in front of Marcello. Luckily, he took the lead this time.

"A vivacious, ripe berry flavor," he complimented Franco. "A hint of plum and cherry. I suspect your blend contains a percentage of good quality merlot."

"Of course, you are right." Franco grinned. "Now, our trebbiano," he said proudly.

He poured white wine into three glasses.

Olivia sipped.

"Oh, wow, this is another relatable wine. Dry, but packed with fruit and flavor. I can imagine how well this would pair with just about any food," she enthused.

Marcello nodded approvingly. "Exactly. The trebbiano is easy-drinking, and one of the most popular wines to accompany food in Italy. There is no restaurant wine list where you will not find a trebbiano, and yours are on a number of them, Franco?"

Franco shrugged modestly.

"We have been fortunate that three local restaurants have started carrying our wine," he said.

Olivia couldn't help it. She sneaked another sip of the delicious white, causing Franco to beam even more widely. What a wine it was! It seemed to beg for food, friends, and family to be added to the table.

For a moment, Olivia felt a pang of regret that she wouldn't be able to run a campaign for these wines. She wished she'd been able to market this wine back in Chicago, rather than the Valley Wines drain-cleaner she'd been in charge of. What a pleasure to find ways of helping the consumer relate to such a fun series of wines, packed with personality.

Marcello stood up.

"I am pleased to announce we have a deal," he said.

Olivia stared, surprised, as he and Franco embraced again and then shook hands firmly.

What did he mean, a deal? What was happening—were they making a collaboration wine? If so, what could it be? Olivia wasn't sure how the La Leggenda wines could combine with these wines, as they were very different in style and taste. She worried that she wasn't understanding well enough how winemaking worked, and that her knowledge was too poor for her to see how the two wineries' products could co-mingle.

She guessed that this was the main reason for Marcello's trip to Pisa. He looked delighted, and both the men were laughing, excited, as Franco lifted a sheaf of papers from the shelf above the sideboard.

Olivia sensed that this was an auspicious occasion, but even though she tried to peer at the pages, she couldn't make head or tail of them as they were all in Italian. Small-print Italian, worse still. If they'd been printed on sandwich boards, she was sure she'd have been able to pick up a few words.

Summoning up her patience, as she perched expectantly on the wooden chair, she hoped Marcello would soon reveal what the purpose of the visit to this modest, yet excellent, winery had been.

CHAPTER SEVEN

Marcello put the black folder containing his copy of the signed papers in the trunk of the SUV and they climbed inside.

Franco, still beaming, stood on the step of his winery as they departed, waving enthusiastically. Marcello buzzed the windows down and they waved back until the small building was out of sight.

"Well!" Marcello said. "I think I may have acted impulsively there, but I knew it was the right decision. Your reactions to the wine helped me to decide." He sighed. "I am very poor, now. Penniless, but happy. And hopeful!"

His elation was contagious. Olivia found herself grinning at him even though she didn't yet know why.

"What was that all about?" she asked.

"Franco is an old family friend," Marcello said. "He has built his business over decades, from nothing, but he had a few setbacks over the years and his wines have never achieved the sales that he hoped for."

"It's not due to lack of quality. Those wines were delicious," Olivia said.

Marcello nodded. "For years, now, he has been asking us if we would invest in it. He is looking to retire soon, and wants to see his creation taken further, marketed more actively, and expanded for increased production. For us, I started to realize that it is a necessary step. These wines are, as you say, relatable. They are easy drinking. This will allow us to break into this very important market, while still offering a quality product."

"So you decided to invest?"

Olivia was excited by the thought, and could see how this would be a win-win situation for the friendly Franco, as well as a strategic move into a new market for La Leggenda.

Marcello nodded. "More than that. We have bought the winery outright."

Olivia gasped. "That's a huge decision! How exciting."

"I am thrilled. Until now, we could not afford it, as we were paying off our existing business loans from the major expansion we did five years ago. I think Franco did not try too hard to sell to others during that time. He was hoping we could take his dream forward. Now, we can afford it—but only just. It will be a squeeze, as the place requires a lot of renovation. There is so much to do. But the potential is there."

"Well, I'm thrilled for you," Olivia said.

"With business done, I believe we should now take some enjoyment from our day. Let us celebrate," Marcello said. "What do you want to do?"

Half an hour later, Olivia stood under the Porta Santa Maria arch, staring at the green lawns and exquisite white-marble buildings that formed part of the Piazza dei Miracoli. This was where her bucket list destination, the Leaning Tower of Pisa, was located. She'd always thought, from friends' photos, that it was a random tower, set in a green lawn. She had never dreamed that it formed part of such a fascinating complex, filled with historic, religious, and cultural significance.

Having Marcello beside her as she entered the Square of Miracles made the experience even more memorable. How lucky was she, to be visiting this incredible destination in the company of the most handsome man in Italy?

"There is so much to see here." Marcello pointed to a strikingly decorated, circular building. "That is the Baptistery of San Giovanni, where the famous Galileo Galilei was baptized. Today, it is empty, but the acoustics are amazing. You will hear the echo it produces when we walk and talk inside. Or perhaps, even try our hand at singing." He smiled. "As a child, coming here, that used to fascinate me the most."

Olivia was enthralled by the spacious, echoing interior of this historic structure. From there, they headed to the eleventh-century Duomo, the cathedral. She had never known that the charming Leaning Tower was simply the cathedral's bell tower, even though its slanting shape meant it claimed so much of the fame and photos.

Entering the coolness of the huge cathedral, Olivia found herself rubbernecking at the incredible detail in the high, tiled ceiling, the magnificent sculptures, and the breathtaking carvings that surrounded the giant, hexagonal pulpit. What passion and artistry must have gone into this project, which had no doubt taken many years to complete.

Then she had the thrill of climbing up the spiral stone staircase within the Leaning Tower itself. She was amazed by how worn the shallow stone stairs were. How many feet must have trampled up and down them, to gradually wear each tread into a subtle, curved dip in its center? The feeling of history enchanted her. She was glad she'd chosen sandals that were easy to walk in, for this twisting climb.

"Wow," Olivia sighed, when she reached the top and stood on the circular walkway surrounding the tower. What a view! For a moment, she wondered if she might even be able to spy her farmhouse on the distant horizon, perched in its hillside setting.

The most memorable part of the whole experience was yet to come.

After descending the tower, Olivia stood on the manicured grass, leaning forward, with her arms stretched out in front of her as she reached into thin air. It was difficult to keep them completely still when she turned her head away. Her muscles were burning.

"Move your right hand back a little. Just a little," Marcello said. "More. No, less. That's it. Smile! Hold still! Smile again."

Olivia beamed at the phone he was holding as Marcello took a few photos in swift succession.

He stared down at the screen and then nodded in approval.

"Come and see," he said.

Olivia practically ran back to him, dodging a group of Japanese tourists who were on their way to stand in the same spot she'd been.

She stared eagerly down at the phone.

The photo was perfect. There was the charming, tilted tower of Pisa—and there was her, leaning forward, her hands perfectly aligned with the edge of the building to look as if she was the one holding it up and stopping it from falling over!

Olivia laughed in delight. What a bucket-list experience. She couldn't wait to Instagram this shot. She'd always dreamed of standing on this green lawn, in the presence of this historic and unique tower, and taking the same fun photo that Marcello had so patiently choreographed today.

Glancing at the pale, stone tower again, she smiled to see the Japanese tourists doing exactly the same thing she'd done. She hoped that their photos were just as successful as hers.

"Now, a selfie of us both," Marcello suggested.

Olivia wondered if it were wrong of her to deliberately take as long as she could to arrange the shot, while Marcello's arm wrapped around her waist and his face pressed against hers. No, she decided, when she finally pressed the button. It wasn't wrong of her and was, in fact, very clever.

To her, this entire experience felt less like a business trip and more like a sightseeing outing, with the opportunity for some light flirting. Especially since there didn't seem to be any more business to be done.

Marcello drove through the town of Pisa, stopping outside a tiny alleyway that led to a restaurant populated only by locals.

"This is one of my favorite spots," he explained. "It is so seldom I am able to enjoy lunch here, especially during the summer, and with such a wonderful companion. I have been looking forward to this occasion ever since I planned the trip."

He stared into her eyes and with a lurch of her stomach, Olivia sensed—no, knew—that he was hinting strongly at how he felt about her.

The owner greeted Marcello, before leading them to a tiny table squeezed into the corner, so cramped that their knees touched from the moment they sat down.

Olivia was thrilled to see a few of the La Leggenda wines on the wine list.

They ordered lunch, including dishes of the local *pici*—a fat, handmade pasta served with tomato and garlic sauce—and sublime portions of grilled cod.

"With this, I think a good white wine would be the perfect accompaniment," Marcello suggested. "Perhaps a vermentino. Although I am tempted to order our own wine, I think this is a great opportunity to taste a competitor's wine. What do you think?"

"That's a brilliant strategy." Olivia was fascinated by the variety on the menu. "How about we choose two different ones from wineries in the wider area? That way, we'll have two chances to snoop on the competition."

Marcello laughed. "A great idea. And we can share both."

As they passed the glasses between each other, while savoring their leisurely lunch, Olivia decided this outing was better than the best date she'd ever been on.

Was it a date?

Marcello was definitely flirting. She could see it in his eyes; the mischievous expression causing the dark blue to sparkle. She could hear it in the way he spoke to her. He touched her arms, and her hands, more often than he needed to during their conversation, and when he did, his fingers lingered on her skin, sending a definite message.

As for her? Well, she was flirting back—subtly yet enticingly, she hoped.

She didn't want to push the situation out of the slowly widening comfort zone that they seemed to have achieved. After all, Marcello was her boss and that complicated any potential relationship.

She didn't want to end up like Gabriella, stalking bad-temperedly around the winery, desperate to keep her job even though her relationship with Marcello hadn't worked out.

Any serious moves would have to come from his side, Olivia decided. Her situation was so idyllic, she didn't want to destroy her happiness by acting rashly.

With a dream job, and a romantic spark with her employer, and her own grapes hopefully sprouting at that moment, Olivia decided her life had reached an all-time high. Life simply couldn't get any better.

Of course, once she'd had that thought, her next immediate concern was that it wouldn't.

What if this moment was as good as it would get?

What if she'd reached her peak, and her life began heading inexorably downhill from here?

CHAPTER EIGHT

Olivia buried her face in her hands, peeking between her fingers to check that the date on her phone was real, and not some dreadful nightmare.

How had this happened?

The weeks had flown by. The days that had felt so endless had melted into the past. They were gone. Summer was coming to an end. What had she done with the time?

She removed her hands from her face to stare up at the farmhouse.

Even though the dust and the spiders were more or less under control, it was nowhere near ready. It didn't even feel livable. The problems with the water supply didn't seem to be an easy fix. It came and went, and worked when it felt like it, usually on the days that it rained, which was no help at all.

She felt terrified about living here on her own. Terrified! It had been years since she'd lived independently and without company. The last time she'd lived on her own, it had been in a small apartment, with people on each side of her.

How would she cope in this quiet, remote farmhouse, with only a goat and a part-time cat for company? The cat wasn't even tamed yet. She had made disappointing progress in that regard.

Olivia couldn't help wondering if her entire venture was a giant, misguided mistake.

Her biggest worry of all was that none of her seeds had sprouted. Not a single grapevine had pushed its way through the surface of the soil.

Her first foray into farming had been an unmitigated disaster.

She buried her face in her hands again. It felt safe in the darkness.

"Aaargh," she groaned.

"What's up?"

Hastily, Olivia raised her head to see that Charlotte had arrived.

"Nothing—much," she admitted.

Charlotte gave her a cynical look.

"Let me guess. You're terrified of what will happen when I leave, and you have to live in this farmhouse all alone. And you feel you haven't done enough work on it, and you will never be happy here, because occasionally there isn't any water in the taps."

Olivia felt tears prickle her eyes. Charlotte understood. Completely!

"Furthermore," Charlotte declared, "you are probably anxious that your grapes have not yet grown. I'm certain that they're just lying fallow. Perhaps they are late-season vines."

Olivia nodded gratefully. Charlotte was right about everything. Except the vines. It was all over for her grape-growing endeavor, but she wasn't going to go there.

"It's true," she sighed. "I feel like this was a bad decision. Plus, I'm filled with guilt that your vacation has turned into a farmhouse DIY project. You've basically removed every single spider! And you've helped with renovating the kitchen, and shared in the cleaning. That's no fun for you!"

Charlotte rolled her eyes. She put a comforting arm around Olivia's quivering shoulders.

"You are so, so wrong," she soothed, and as Olivia gave her a dubious glance, she hurried to explain.

"I love doing this kind of thing. And I'm never going to get the chance. My little pad is suburban bliss, and there's not a thing wrong with it! I haven't had to do more than change a light bulb, and I never will. This has been the biggest DIY adventure of my dreams. I've loved every minute."

She stared at Olivia more closely.

"Also, you'd better realize that this is an investment. I'm going to be calling you in June next year, reminding you how much labor I put into this place, and that the spare bedroom might need occupying for a couple of weeks."

Olivia laughed shakily.

"You're right. Sorry. I just had a moment. And I can't wait for June next year. The bedroom is yours, for as long as you want. The whole summer, preferably."

Charlotte nodded, seemingly content that Olivia had calmed down at last.

"Now, you'd better get to work. I will wait here for the paving stones to arrive, so we can construct your kitchen courtyard tomorrow. And I'll keep a special lookout for the cat. I know you must be worried about him, too."

After unburdening to Charlotte, Olivia felt lighter. The walk to work passed in a flash, and as she headed into the winery, she was reminded how grateful she felt to have turned her life around. Here she was, living an adventure that she'd never dreamed would become her reality. Although her family and colleagues had all known about her love for Italy and her passion for wine, none of the people who knew her would have guessed she'd take this giant leap into a different world.

Her mother was still taking herbal tranquilizers to try and come to terms with Olivia's life change. Olivia heard all about their dosage and effects during her weekly phone calls. Her mother gave her a detailed account every time, subtly hinting that the side effect of occasional diarrhea could be directly attributed to her daughter's reckless behavior.

Olivia resolved that she wasn't going to let her mother's nervousness and fear affect her own optimism. Of course there were going to be hiccups. It was inevitable. What mattered was that she didn't get demoralized by them.

She was so used to Erba trotting behind her that she barely noticed the goat peel off and join the winding, sandy track lined with wild rose bushes and lavender plants. The little animal was heading toward the dairy at the top of the hill, to hang out with her friends for the day.

As she walked into the tasting room, Marcello arrived. Olivia admired how well his dark jacket and white scarf suited him. Although the days were sunny, the mornings were starting to become chilly.

Marcello's office, in particular, was exposed to the cool breeze coming off the hillside.

He smiled when he saw her, giving her a frisson of happiness.

Since the purchase of the Pisa winery had gotten underway, Marcello had been doubly busy. Olivia was grateful for the day out they'd enjoyed, because she hadn't been able to spend any quality time with him since then. If he wasn't at the new winery, he was at the bank, or visiting wine stores and restaurants, or in handover sessions with Franco.

She treasured the memory of their wonderful, flirtatious day out, but couldn't stop herself from wondering if it would ever happen again.

"I have some good news for you," he told her.

Olivia had learned to read Marcello's tone of voice since she'd been working as head sommelier. The moment he started to speak, she intuited that this was work-related news.

In other words, Marcello wasn't about to tell her that he'd booked a week's holiday in the South of France and ask if she wanted to come along.

Even so, when he told her the news, Olivia was captivated by his words.

"We have a celebrity guest visiting us for a few days, which will present an incredible opportunity for you," Marcello said.

He sounded beside himself with expectation.

"Who?" Olivia asked.

"Alexander Schwarz. You may have heard of him."

Olivia nodded. She had heard the name, and her eyes widened as she remembered where.

"Did he write *Become a Sommelier*? That book you loaned me? It was excellent. Of all the books I've read, that one stood out."

Marcello nodded, smiling.

"He is a prolific author, who is an award-winning winemaker, as well as a world-renowned expert and mentor. We are very privileged to welcome him here."

"Oh, how wonderful," Olivia breathed.

Would she be able to learn from this icon's expertise? she wondered. Before she could even voice the question, Marcello continued.

"He will spend a morning with you, teaching you about flavors and nuances and the intricacies of tasting. I will attend, too. I cannot wait," Marcello said.

Olivia felt her heart speed up. What an opportunity! To be coached by one of the winemaking greats. She could learn so much, and ask all the questions she needed to. Perhaps this icon might even have some pointers on the making and blending of wine.

"I can't wait, either. Thank you." She smiled.

Olivia took her position behind the tasting counter, feeling elated as she stared across the spacious room, at the oak barrels and wooden shelves whose presence she loved, as it helped her feel connected to the process of winemaking. It was so kind of Marcello to have set aside this expert's time to help her. And how fortunate she was, to be working at a caliber of winery that was frequented by such experts.

She'd better brush up on her tasting, Olivia told herself. She hoped she could impress Alexander Schwarz by how much she had learned so far.

Olivia wondered if she should ask Nadia, the head vintner, for a tutorial on blending wines. That might be helpful to her before her session with the legendary mentor.

At that moment, Nadia rushed in.

The short, dark-haired, energetic woman looked stressed and disheveled, but that was par for the course. Nadia had the most tempestuous personality of the three siblings. Olivia was about to call out to her and ask if she could book some time with her.

Then she saw the winemaker's face and realized, with a chill, that something was very wrong.

She had never seen Nadia look so distraught.

"Marcello!" Nadia shouted. "Where is Marcello? Quick, there has been a disaster."

Chapter Nine

A lerted by Nadia's words and frantic tone, Marcello sprinted out of his office.

"What is it?" he called.

The torrent of Italian that Nadia shouted in reply was too fast and complicated for Olivia to pick up on. She didn't understand what was happening at all.

To her dismay, Marcello now looked as devastated as Nadia.

Olivia twisted her fingers together anxiously, hoping that one of them would stop speaking Italian long enough to update her on the exact details of this catastrophe.

"Call Antonio," Marcello told Nadia. "Quick, phone him, tell him to drop everything and come to my office."

Then he turned to Olivia.

"Will you join us, please?"

Olivia nodded, tense with expectation. She glanced at the wooden clock on the side wall, noticing that its gold hands were just touching ten a.m.

She couldn't leave the tasting room unattended after opening. Perhaps Paolo would be able to stand in for a while.

As Nadia stabbed at her phone's screen before embarking on a one-sided and shouted conversation with Antonio, Olivia ran to the restaurant.

There was Paolo, polishing glasses, his neatly combed dark head bent diligently over the shelves.

"Can you help me for a half hour?" she asked, and saw his face light up.

"Of course," he replied immediately. "I would love to."

Then an angry finger jabbed into Olivia's shoulder blade.

"What is this about?" Gabriella screeched.

Olivia hadn't even seen the restaurant manager when she'd rushed in, and had assumed that she hadn't yet arrived for the day. Of course, she had materialized, as if summoned by Olivia's voice.

Gabriella's tortoiseshell hair was elegantly pinned back, and her perfectly made-up face looked thunderous. The French-manicured finger that she'd used to poke Olivia so rudely in the back was still pointed at her accusingly.

"You will not poach my waiters," she insisted. "Paolo works for me. Not for you! And he is very busy now, polishing."

"It's an emergency," Olivia explained politely.

"I do not care!" Gabriella steamrollered over her, but Olivia stood her ground.

"I have been called into an urgent meeting with Marcello," she said. Although her voice was calm, she couldn't resist emphasizing the word *Marcello*, as his word was law, even though she knew the mention of his name was likely to trigger Gabriella.

It did. Her lips tightened and her face darkened, and she stared at Olivia with a gaze full of poison barbs. But there was nothing she could do.

"I need him back in half an hour," Gabriella spat.

Olivia smiled understandingly.

"He'll be back with you as soon as possible," she soothed, feeling inwardly gleeful that she'd managed to discombobulate the restaurant manager so early in the morning. She'd never forgotten how Gabriella had viciously insulted her in front of guests soon after she'd started working at the winery.

Every small victory formed part of the payback, Olivia decided.

As Paolo practically capered out of the restaurant to the tasting desk, Olivia rushed down the corridor to Marcello's office.

Petty triumphs aside, there was a situation afoot, and she felt increasingly nervous as she stepped inside. Marcello looked as serious as she'd ever seen him, and Nadia was in tears, groping for the box of Kleenex on the polished wooden desk as she sobbed.

Quickly, Olivia grabbed a handful and passed them to Nadia, before sitting next to her.

A moment later, Antonio hustled in, still in his dusty work boots, with a flask of coffee in one hand and his faded baseball cap in the other.

"*Salve, salve*," he greeted everyone. "What has happened?"

Marcello glanced anxiously at Nadia, but the winemaker was still in tears. She waved for him to continue.

"An entire batch of our sangiovese wine has been affected by TCA taint," Marcello explained solemnly. Olivia's eyes widened as she heard Antonio's indrawn breath of horror.

"What's that?" Olivia asked. She hated sounding ignorant, but she'd never heard of the problem. It seemed that winemaking was full of unexpected risks. The more she learned, the more she realized she didn't know. To think that she'd blithely assumed that it was an easy activity where nothing could go wrong. It seemed that the process was fraught with calamity.

"TCA is a chemical compound that sometimes occurs in winemaking facilities. Commonly, it is found in corks—that is why people refer to a wine as being 'corked.' Although it is harmless, it gives the wine a musty aroma and spoils the flavor completely," Marcello explained solemnly. "It can affect not only corks, but any surface that comes into contact with wine, usually wood. This time, it has tainted wooden barrels."

"Ten of the special five-hundred-liter barrels," Nadia sobbed. "All the late-season sangiovese harvest has been affected. Every drop."

Marcello paled visibly. He pressed his lips together, scraping his fingers distractedly through his hair. Olivia could see how shaken he was.

"Those were the barrels we bought last year?" Antonio asked, and Nadia nodded.

"I thought we had checked and cleaned them," she sobbed. "But not well enough."

Marcello took a deep breath and Olivia could see he was struggling to speak, and probably think, calmly in the face of this panic.

"These are the risks of our profession," he said after a pause. "Sometimes it cannot be prevented. What wines will be affected?"

Nadia counted on her fingers. "Our late-season sangiovese, obviously. Our late-season Miracolo blend. Our special cabernet-merlot blend, which also contains a little sangiovese—it is vital to the blend's character and cannot be made without it. In total, about thirty thousand bottles cannot be made."

Olivia's hand flew to her mouth. Now she understood the scale of the disaster. This was a catastrophe which would have a major impact on the winery's end-of-season sales. Many of La Leggenda's most profitable bestsellers would be unable to go to market.

Her heart thudded into her shoes as she remembered that Marcello had just made the huge investment of acquiring Franco's vineyard.

This could not have happened at a worse time. The winery's commitments were overextended, and there was no spare cash to be had.

Antonio bowed his head, massaging his temples with his fingertips.

"We needed those sales," Marcello said, as if to himself, but Olivia could hear the desperation in his voice.

"We still have two hundred cases of the mid-season Miracolo in the warehouse," Antonio said.

"We can raise the price on that," Marcello said. "Scarcity brings value. But it will not be enough to save us."

Save us? Olivia swallowed hard. This was even more critical than she had thought.

"I can increase the cabernet sauvignon and merlot totals," Nadia sniffed. "We can bottle the wine we had kept aside for the blends."

"That, too, will help." Marcello's voice was heavy. "But we need more."

There was a silence in the room.

"We will have to hold an auction," he said eventually.

"No!" Nadia and Antonio shouted the word in unison.

An auction? What for? Why had this suggestion been met with such an instant veto? Olivia stared in confusion from one of the Vescovi siblings to the other. Clearly they knew what he meant, and were appalled by the idea.

What could it be? she wondered.

Marcello raised his hands.

"Please, do not let emotion prevail here."

"We will be selling off our heritage! Our history!" Nadia pleaded.

Turning to Olivia, Marcello explained.

"We are talking about the historic bottle of wine, from the very earliest vintage produced on my great-grandfather's original farm, long before La Leggenda came into being. For decades, we have safely kept it in the vault. It represents an irreplaceable part of our past and will be extremely valuable to a collector."

"No, we cannot!" Nadia implored, but Marcello shook his head.

"I know this bottle is a part of our history, but we have to think of our future, not only our past. Painful as it is, this will have to be done. With the purchase of the second farm, an auction at this time will be good for the winery and will create valuable media attention. It will result in a favorable outcome," he emphasized firmly. "We can hold it while Alexander is visiting. Having this legendary VIP present will be a draw card. We can display and sell his books."

Although his words were encouraging, Olivia could sense the agony he felt at having to part with his family heritage.

"What type of wine is this special bottle?" Olivia asked in a small voice.

"It is a magnificent Brunello di Montalcino red wine. Two years after it was launched, a new wine awards started in Italy and this vintage was its first-ever gold-medal winner."

Nadia buried her face in her hands. Feeling that she needed support, Olivia rubbed her back gently. She felt terrible to see the other woman's genuine devastation. It brought home to her how much more than a business this winery was. It was their life and their soul.

Marcello sat straighter and spoke with authority.

"I will confirm the date now and start the process," he said, and his tone brooked no further argument.

After work, Olivia headed straight back to the farm. She had a date there with Charlotte, a pile of gravel, and approximately twenty granite tiles.

This would be their final DIY project—creating a courtyard herb garden similar to the one at the villa.

Excited as she was to be embarking on this project, Olivia felt heavy-hearted about the Vescovi family's predicament, and not even Erba's antics as she gamboled alongside her could improve her mood. Marcello, Nadia, and Antonio had become a part of her extended family, and she keenly felt their pain.

It also brought home to her what a risky endeavor wine farming was. She hadn't realized she was embarking on a venture with so much potential for problems and even failure.

Ignorance was bliss, Olivia decided sadly.

When she reached her farm, and saw the pile of granite tiles waiting near the front door, her spirits lifted. At least this would be achievable, after just a few hours of hard work. She couldn't wait to have a courtyard garden. Olivia imagined it with a table and chairs in the corner, sheltered by a wooden fence lined with vegetable and herb beds. It would be a peaceful and beautiful place, and the herbs would allow her to experiment with cooking many of the Italian dishes she'd grown to love.

"I brought us some Prosecco sparkling wine," Charlotte said. "And some picnic food. Ciabatta, Parma ham, mozzarella, olives, and artichokes. I know you don't have furniture yet, but I thought we could sit on a blanket, which I also packed."

Olivia felt her heart soar. Somehow, this stressful day had tipped back into balance and she felt as if her usual happy state was prevailing once again.

"What a star you are!" she said. "Now, we'd better start laying out these paving stones and bringing the gravel here in the wheelbarrow."

Olivia set the stones into place—carefully, but not too precisely. She wanted her garden to look natural, with a hint of Italian chaos to it, as if it were an organic part of the landscape rather than being superimposed onto it.

It also meant that by eyeballing the alignment of the stones, instead of painstakingly measuring them out, the work was able to proceed a lot faster.

The stones looked like a playground checkerboard with wide gaps between them once they were in place, and Olivia's arms ached from lifting, moving and lowering them. Charlotte, who had taken the other side of each granite slab, was shaking her fingers out and rubbing her biceps.

"I didn't realize today was arm day on the Tuscan fitness calendar," she complained good-naturedly.

Olivia had opted for gravel between the tiles, rather than a ground cover plant, because the area was small and cozy, and she didn't want plant growth to overwhelm the tiles. As they carted barrow loads of gravel around the side of the house, poured them into place, and then raked and swept them into the gaps between the tiles, she was confident it had been the right choice. It would be easy to maintain, and the silvery pea gravel looked beautiful in between the gray-gold tiles.

Olivia imagined herself treading barefoot over the smooth stone in the morning sun, heading out to pick spinach and chives from the surrounding beds for her morning frittata.

She felt elated by what they had achieved.

The sun was setting as they cracked open the Prosecco and collapsed gratefully down on the blanket to enjoy their first-ever picnic on the farm.

As Olivia clinked glasses with her best friend, cross-legged on the tiles they had so carefully placed, she knew that she could not be happier. Of course there would be hurdles. She would be mad to think otherwise! But what a start she had made, with the house gradually returning to order, and the herb garden she'd always longed for now a reality.

It was almost dark by the time they packed the remainders of the picnic away. There wasn't much food left over at all. The hard manual labor had given them both a good appetite for their meal.

As they closed up and headed back to the villa in the late evening gloom, Olivia couldn't help casting yet another anxious glance at the nearest beds where she'd planted her vine seeds. There hadn't been as much as a tiny shoot emerging since then. If anxious glances could germinate these seeds, Olivia was sure they would have grown six feet tall by now. That was roughly the two-hundredth time she'd stared in their direction with a worried frown.

She must have done something very wrong, but what?

She wished she could ask Marcello, but it didn't feel ethical to do so, and especially not now, when the family was so stressed after the disaster of the wine spoilage.

Olivia decided that she simply couldn't bring herself to burden the Vescovi family with her selfish issues.

There was one other person she could get advice from. In fact, he'd freely offered it.

Olivia sighed.

Did it have to turn out this way? Seriously?

She rolled her eyes in frustration.

Much as she didn't ever want to see the annoying Danilo again, it looked as if she would have to swallow her pride and ask for his help, if she wanted to have any hope of a viable harvest next year.

CHAPTER TEN

O livia had forgotten what she'd done with Danilo's card, and as she frantically searched her purse and car, she started to wonder if she'd thrown it away in annoyance over his interfering ways.

Eventually, to her shamed relief, the card turned up in the farm-house's bedroom. Thinking back, she remembered she had put it in the pocket of her scruffy sweatpants. When she'd taken them off, the card must have fluttered out of sight and lodged in a loose skirting board under the dust-lined windowsill.

Danilo was a carpenter and woodworker by trade, according to his business card.

In this village, where everything was all about wood and warmth and natural surfaces, Olivia was sure he must be very busy. She wasn't sure how he had acquired his wine knowledge, though. Perhaps he lived on a farm.

As she dialed his number, she had a sudden suspicion that Danilo was expecting her call. Probably, he'd been waiting for it ever since she'd thrown him off her property.

"*Salve, turista* farm lady?" he answered.

He sounded guarded yet smug. Despite her best intentions, Olivia felt another surge of annoyance. There was something about him that rubbed her the wrong way. Why did the one person who scored a ten out of ten on her irritation scale have to be the one offering free advice?

"Hello, Danilo. My name's Olivia," she said coolly, deciding to opt for an icily professional approach.

"Olivia!" He sounded thrilled to be on first-name terms. Well, so was she. Anything was better than *turista* farm lady.

She decided to get straight to the point.

"My seeds haven't grown," she admitted.

"No, of course not," he agreed.

Olivia sighed.

"I would appreciate it if you could give me some advice," she said.

"Gladly!" He sounded happy—thrilled, in fact. "When can I meet you?"

"As soon as possible. This evening, if that will suit you?" she asked. She needed this problem resolved as soon as she could. Her vineyard's lack of productivity was weighing on her mind.

"I will be there at six p.m.," he promised.

Oliva disconnected, feeling a mixture of excitement, trepidation, and annoyance that she would, at last, be able to troubleshoot her grape-growing problems, even though she would also be forced to confront her own stubborn non-expertise.

At La Leggenda, Olivia found the place was abuzz. Nadia and Antonio had clearly overcome their initial resistance to the idea of holding an auction. Now, everyone was enthusiastically involved, although they all seemed to be taking a different approach.

When Olivia arrived, they were in the midst of a huge argument—or rather, a discussion, as she knew they would all insist if she accused them of arguing.

The three siblings were standing in the middle of the spacious tasting room. Nadia held a notepad and pen, Marcello was brandishing a tape measure, while Antonio was pacing around the room.

"So if we have the auction podium here, then guests can be seated around the outside of the room, and there will be more space," Marcello was saying in a tone of forced reasonableness.

"But if we have the podium by the tasting counter, guests can look at the backdrop of wood and barrels. It will be exciting for them! They will spend more money!" Nadia insisted, waving her arms.

Antonio clutched at his head, shouting in exasperation. "No, no, no! We should not have the auction here at all. Why not hold it in the wine-making room?"

Both Marcello and Nadia yelled at him in unison.

"There is no space in the winemaking room! You think only ten guests will attend?"

"I have already had one tainted batch. I am not having rich obnoxious people wandering around and contaminating another!"

As they saw Olivia standing there, silence fell.

Antonio scuffed the ground with his shoe, as if he were embarrassed to have been caught arguing, while Nadia developed a sudden interest in the tasting room's vaulted ceiling.

"What do you think, Olivia?" Marcello asked. "Where should we hold the auction?"

"Um," Olivia said. She felt she was treading on thin ice here. There was no way she could please everybody, and a very high likelihood that she wouldn't manage to placate anybody.

"Well, I don't know anything about auctions," she said, grateful for her recent experience with Danilo that had at least empowered her to own up to ignorance. "How does it work? How many people will attend? Are there snacks?"

"Snacks, good point," Nadia said. "We will need food as well as wine."

"Food is essential," Antonio agreed.

"Absolutely," Marcello confirmed. "In terms of numbers, we expect about a hundred guests to attend, including buyers, VIP invitees, dealers, and the media."

Grateful that she'd managed to say something helpful and that hadn't gotten everyone embroiled in an even worse argument, Olivia sneaked through the side door and busied herself behind the tasting counter, organizing bottles and tasting sheets for the day ahead.

"If there are food tables, they will have to be set up along the side of the room," Marcello said. "In which case, you are right, Nadia. The auction must take place at the counter, with the backdrop of barrels. That will work best. Let's plan the layout and we can then decide what other items we can include in the sale."

Olivia was sure everyone would have strong opinions on the other items, too. She hoped they would be able to get the auction inventory agreed upon before the day's guests started to arrive for their tasting.

As Olivia watched the three Vescovis measuring the room and writing down numbers of chairs and tables needed, she felt a flicker of excitement. Even though it was soul-destroying for the family to have to part with a precious, historical artifact, the event would highlight La Leggenda's presence on the winemaking map.

Attending a high-end wine auction would be a brand new experience for her.

The last guests of the day left the tasting room just after five p.m., and it was five-thirty by the time Olivia had finished tidying the counter and preparing for the following morning.

She realized that she wouldn't have time to go back to the villa, or else she would be late for her meeting with Danilo. She would have to head straight to her farm in her work clothes. Hopefully, Danilo's advice wouldn't involve too much digging, because her pretty silver sandals wouldn't stand up to the job.

Erba was waiting for her at the winery's service gate, and they headed onto the quiet back roads together.

As soon as Erba realized which way Olivia was heading, her pace quickened. The goat loved the farm, and was at her happiest when heading up the steep hill and onto the sandy access road.

"You're a real mountain goat," Olivia praised her, as Erba leaped up the rocky sidewalk to steal a mouthful of lavender from a fragrant bush.

She felt a stab of nerves as she saw Danilo's truck already parked by the gate. She hoped this meeting would go well, and that her vines would be salvageable.

"*Buon giorno*," he called, climbing out when he saw her.

To her surprise, she saw his hairstyle had changed. Now it was parted on the other side, and longer, and the top of his head was lighter, with warm chestnut streaks in the dark hair. Clearly, Danilo spent a lot of time at his hairdresser.

Olivia noticed that on the back of the truck was an exquisite wooden cabinet. He must have handcrafted this item, and be on his way to deliver it.

"*Buon giorno*," she replied. She took a deep breath. Better to get the apology over with. "I'm sorry I was rude to you when we last met. I wanted to try it my way."

White teeth flashed in Danilo's tanned face as he grinned. "Surely we all do! But you also want your vines to grow, no?"

Olivia sighed.

"I have no idea why they haven't even sprouted. I can't believe I did it so wrong." She stared appealingly at Danilo. "Okay, what was it? Too deep, too shallow, not enough fertilizer? Should I have added compost?"

"None of the above," he explained, still smiling widely.

"What, then?"

"Come with me, and I will show you," he explained.

Danilo took a leather satchel from his truck. He walked through the wrought iron gate, toward the closest plantation, with Olivia following anxiously. Her silver sandals scrunched over the sandy soil as she reached her non-yielding vine plantation.

Danilo looked down at the bed.

"What have you planted here?" he asked.

"These were my sangiovese grapes." Olivia spread her arms in frustration. "The most common local varietal, and they haven't grown!"

She'd said "were," she realized. Was it wrong of her to have already given up on these seeds?

Danilo nodded.

He rummaged in his satchel and produced a plastic packet of seeds.

"Grape seeds do not germinate easily," he explained. "They need first to think that it is winter. So, either you can wait, and these seeds that are now in the ground will go through winter and will start to sprout in the spring, or else you can plant seeds that have been through the process already, as these have. That way you will have small plants before winter comes, and might even have a harvest next summer."

Olivia blinked.

Who would have thought you needed to do such a thing? She'd never dreamed of this simple, basic, but not necessarily logical step.

"Sometimes you can be lucky," Danilo explained. "Some seeds will germinate and grow without this step. But usually, the majority will only grow if you do it first."

"How did you take them through the process?" she asked curiously.

"You ensure the seeds are good and healthy. Then you wet them and put them in a plastic bag in the fridge. You can add some damp cotton wool or moss. I use cotton wool. You need to leave them there for at least three months. Voila, you have just made the seed think it has been through winter," Danilo explained.

"Oh, my goodness," Olivia said.

"Compost will help their growth," he said. "I will message you a list of what you can buy. But since your seeds have not had winter yet, they may only start growing next summer."

Olivia nodded sadly.

If she'd only known. Now there would be a lengthy wait before she saw any results. It took a lot of patience to farm grapes, that was for sure.

But Danilo was holding out the packet to her.

"Here, plant these sangiovese seeds," he said. "They are ready, and have been in the fridge. Put them into the ground in between the ones you have already planted. Then you can move the new seedlings when they sprout."

Olivia was taken aback by his generosity.

"I must pay you for them," she insisted, but Danilo shook his perfectly gelled head.

"Not necessary," he said. "They are left over, and in any case, it is late in the season now. It is risky. If there is an early frost, it could be a disaster."

Olivia frowned at him, worried, as he continued. "I have a small farm and have planted my new vines already. These were left over. I think they were meant to be a gift, for a beginner who does not like to listen."

He winked at her and Olivia felt herself bristle instantly.

What did he mean, she didn't like to listen? Of course she did. She was excellent at listening. She just hadn't been ready to do it at that particular time.

"So let's see what you have done with the place."

Danilo strode toward the farmhouse and Olivia stomped after him, angry all over again. She hadn't invited him in. Why hadn't he waited for an invitation before pushing his way into her still-ramshackle and unfurnished farmhouse? What rudeness!

Pressing her lips together, she did her best to swallow down her annoyance. This sharply groomed man had just, very generously, given her seeds so that she might have a harvest next year. Now here she was, already wanting to throw him off the farm again.

Olivia reminded herself to stop being so short-tempered. Patience was a virtue for a winemaker, and she needed to start applying it to other areas of her life, too.

"Hello, you have a cat?" Danilo stopped in his tracks, almost causing Olivia to cannon into him. "I love cats!"

There was the black-and-white cat, sitting on the porch, blinking nervously as they approached.

"He, or she, is still very wild," Olivia explained. "I've been leaving food out nightly. I'm busy taming him, or her."

"Psspsspss," Danilo said, dropping down to his hands and knees and leopard crawling toward the cat as he cooed endearments. "What a lovely kitty. Are you so clever? How cute you are. You look like you are about to rob a bank with that mask over your eyes."

To Olivia's disbelief, when Danilo held out his hand, the cat stood its ground.

It flinched away as Danilo stroked it with the very tip of his fingers, and then arched its back, pushing its head against his hand as he caressed its back.

Olivia couldn't help feeling put out by this disloyal behavior. She'd spent months patiently feeding the stray. Months! And it hadn't let her get close. Now, here it was, rubbing its whiskers against Danilo's fingers as if Olivia had been the one with the problem, not it!

Danilo got to his feet.

"I think your kitty will be tamed very soon," he said. "Soon, it will be as tame as the orange goat on your windowsill."

He strode inside.

"Lovely place," he said approvingly. "It feels bigger inside than it looks. The bedrooms are upstairs, yes?"

He headed through to the kitchen, and Olivia followed, feeling anxious and defensive. Seeing this place through a stranger's eyes was reminding her how much there still was to do. She had to buy all the furniture. And deep clean the place! Charlotte was leaving next week, and the villa's rental expired the day after she left.

Now, Danilo was looking out of the grimy kitchen window at the herb garden she and Charlotte had arranged so proudly the previous day.

Looking at the artfully chaotic tiles surrounded by gravel, and remembering the precision of the wooden cabinet in his truck, Olivia steeled herself for more stinging criticism.

But to her surprise, Danilo smiled.

"Beautiful," he said approvingly. "The natural look works well there. Organic, in harmony with its surroundings. You did it yourself? I love it."

"Yes, it's my first project," Olivia said, feeling mollified by his praise. Then she shrieked.

An arm's length away from her, on the kitchen wall, was another large spider.

"What?" Danilo whirled around in alarm, as Olivia backed away.

"There—there—" she stammered, pointing a shaking finger at the threatening arachnid.

"You want me to remove it?" Danilo sounded unsure.

"Please don't kill it!" Olivia entreated. "I feel so sorry for them but I'm so scared. I just want it to be somewhere else!"

"I won't kill it." Carefully, Danilo removed the checkered shirt he wore, revealing a tanned and well-defined torso. "I will just try to shoo it out."

He stepped forward and breathed in deeply, flexing his muscles as if preparing himself for a challenging task.

Olivia watched, frozen to the spot in horror. What if his maneuver didn't work, and he ended up chasing the spider upstairs? She'd never be able to sleep in her farmhouse again.

Gently, Danilo flicked the shirt at the spider.

To Olivia's relief, it scuttled across the wall and climbed out the open kitchen window.

She let out a breath of relief, realizing she was shaking all over.

"That was so scary. Thank you."

"No problem."

Danilo shook out his shirt very thoroughly before putting it back on. He spent quite some time on the task.

Then he hurried outside.

It seemed as if he'd had enough of exploring her farmhouse, or perhaps he'd remembered he needed to make his furniture delivery urgently.

At any rate, he was leaving far more suddenly than she'd expected.

"Thank you," she called.

"I'll see you later," he shouted back.

He climbed into his truck and sped away, leaving Olivia confused.

Had it been her turn to offend *him* somehow? Had she said, or done, something that he'd taken the wrong way? Had he been angry that he'd gotten his shirt dusty while dealing with the spider?

She replayed the encounter in her head but couldn't think of any reasonable explanation.

Sighing, she decided to leave it be.

For now, she had a packet of viable seeds, and a single chance at getting seedlings out of the ground this year.

Whether they grew would be up to fate, frost, and timing.

CHAPTER ELEVEN

It was the day before the auction, and the winery was transformed.

The parking lot had been spruced up and swept clear of stray leaves, and the hallway had become a temporary reception area, with a polished oak desk flanked by potted plants and beautiful arrangements of flowers.

Olivia breathed in their scent as she weaved past the desk and into the tasting room. This, too, had been painstakingly prepared. Although the chairs would only be brought in on the day of the auction, the large wooden tables for catering already lined the right-hand wall, interspersed by more plants and flowers. Everything looked clean and shiny, scrubbed and polished to within an inch of its life. The gold "La Leggenda" lettering on the back wall of the tasting room gleamed so brightly it was blinding.

Tomorrow the tasting room would be closed in the afternoon, to prepare for the auction which would commence at 6 p.m.

Olivia was distributing the tasting sheets along the counter when she realized an early customer had arrived.

An urbane, gray-haired man in a perfectly cut black jacket was waiting at the far end of the counter.

Even though opening time was still half an hour hence, Olivia would never turn away anyone ready and eager for the bucket-list La Leggenda tasting experience. She was only too glad to help this early arrival.

"Hello and welcome," she said with a smile, picking up a tasting sheet as she hastened over to him. "*Buon giorno*. Would you like to see our wine menu?"

To her surprise, the man returned her warm smile.

"You must be Olivia," he said. "How nice to meet you."

She stared at him, surprised. She didn't know this man. His beaky nose, bushy eyebrows, and craggy bone structure were distinctive and memorable. Who could he be?

"That's me," she admitted. "May I ask your name?"

"I am Alexander Schwarz. I am fortunate to be visiting this wonderful winery for a few days. Your tasting room is my first port of call."

Olivia gasped. This was the renowned mentor whose arrival everyone had been anticipating.

His English was excellent, although she picked up a slight accent. Not Italian, something else. German? Austrian? And he was far nicer than she'd assumed a world-renowned wine expert would be. He wasn't snobbish at all, although she couldn't help being intimidated in the presence of such an expert.

Her nerves came rushing back. She hoped he wouldn't think she was useless.

At that moment, Marcello hurried into the tasting room with a charming smile.

"Ah, Alexander. I see you have already found our lovely head sommelier."

Olivia remembered, with a frisson of expectation, that Marcello had said he would also participate in the tasting. Was this why he had arrived? Or would he cancel the commitment and say he was too busy?

Her heart leaped as Marcello reached across the counter, clasped her hand in his warm grasp, and said to Alexander, "It is time for us to have our private lesson with the maestro. What wines do you have for us to learn about?"

"I have prepared five different wines for this tasting journey," Alexander replied.

"We should hold it in the restaurant," Marcello said, and Olivia's heart sped up again, but this time for different reasons.

Gabriella would explode with jealousy to see her participating in this session with Marcello. Not to mention that Paolo would need to look after the tasting room, making Gabriella even more livid.

Well, there was nothing she could do about it.

Even so, she averted her eyes from the reception desk when she walked into the restaurant. She didn't want to be pierced by Gabriella's dagger-like stare.

"Let us sit here," Alexander suggested, indicating a table in the corner.

Quickly, Olivia took the seat with her back to the room.

She noticed Marcello's lips twitch, and wondered if he had picked up on the furious vibes that were practically burning a hole in her spine. At any rate, she thought he'd worked out why she'd chosen that seat.

"We have three main senses when it comes to wine tasting," Alexander began. "Each one is important. Firstly, sight, which gives us a good idea of the age and type of wine. Secondly, smell—a critical sense. Thirdly, taste, which also brings a second opportunity to smell. It takes all these to form an opinion on the wine, and to learn to sense the flavors which we then describe as other relatable experiences—as fruits, grasses—even though we do not eat grass, spices, tobacco, and so the list goes on."

Olivia nodded, enraptured.

"When you smell wine, you are smelling hundreds of different nuances that are carried to you as the alcohol evaporates. Each one has a different effect, and each can affect the flavor of the wine when you taste it." Alexander smiled. "To complicate things, no two tasters will ever have an identical experience, as everybody's nose translates the bouquet differently. One person's nose can smell peaches, while another identifies nectarines, but both will agree, when they taste, that they pick up stone fruit."

Olivia caught her breath, as Marcello's foot found hers under the table.

His foot pressed against hers. There was no way this was accidental. He was deliberately flirting with her, in an innocent way that was sending a very clear message.

Shivers of anticipation prickled her spine.

As Olivia smelled the first wine Alexander poured, an exquisite cold-climate sauvignon blanc from France, she wondered if she'd ever be able to drink sauvignon blanc again without flashing back to this unforgettable moment.

❧ ❧ ❧

Olivia walked home that evening feeling as if she were floating on a cloud. She felt far more knowledgeable about identifying flavors, as well as the age of the wine, the quality, and so much more. She knew she had progressed a few steps in her education. Still near the bottom of the ladder, but high enough to start enjoying the view.

Of course, having Marcello's foot, and then his knee, pressed against hers had added a huge thrill to the experience.

She felt short of breath when she wondered if, one day, they might end up dating. Perhaps he would relax his rules about romance with employees, over time.

Olivia couldn't wait to walk down to the restaurant with Charlotte, order a bottle of wine she'd never tried before, and wow her friend with her newfound knowledge on top notes and nuances and aromas.

"Let's go," Charlotte agreed, as soon as Olivia had bounced through the front door and proposed the outing.

"I'll lock up, if you go around to the kitchen garden and lure Erba with carrots," Olivia said. The goat loved the restaurant, too, but was lacking in etiquette and had a bad habit of eating directly from people's salad bowls. She inevitably caused havoc and had to be escorted home in shame.

The carrots would keep her occupied while they left.

As they walked briskly down the road, Olivia enthralled Charlotte with an account of her day's adventures.

But as they reached the restaurant, they slowed, staring in surprise at the ranks of shiny SUVs and sports cars that were parked so poorly, they were just about blocking the road.

"What's going on?" Olivia wondered.

As they headed down the paved path, the owner rushed to meet them. Usually full of cheerful smiles, the pleasant, middle-aged woman looked harassed this evening.

"Ciao, my lovely friends, ciao. I am so sorry. We are fully booked, with many people waiting at the bar."

"What's the occasion?" Olivia asked, perplexed. This wasn't usually an especially busy night.

The owner waved her arms.

"We have so many people in town for the auction tomorrow night. And it seems most of them have come here." Her voice dropped. "These are foreigners, so different from our local people. So rude! Do we have imported salami? Imported from where? We use the finest *salame* Milano from Milan!" She rolled her eyes.

Olivia nodded sympathetically. "It's no problem," she reassured the owner, who then rushed back to her guests.

Olivia could hear the background buzz of conversation and picked up a few phrases floating toward her on the breeze.

"I enlarged my cellar because I acquired a few more highly sought-after bottles. It cost two hundred thousand dollars, as they had to blast through solid rock. Is this the pizza that's supposedly so famous? It doesn't look like much compared to the Michelin-starred one we had in Milan."

Olivia recognized the American drawl and craned her neck to see the speaker—a heavily built, dark-haired man wearing gold-framed eye-glasses. She sighed. Her fellow countrymen should know better than to make a spectacle of themselves, being loud and obnoxious in public.

He wasn't the only one. She heard a French accent from another direction.

"Yes, we are attending the Grand Prix this year. We have VIP seats in the front row, of course, and special entry to the pits. Waiter! This wine is undrinkable. I believe it is corked. Do you not know how to manage your cellar? Bring me a different bottle."

Who was this lean, balding man? Olivia wondered. Was he in the wine business or was it just his hobby?

And her head turned sharply as she heard, from elsewhere, "Well, Harold and I have been thinking of selling our London home, but it's so central. Being permanently based in our Marbella beachfront man-sion would be an inconvenience for skiing trips, as well as international travel."

The blond woman who spoke in a plummy British accent was wear-ing a strapless top that showed off her deeply tanned, well-toned arms. One of them was slung around her husband's shoulder. He was puffing on a cigar, the smoke pluming toward the No Smoking sign on the wall above their table.

Olivia had heard enough, and from her expression, so had Charlotte.

"Let's go," she suggested.

As she turned away, Olivia couldn't help feeling nervous that tomorrow, these unpleasant people would converge on the winery. This auction was going to be a more challenging experience than she had thought.

"There are two bottles of wine in the fridge," Charlotte said. "That lovely vermentino we bought from the market, and the sauvignon blanc that we picked up from the wine shop. You can demonstrate your tasting skills with them."

They turned away and walked back down the path between the quiet vegetable beds, relieved that the hiss of the irrigation was the only sound.

"There's pasta in the cupboard," Olivia remembered.

"And those fresh clams I bought at the market today. We've been saying for ages we should make pasta vongole. We have all the ingredients, including parsley and garlic and chilis, and we could put some crushed tomatoes in, too. This is our chance," Charlotte agreed. "It's the ideal dish to use up leftover wine."

"What's leftover wine?" Olivia joked, and they dissolved into giggles.

"Before we start our dinner, let's do the tasting," Charlotte decided.

She took the two bottles from the fridge and placed two glasses in front of Olivia.

"I think you should do a blind tasting," Charlotte decided. "Let me get a scarf. Don't read the labels while I'm gone!"

She ran through to the bedroom, and Olivia stared at the floor, determined not to cast a stray glance at either of the bottles, in case she accidentally picked up a detail that could help her.

"Here you go!" Charlotte passed her a black and silver scarf. "Wrap this around your eyes."

Olivia tied the scarf so tightly that she couldn't see as much as a sliver of light.

"Pass me the first one," she said.

She heard the sound of a bottle opening, and wine pouring. Then a glass touched her outstretched fingers.

"There you go!"

Buoyed by the confidence from her earlier session, Olivia breathed in the wine's bouquet, analyzing it carefully before sipping.

"This is a lovely sauvignon blanc," she stated with authority. "I'm picking up strong herbaceous, grassy flavors as well as hints of citrus."

"Very good," Charlotte praised her. "That's pretty much what the label says. Would you like a sip of water before the next one?"

"Yes, please." Olivia had learned that bread was the most effective palate clearer, but she was sure that with only two wines to taste, water would do the job.

She sipped from the proffered water glass, and then listened to the next wine being poured.

Olivia frowned as she breathed in the aroma. She sipped, feeling her confidence evaporate. This wasn't what she had expected from a vermentino, which had a characteristic bitter finish—or occasionally, as Alexander had explained, fresh almonds could be tasted.

What was wrong with her palate? Why couldn't she pick up the basic flavors and nuances that characterized this delicious and distinctive wine varietal?

"Um," she said.

Perhaps she was never going to make it as a sommelier.

Why did this vermentino taste exactly like a sauvignon blanc?

The answer came to Olivia in a flash, together with the realization that she hadn't heard the second bottle open.

"Charlotte!" she exclaimed. "You're trying to trick me!"

She tore the blindfold away to see her friend collapsing in giggles at the other side of the table, with the unopened vermentino in her hand.

"I couldn't resist it!" she spluttered, as Olivia started laughing too. Charlotte's mirth was contagious. "You passed with flying colors. They should give you a raise at La Leggenda. Master sommelier, I say!"

"I declare the blind tasting an unqualified success, thanks purely to the quick thinking of the taster." Olivia grinned. "Let's start dinner."

She filled two glasses with the sauvignon blanc, while Charlotte assembled the ingredients.

Delicious aromas permeated the air as she quickly cooked the garlic, chilis and tomato in olive oil, before adding the well-rinsed clams and a liberal splash of the wine.

Olivia couldn't imagine a nicer setting than this home-cooked meal, in the beautiful villa, with the company of her friend. It was the ideal dinner before the stress of the following day.

She hoped nothing would go wrong tomorrow that might ruin the success of the carefully planned auction.

Even so, she couldn't help having a shiver of premonition that, with so many entitled individuals, all used to getting exactly what they wanted, something would.

CHAPTER TWELVE

The following afternoon, La Leggenda was abuzz with activity. Everyone was feverishly preparing for the event.

The chairs were delivered late, and Marcello and Antonio were rushing to place the plush, upholstered seats in organized, even rows. Not too close together—the wealthy liked their space. The tasting room was filled with clangs and clatters and shouts of advice as the brothers worked together. Olivia had realized soon after starting her job that nothing was done quietly when two or more members of an Italian family were involved.

Olivia was hurrying back and forth, taking the food platters from the restaurant to the tables in the tasting room. It wasn't where she would have chosen to work, but someone had to help out with the food, and she was the only one available.

The elegant trays of canapes looked mouthwatering. Gabriella had opted to create an international spread of food, rather than traditional Italian. Olivia felt this was a good choice, given that guests from every corner of the world were arriving.

She wished for some friendly conversation as she waited for the colorful trays of sushi, with the gleaming pink salmon, deep-red tuna, and bright green avocado. But Gabriella worked in stony silence, barely even glancing at Olivia as she checked each display.

Olivia returned for another tray of delicacies—king prawn skewers, cooked in honey and garlic, and mini lobster burgers, with generous chunks of meat sandwiched between golden-brown, seeded rolls.

"Wait," Gabriella told her. "You can take the tray with the caviar crackers, also."

Even though Olivia had no love for Gabriella, she had to admit these were a catering triumph. Perfectly browned crackers were topped with a flake of gold leaf, a sprig of arugula, and a sumptuous pile of black caviar.

Olivia felt relieved that the catering would surely meet the guests' high expectations.

She placed the trays onto the table and hurried back to where Gabriella was finalizing another masterpiece—slices of toasted ciabatta topped with rare Wagyu beef, truffle mayonnaise, and shaved pecorino cheese.

Using tweezers, Gabriella was adding a sprig of mustard cress to each one.

"We are running late," she said, sounding frustrated. "I can hear the first guests have arrived."

Olivia listened and picked up the sound of voices—hearty greetings in loud, confident tones. The scraping of chairs had stopped. Hopefully the seats were in place and the tasting room arranged to perfection.

"Marcello will look after them. He is serving champagne," she reassured Gabriella, but realized too late that the mention of Marcello's name would only put her in a fouler mood.

She glared at Olivia, shoving the trays of roasted cinnamon pear bruschetta in her direction, before picking up the final two trays of deviled quail eggs.

"I will need some uninterrupted time to arrange the desserts," she snapped.

Olivia interpreted this as "Get out of my kitchen."

As they were placing the last trays on the table, decorated with colorful arrangements of roses and gardenia, and with the display of Alexander's books at the far end, the first guests began eagerly making their way to the spread of food.

"So, Vernon, I'm here to buy the antique wine barrel as a feature for my new, enlarged cellar. I hope this event starts on time, as I'm flying to London straight afterward. My private jet is waiting. What are you bidding on?"

The speaker was the heavyset American man she'd overheard the previous night. Olivia remembered, with a pang of annoyance, that he'd bragged about the ridiculous renovations to his wine cellar, while insulting the pizza.

Olivia wouldn't hear a bad word about that pizza. It was fabulous, and if anyone thought otherwise, the problem lay with them, and not with those perfectly browned, crispy-based, tomato-rich delights, oozing with high-quality cheese.

"Well, Patrick, I'm bidding on the big one. I have a very exciting launch ahead."

Olivia whirled around, feeling her heart speed up.

She recognized this voice. She knew who the speaker was. The name—Vernon—had rung a bell but she'd thought nothing of it.

She found herself staring, horrified, at Vernon Carrington, the ex-CEO of Valley Wines.

The suave, slim man, who had always reminded her of a snake, was looking directly back at her. Olivia couldn't breathe. Hastily, she lowered her head. They'd sat in a few meetings together. Without a doubt, he'd recognize her if he looked at her for long enough.

However, she was out of context here, working in an Italian winery, with her hair pinned back. He wouldn't expect to see her, and she might be able to stay below his radar if she were cautious.

Vernon Carrington was here?

Why?

She wouldn't have thought anyone whose evil mind had come up with the idea of the Valley Wines battery-acid slop would know red from white, never mind chardonnay from sauvignon blanc.

If he were here to bid for the priceless collector's item, there had to be a nefarious motive. What could it be?

Olivia had to know. If she kept her back to him, she could listen in on what he was saying to Patrick, who was clearly a business acquaintance.

"I'm going to start a new venture, similar to my last project."

Olivia drew in a horrified breath. The world was going to be subjected to more Valley Wines horror?

"But I've learned my lessons from last time," Vernon continued in the oily voice that was so familiar to her.

Olivia felt her stomach uncurl a little. If he'd learned, that must be a good thing, right?

"For a start," Vernon explained, "I'm separating myself from Kansas Foods and operating independently. And I'm moving my manufacturing plant out of the States. Having the FDA do that pesky raid put a real spoke in my wheel. Power-hungry, interfering government lackeys! I'm sure they planted that rat. There are many other locations which are much more manufacturer-friendly and where the authorities know to turn a blind eye, for the right price."

His voice dropped and Olivia strained to hear his final words. What was he saying? He was starting up all over again, doing the same thing, only this time, making sure nobody would find out how badly made the wine was.

She sidled closer, desperate to know what he was planning.

"Anyway," Vernon continued more loudly, "I am positioning this new wine as a higher-end product, for better profitability. Buying this bottle tonight is going to be part of my brand story, all about heritage and quality. It will imply a rich, noble lineage."

Imply? Olivia wanted to choke with anger. He was going to use this prestigious bottle as part of the fake brand story?

She would never have allowed that if she'd been in charge of the account. Never!

But then, Olivia realized, Vernon might not tell the truth when briefing his new agency. After all, he hadn't told her the truth.

Then, from behind her, she heard Gabriella's angry voice.

"Olivia, what are you doing there? We need you back in the kitchen. We are ready to bring out the chocolate profiteroles and mini berry cheesecakes."

Thanks to Gabriella's sharp-voiced reprimand, she found herself staring in Vernon's direction again.

This time, the combination of her face and name rang a bell and to her horror, she saw recognition in his eyes.

"Olivia Glass?" he asked in surprise. "What a coincidence. I was just talking about Valley Wines. I didn't expect to see you here. Are you running campaigns for any of the buyers?"

Panic surged inside Olivia as she saw Gabriella sidle closer, the same way she had done. Clearly, the restaurant manager had picked up that there might be a juicy scandal emerging.

"Lovely to see you, too," Olivia replied in tones of fake enthusiasm. "I'm actually working for the winery." Keen to deflect the conversation, she continued. "There are some amazing wines at the tasting table. I see you have finished your champagne. Can I introduce you to them?"

But Vernon would not be deflected.

Speaking clearly, he explained to Patrick.

"Olivia used to work for the advertising agency we used. She was responsible for bringing Valley Wines to market, and did a great job. The brand achieved extraordinary success in a short time." He gave her a faux-sympathetic smile. "I suppose you were fired after the FDA targeted my factory so unfairly. I personally think a rival was out to get me. Everyone cuts corners, don't they? It's the name of the game."

Olivia felt rooted to the spot with horror. This was spiraling totally out of control. Worst of all, Gabriella was looking more gleeful than she'd ever seen her.

"I have to go," Olivia said in a small voice. "Enjoy the auction. Good luck with your bidding."

This was it. Her secret had been revealed at the worst possible time. It would mean the end of her job here; she was certain. Worse still, Marcello would be devastated that Olivia hadn't been honest about her diabolical role in promoting the worst wine in the world.

The thought of his disappointment felt like a knife in her heart.

She turned away and trailed back to the kitchen, conscious of Gabriella's high heels clicking purposefully behind her.

"Well!" Gabriella said, as soon as they were in the privacy of the kitchen.

Olivia didn't know what she could say in response. She waited for Gabriella to drag Olivia back to the tasting room and announce the disastrous news for all to hear.

But instead, Gabriella just gave her a sly, knowing smile.

With a sinking feeling, Olivia realized that Gabriella was enjoying having something on her, to keep a secret until the time was right.

Knowing that Gabriella was waiting for the most damaging moment to drop the bombshell made Olivia feel even more afraid of what might happen next.

CHAPTER THIRTEEN

Olivia picked up the final trays of petit-fours, glossily iced in pastel shades, and the brightly colored macarons. Carrying them to the food tables, she placed them beside the mini chocolate gateaux.

Tempting as the array of desserts looked, Olivia felt sick inside. Thanks to Vernon recognizing her at the worst possible time, her well-coiffed rival knew her shameful secret.

There was nothing Olivia could do to stop her from revealing it.

She guessed that Gabriella would bide her time. After all, waiting would give her more time to gloat. But maybe some fortuitous intervention might occur.

For a moment, Olivia entertained the vain hope that Gabriella would simply forget about what she had heard.

Fat chance, she told herself, knowing the restaurant manager had etched every word of that conversation into her memory.

Olivia decided she urgently needed wine.

She headed to the magnificent display set out along the counter of the tasting room. The bottles were displayed in sections. Each bottle had a gold-framed description of the wine, and several filled glasses, alongside.

Nadia was manning the wine display, rushing from section to section to put out fresh glasses and keep them filled. Paolo had the job of removing the empty glasses. He was working almost as fast.

Olivia chose a glass of the famous Miracolo blend. That was what she needed now. A miracle.

Quickly, she stepped aside as the blond woman she'd seen at the restaurant yesterday made a beeline for the display. She was draped in a shimmering gown, and heavily made up. Behind her followed her husband, resplendent in a tuxedo.

Shouldering Olivia out of the way, she picked up two glasses of the Miracolo.

"Try this, Harold," she ordered her husband. "It's supposedly very famous." She sipped and grimaced. "It's very dry. Do you think they have any lemonade here?" She waved at Nadia, shouting, "*Scusi, senorita. Limonado?*"

Olivia felt a rush of sympathy as she saw Nadia wordlessly hand the woman a small can of lemonade. She could see that the winemaker had to use every ounce of restraint she possessed to keep quiet.

"Hopefully this whole boring event won't take too long and we can go home with the special wine," the blonde continued. "From the pictures of it, it'll work perfectly in our dining room. I'm thinking we display it in a frame, next to our Jenny Saville painting? What a talking point it will be for our guests." She topped off her wineglass to the brim with lemonade. "We'll definitely be one up on Brian and Michelle, with that antique whiskey bottle they bought last summer."

Deciding she could listen to no more of this conversation, Olivia moved away.

Then, to her alarm, she heard Vernon's oily voice cutting through the background chatter. He was standing at the next-door station where the cabernet sauvignon was on display.

"I pick up top notes of citronella and jasmine," he announced to Patrick.

He was a wine expert? How could that be?

Olivia's mind reeled at the idea that anyone who truly loved wine could deliberately bring cheap, toxic rubbish to market. He'd done it with Valley Wines and planned to do it again, even worse—and here he was, offering an educated opinion?

What kind of insanity was that?

She heard a polite throat-clearing.

"I don't think so, *signor*," a respectful voice corrected Vernon.

Alexander, with his gray hair impeccably styled, and wearing an elegant black dinner jacket, had joined Vernon at the tasting station.

The expert had clearly been unable to stop himself from speaking out.

"The main flavors in this vintage are distinctive dark fruits," Alexander explained, politely but firmly. "The strong notes of plum and black cherry are almost overpowering, but very finely balanced with vanilla and just a hint of black pepper. It is an exceptionally made wine."

Vernon stared at him in astonishment.

Olivia could see he was incensed by the criticism.

His voice sounded even more oily and silky than usual as he replied, but it had a carrying power that caused a few nearby heads to turn.

"As the CEO of a major corporation, I'm accustomed to having my word respected, old man," he retorted. "I guess you fancy yourself as an expert. I'd like to remind you that wine tasting is all about opinion."

"It's not so," Alexander replied, and now there was an edge to his voice. "A palate has to be trained to assess predominant flavors, but when trained, these are unmistakable."

Vernon laughed.

"Opinion, old man. Mine is as valid as yours. In fact, more so, because I'm here to bid on the big bottle and it's clear you're not in the same league." He laughed.

Olivia clapped her hand over her mouth. She'd never realized that Vernon was so easily insulted, or such a vicious adversary.

Alexander had clearly had enough.

He turned away, but Vernon grabbed his shoulder and yanked him back.

"Taste this, old man." He flicked the glass and sent a stream of wine splashing onto Alexander's chin. "I will tell you what it tastes of. It tastes of shut the hell up and mind your business."

He released Alexander's jacket and stalked away. Patrick roared with laughter as he followed.

Olivia saw a flash of real fury in Alexander's eyes.

Nadia, who had also watched this drama play out, abandoned her post at the tasting counter and rushed over.

"Olivia, please take my place," she begged, clearly distressed that their VIP guest had borne the brunt of such abuse. "Maestro, come with me. I see there is a stain on your shirt. We shall rinse it immediately so it does not set. Antonio has many dress shirts, he collects them but never wears them. It is his fetish! Can we loan you one to your liking?"

Protectively, she ushered Alexander out of the room.

As she passed Olivia, Nadia muttered furiously under her breath.

"*Bastardo!*" Olivia heard her hiss, as she rushed to take her place behind the counter.

The balding French man she'd overheard complaining about the restaurant wine headed over to the tasting counter. Olivia watched him nervously as he selected a glass from the chardonnay display.

However, the Frenchman seemed distracted, conversing in low tones with another man that Olivia guessed, from the way he kept saying, "*Oui, monsieur,*" was one of his staff.

"It is essential that we win this bottle tonight," the French man explained.

"*Oui, monsieur,*" the other man agreed, nodding vigorously.

"It will be a massive coup for our antique dealership," the man explained. "This auction was poorly planned, at short notice. Typical of the Italians, but it gives us an opportunity. If the bidding is low, as I believe it will be, we can resell this for double its price. I already have private collectors interested and one firm offer on the table."

"*Oui, monsieur.*"

"You remember our strategy? You begin our war, remaining in the bidding until I nod to you. Then, from there, I will come in. As a brand new bidder starting high, I predict that the individuals currently in the war will become intimidated and drop out."

"*Oui, monsieur.*"

They moved away, leaving Olivia wondering what the outcome of this auction would be. There seemed to be many people lusting after this bottle, for many different reasons.

At that moment, the bang of a gavel made her jump.

The buzz of conversation around the room fell silent.

Marcello had taken his place at the podium.

"Does everyone have their bidder's cards? Please raise your hand if you need any assistance."

As a couple of hands lifted, Olivia saw the guests glance at each other with expressions of dislike and distrust.

An uneasy certainty filled Olivia. This auction was going to be exactly as the Frenchman had described it—a war.

Chapter Fourteen

"Are we ready to start?" Marcello opened the printed catalog and stared down at it.

Although his deep voice was perfectly neutral, and his appearance immaculate, Olivia could see that he looked far more somber than usual. There was no sparkle at all in his deep-blue eyes. This was a painfully necessary event, which would bring the family much-needed financial gain, but significant emotional loss.

She glanced at the side door. Alexander had returned, wearing a fresh shirt. Behind him stood Nadia, wringing her hands, clearly unable to control her dismay at what was about to unfold.

While some of La Leggenda's memorabilia was up for sale, the auction also included several collector's items from neighboring wine farms—La Leggenda had opened the auction to others in a spirit of cooperation.

"Item one: an antique oak wine barrel, purchased as a collector's item by the founder of La Leggenda."

The bidding started briskly, with local farmers leading the war until the price grew too high. Then Vernon's friend Patrick entered the fray with a large bid. To Olivia's disappointment, he won the barrel. Looking pleased with himself, he completed the shipping form before checking the time and hurrying out.

"Item two: a late-nineteenth-century brass corkscrew, in perfect condition."

As the auction continued, Olivia was relieved to see Marcello's natural character and showmanship prevail. He warmed to his job, including interesting details on the items, as well as flashes of his trademark sense of humor.

In turn, the audience became more animated, clapping and cheering when the hammer fell, and Olivia began to realize what an entertaining occasion this was. The local wineries might be parting with historical items, but they were going to new owners who would value and appreciate them. She was thrilled to see the joy in the eyes of the woman who won the bid on a magnificent oil painting of a wine farmer at work. Olivia had no doubt this spectacular item would be proudly displayed at her home.

Then a hush fell.

It was time for item number twenty-one, the drawcard of the auction; the rare bottle of Brunello di Montalcino.

All the joy had leached out of Marcello's voice as he announced the final item.

In contrast, Olivia could see the potential bidders were alert, their eyes gleaming, their cards held at the ready.

Nadia brought the bottle into the winery, holding it with loving care, and as she walked to the podium to display it, all eyes followed her. Olivia found she couldn't tear her gaze away from this noble, ancient wine with its dark glass and yellowed label.

"What am I bid?" Marcello announced tonelessly.

"Ten thousand dollars," someone called from the back of the room.

The British blonde casually raised her card.

"Fifteen," she announced.

"Twenty," the "Yes, Monsieur" employee offered, with an anxious glance at his boss.

With an expression of disgust, Vernon raised his card.

"Stop playing in the little leagues, folks. I'll take it at fifty."

Fifty thousand dollars?

Olivia cringed at the thought that he would win the bottle. It would not be used for any good, but to create a false story for a vastly inferior, trash wine. She was sure that was not what the original winemaker had ever wanted! She stared around anxiously.

"Sixty," the blonde offered, giving Vernon a scathing glance.

Olivia was filled with relief.

"Seventy," the Frenchman's employee shouted.

"Eighty!" Olivia couldn't see the speaker, but he was at the back of the room.

"Ninety," another stranger called from the opposite side.

Olivia couldn't believe what these people were willing to pay. She'd never dreamed the bidding would go so high. Marcello had told her that they were hoping for eighty thousand, but would be happy with anything over fifty.

Hopefully, the money would ease the pain of having to part with this bottle.

"One hundred," the blonde continued, after a pause to confer with her husband. Clearly, having a collector's item to trump Brian and Michelle's whiskey bottle at dinner parties was worth any price.

There was a pause.

"One hundred thousand dollars. Going once." Marcello gazed around the room.

"One hundred and twenty. The poor people can go home now. Leave the bidding to those of us with means."

Vernon's smooth voice upped the bidding again. He was smiling, gloating, looking delighted with himself as he spoke the scathing words. Clearly, he believed victory, in the form of the precious bottle, was already in his grasp.

Olivia felt worried that other bidders were becoming intimidated by his insults. Someone else needed to win this. They must!

"Going once. Going twice," Marcello said.

Olivia twisted her fingers together, desperate for someone else to bid.

"One hundred and forty," the Frenchman's employee offered, and she nearly fell over with relief. She noticed the nod pass between him and his boss. The Frenchman clearly thought it was his time to step in and take over the war.

"Two hundred," the bidder from the back of the room shouted, and Olivia gaped in amazement. Two hundred thousand dollars?

"Two hundred and ten," the Frenchman announced confidently.

Now the blonde and her husband seemed to be arguing.

"Two-twenty," she yelled, before they continued their furiously whispered debate.

"Two hundred and thirty!" The voice from the back of the room sounded desperate.

"Two hundred and forty," the Frenchman said.

Marcello glanced at the blonde. Her husband shook his head firmly.

"Two hundred and forty thousand dollars," Marcello said. "Going once. Going twice."

Vernon cleared his throat, sending ice-water shivers down Olivia's spine.

"Three hundred," he said, calmly, turning so that all the onlookers could see his confident smirk. "The rest of you can pack up and go home now. I want this bottle, and whatever you say, I will outbid you. I'm in it to win it, and I'm not scared, like the rest of you are."

A shocked hush followed.

Nadia drew in a hiss of breath. She looked furious.

Alexander's face was like thunder.

"Going once. Going twice. And sold, for three hundred thousand dollars, to the bidder on my right."

Marcello's voice was flat with despair.

The hammer fell with a bang.

Arriving at the winery the next day, Olivia could sense the atmosphere as soon as she walked in. Anger and gloom seemed to fill the spacious tasting room.

Marcello and Antonio were removing the last of the chairs, while Nadia tidied the counter, wiping the stains and spills from the previous night. Nobody had been motivated to do any cleaning up after the bombshell of Vernon's winning bid. A sense of anticlimax had prevailed, and most of the guests had left soon afterward.

"Morning," she said softly.

Marcello put down the stack of chairs he was carrying and walked over to her.

"Good morning. Thank you for your hard work last night. It was a great success. Financially, at least."

He slid his arm around her waist and kissed her on her cheeks.

That greeting made Olivia feel a little better about the dreadful outcome. She hoped it had cheered Marcello slightly, too.

"Do we have the payment?" Nadia asked suspiciously, as if she didn't trust Vernon to stand by his word.

Marcello nodded. "The money was wired to us straight after the auction, before the bottle was released."

"What about the paperwork? He was supposed to sign the handover form that he received it in good order."

Marcello and Antonio exchanged glances, and Marcello shook his head reluctantly.

"I forgot all about that. I am sorry."

Nadia tossed her cleaning cloth into the bucket.

"Well, someone needs to go and get it signed this morning. Not me. I refuse to speak to that monster again."

She marched out.

Antonio and Marcello exchanged another glance. Olivia could tell neither of them wanted to go, but neither wanted to say no, either.

"I'll take it," she said. "Is he staying nearby?"

Marcello sighed in relief.

"Thank you, Olivia. Yes, he is residing at a villa in the area. Would you mind? My car is outside. You can use it. Here are the keys."

He gave them to her, together with the necessary paperwork for Vernon to sign.

Olivia felt relieved to be able to leave La Leggenda and head out on this errand. It was depressing to see all the Vescovis in such a bad mood. She hoped that by the time she returned, the atmosphere would have lightened.

She wasn't thrilled by the idea of seeing Vernon again. She had forgotten how evil and arrogant he was. Having won the bottle, she was sure his big-headedness would be out of control. She'd probably have to listen to an hour of his boasting before he was ready to sign the forms.

Better she endured it, than one of the brothers, Olivia thought, adjusting the SUV's seat before heading out. Vernon's instincts for identifying weakness in his adversaries were finely tuned. If he suspected that the sale of this great wine had caused them pain, he'd spend two hours rubbing it in before agreeing to sign.

Vernon had rented a villa in the expensive side of town. The villa she and Charlotte were occupying, though spacious and sumptuously furnished, was reasonably priced. Just after the village of Collina, a narrow tar road climbed into the hills. This was where the larger, luxury residences were located, standing shoulder to spacious shoulder in their private settings, the houses set far back from the cypress-lined road.

Olivia slowed down as she approached the ornate, marble gateposts of Villa Diamante, where Vernon was residing.

Uneasily, she wondered how much longer he would stay in town. Charlotte was leaving soon. Would they be able to go for a final meal at their local restaurant without bumping into him?

She drove up the long, winding, immaculately paved driveway until the splendid, three-story villa came into view.

Olivia's first, uncharitable thought was that it looked like an iced cake. The pale yellow walls and bright-white detail weren't authentically Italian at all, and seemed overdone. She guessed that the rich guests who booked this villa didn't want authentic, and preferred overdone.

She climbed out of the SUV and walked up the shallow stone stairs, heading between the marble pillars into the shade of the massive porch. Ahead was the gold-painted front door.

Olivia knocked.

There was no answer.

Was Vernon out?

She checked the papers in the folder she was carrying with her and saw there was a phone number provided.

Steeling herself to hear his oily voice in her ear, she called the number.

It rang and rang.

As it did, Olivia noticed something strange.

From inside the house, she could hear a faint trilling.

If his phone was there, so was he. She guessed this villa would have a huge yard, probably equipped with an Olympic sized swimming pool and tennis court. No doubt, he was outside on a sun-lounger, perhaps in a Speedo—Olivia winced at the image this conjured up—with a cocktail by his side as he celebrated his victory.

She tried the door.

To her relief, it opened.

"Hello," she called as she stepped inside, in case he was just out of the shower and prowling around without any clothes on, which conjured up an even worse image in her mind.

"Hello, Vernon? It's Olivia from the winery. I'm here with your papers."

She walked through the ornate hallway, breathing in the cool air, fragrant with the undertone of lemon-scented polish.

"Vernon?" she called.

What would be the best way to get to the swimming pool? she wondered. She headed through a white-painted archway at random and found herself in an enormous dining room, with a long, white table that could probably seat fourteen people. Colorful modern art covered the walls, and the room was studded with faux-Greek statues, with various limbs and appendages missing.

"Um, well!" Olivia muttered, feeling she had to say something to herself about this strange room. How the rich lived!

At the far end of the room was another archway. Hopefully, this would lead into a lounge or kitchen, and from there, she could head outside.

The archway led down a short corridor, and at its end, Olivia saw an enormous lounge on the left, and a fully equipped chef's kitchen on the right.

The kitchen was so full of bright silver and polished chrome, the reflections hurt her eyes. There was a massive silver fridge, a stove the size of a car with chrome buttons, ranks of cupboards with chrome finishes, and silver ceiling lamps.

The floor was bright, polished white, apart from the shoe on it, lying on the far side of the center island, where a wineglass and bottle were standing.

Olivia stared at the shoe for a surprised moment, before her brain caught up with her eyes and she realized the shoe was attached to a leg.

Swallowing hard, Olivia took a step forward and peered around the chrome-topped island.

The leg was attached to a body.

Olivia gasped, clutching the chrome surface as she looked down at the appalling sight.

The body was Vernon Carrington's.

He was still wearing the sharp dinner jacket and black pants he'd had on the previous day.

He was lying face-down, with his arms out-flung.

His skin was pale, and his body was immobile. She couldn't see so much as a flutter of movement from him.

Olivia let out a tiny whimper as she gaped, wide-eyed, at the prone body.

Without a doubt, Vernon Carrington was dead.

CHAPTER FIFTEEN

Olivia backed away until she was standing by the kitchen door. She didn't want to look at the disturbing sight, but at the same time, couldn't tear her gaze away.

"Be calm," Olivia advised herself, her breathy squeak signaling that calmness was not in any way being achieved.

She felt responsible! She wished she hadn't been the person to find this deceased man, alone in his massive villa, but she had been. Even though her spine was crawling, she knew she had to try to think clearly.

What would the best course of action be, given this unforeseen emergency?

Quickly, Olivia took out her phone and dialed Marcello. Calling him seemed like the most sensible solution at this moment.

"*Salve*, Olivia. Is everything all right?" he answered. She picked up anxiety in his tone. He'd obviously feared that getting the papers signed wouldn't be plain sailing.

"No. Not really," she said, hyperventilating, unable to take her eyes off the shoe that was all she could see from her relatively safe vantage point in the doorway. "Vernon is dead!"

"What?" Marcello's exclamation blasted down the phone. "Olivia, this is shocking. Do you know what happened?"

"I've no idea. He's lying in the kitchen. I guess he might have had a heart attack," she said doubtfully.

Until now, she'd been pretty certain Vernon Carrington didn't have a heart at all.

"I will call the ambulance, and the police," Marcello said. "And I will be on my way there now."

"Thank you," Olivia said.

She felt vastly relieved that Marcello would be arriving in a few minutes. The whole scenario felt spooky. Only now did she pick up on the resounding silence that filled the villa. The only breathing, the only tiny sounds, were hers.

In another minute, she heard the screaming of a sports car engine. Marcello had arrived in Nadia's Fiat Spider.

Olivia rushed to the front door to meet him.

Marcello enfolded her in a tight, warm hug.

"What a terrible catastrophe," he said. "I cannot believe such a thing has happened. Are you all right?"

"I'm okay," Olivia insisted bravely, even though she was shaking a lot more than she would have liked.

"The police are on their way. Where did you find him?" Marcello asked.

Quickly, Olivia led him through the faux-Greek dining room, hesitating when she reached the kitchen door.

"He's in there," she told Marcello, expecting that he would go and check Vernon's pulse.

Marcello took a few steps forward and then stopped.

He returned to the door.

"Let us wait here," he said. "Just in case there has been any foul play, it will be better for the first responders to find the scene undisturbed."

That jolted Olivia's heart to an even faster speed.

Foul play?

It hadn't crossed her mind that this could be the case. Now that Marcello mentioned it, she had to acknowledge that it could be true. After all, Vernon Carrington was probably in his mid-forties. That was young to die from natural causes. And he had many enemies, Olivia guessed, based on how he treated people. During the auction alone, his obnoxious behavior had lengthened the list of people who despised him.

And, of course, he'd made the winning bid on a rare and sought-after bottle, which others had desired for their own reasons.

"Oh, dear," she said.

Marcello nodded, his face serious.

A few minutes later, Olivia found herself standing in the spacious hallway and staring into the stern, dark eyes of a woman she'd hoped never to see again.

The sharp-voiced Detective Caputi headed up the local investigation team.

Just a couple of months ago, Olivia had been a suspect when the sommelier at La Leggenda had been murdered. In fact, Detective Caputi had nearly arrested her. Luckily, Olivia had done her own urgent investigation. In her attempt to clear her name, she had identified who the real culprit was.

Now, here she was, in the detective's cross-hairs once more.

She felt deeply uneasy about the situation.

To be fair, Detective Caputi didn't look thrilled to see her, either.

"You?" she said, raising her perfectly penciled eyebrows.

Her gray, bobbed hair was as neat and shiny as Olivia remembered it. The detective hadn't changed at all in the time since they'd last met. Clearly, her inherent dislike of Olivia was just as strong as it had been. Which, Olivia realized with a pang of irritation, was extremely unfair since she'd solved the previous case. Practically single-handedly, she had done Detective Caputi's job for her.

And now, the detective was regarding her as if she were a guilty criminal who would only need the right prodding to spill out a confession.

"Yes," Olivia said coldly. "Me."

"You found the body of the deceased?"

"I did."

"Why were you here?"

"I came to bring him papers to sign."

What was it about Caputi? Olivia wondered. She could make the most innocent person start feeling guilty, even while telling a perfectly truthful story. Perhaps it was that hawk-like stare. Since she'd last seen her, Olivia had forgotten how disconcerting it was.

"And you just walked in?" The detective sounded incredulous.

Olivia felt like rolling her eyes. The quiet Tuscan countryside was a safe part of Italy! Well, apart from the occasional murder. But she and Charlotte didn't lock up during the day, either. Only at night, if they remembered. Quite often, they would go to bed without turning the front door key. She was certain most people in this area did the same, and Detective Caputi must surely know that.

"I knocked first," she retorted. "As you can imagine, there was no reply."

She saw the detective's eyes narrow and reminded herself hastily not to get defensive. Caputi didn't take well to sarcasm, even if it slipped out inadvertently.

"Describe to me why you arrived at Vernon Carrington's rented villa," the detective snapped.

"Well, I volunteered to take the paperwork to him. From the auction last night, where he bid on a bottle of wine. Are you sure he couldn't have died of natural causes? He had quite a stressful job, and the bidding was competitive."

"The auction? What auction?"

Olivia suppressed a sigh. The gaps in this story were going to need a lot of filling in. Clearly, the detective thought so too.

"Walk me through your movements from the time you entered this house, until the time you found the deceased," she said impatiently. "We will conduct proper interviews later this afternoon, at the winery, once we have finished up at the villa."

The detective's tone gave Olivia an uneasy feeling in her stomach. She sensed that Caputi was sure there had been foul play. She guessed that the detective's instincts would be accurate. After all, she was experienced in her field, and knew what to look out for.

An otherwise healthy, though obnoxious, forty-something-year-old man lying dead in his sumptuous rented villa ticked all her boxes for "suspicious death."

Seeing she had been the first person on the scene, Olivia knew that the detective already suspected her of being involved and might even believe that she was involved in the untoward events that had caused his death.

Proving her innocence was going to be challenging, especially given her previous association with Vernon Carrington.

She would have to be careful about what she said to Detective Caputi. Remembering her previous experience with the bad-tempered investigator, Olivia was sure she would try every trick in the book to trap her into making an inadvertent confession.

Half an hour later, after walking the detective every step of her journey through the grand villa, Olivia stepped outside, feeling simultaneously relieved and nervous.

She was glad to see Marcello was waiting for her, leaning against the SUV's door and messaging on his phone, his dark hair gleaming in the morning sun.

"Are you okay to drive?" he asked. "I can come back later for the other car, if you want to ride with me."

"Thanks," Olivia said. A ride home with Marcello felt like exactly the moral support she needed. "I'll take you up on that."

She climbed into the SUV's passenger seat and they headed out of the villa's imposing gateway, the opera music providing a soothing accompaniment. By the time they reached the winery, Olivia's nerves felt less frazzled. It was a relief to have some distance between her and that villa.

"We have closed the tasting room for the day," Marcello said, slowing the car as he turned down La Leggenda's long, winding driveway. "It seemed wisest. However I think you should stay here so that we are all available when the police arrive. It will be best to get the interviews over as soon as possible."

Olivia nodded. Detective Caputi's timeframe would be uncertain. It would be better to get the questioning out of the way, so that things could return to normal. She hoped that the police might already have solved the case by the time they arrived. Perhaps the interviews would be no more than a formality.

"I'll do some studying," she said, remembering the bookcase in Marcello's office. There were a few English books on winemaking and flavors that she had yet to read.

"I will ask Gabriella to prepare us a light lunch," Marcello said. "The restaurant is remaining open as usual today."

He parked under the sprawling olive tree near the winery's front door.

The tasting room door was closed. It always stood open and seeing the heavy wooden door barring her way gave her another twinge of unease. The sooner all of this was over, the better.

Probably, it had been natural causes, she told herself, pushing the big door open and heading down the corridor to Marcello's office. Quickly, she selected a couple of books to keep her occupied for the day.

As she returned to the tasting room, Marcello was briefing Gabriella on lunch. The restaurateur, wearing a crimson jacket, was listening attentively but glanced in Olivia's direction as soon as she saw her.

"Nothing fancy," Marcello explained. "Ciabatta and cheese, maybe an Italian salad."

"How about a light pasta to start?" Gabriella suggested. "Salmon ravioli with a dill butter sauce?"

"Perfect," Marcello said. "Enough for four."

"Shall I set the table in the corner of the restaurant?" Gabriella cast another sidelong glance at Olivia. "The one overlooking the valley?"

She emphasized the last word, giving Olivia such a fright that she dropped her books with a thud.

In the craziness of the morning, she'd all but forgotten that Gabriella had learned her terrible secret, and knew all about her association with Valley Wines.

Now, the restaurant manager was taunting her with the knowledge, knowing full well that Olivia could do nothing to stop her.

Olivia picked up the books, conscious that her face was burning and that Marcello was glancing between her and Gabriella in a puzzled way, as if aware that some message had passed between them, but not understanding what it was.

Yet.

Olivia hurried through to the restaurant, hoping she could hide away in the corner and bury herself in her book.

She felt as if she was already firmly on the back foot, and she hadn't even gotten to her interview with Detective Caputi.

Chapter Sixteen

After lunch, Olivia managed to immerse herself in the book. She read with fascination about buying and storing wine, as well as what went into creating a good wine list. Broadening her wine knowledge was exciting, because she knew she'd need to understand every facet of the business, as a winemaker-to-be.

Suddenly, she felt the atmosphere darken.

She glanced up. The ornate hands of the clock on the restaurant wall were pointing to four p.m.

The tasting room door banged open and she heard the officious tramp of feet. Detective Caputi and her team had arrived.

Nadia got up from the table and ran to Marcello's office to call him.

Within five minutes, the three Vescovi siblings and Olivia were seated at the table, with Detective Caputi at the head.

She looked even more stern than usual. Olivia glanced nervously at the thick folder she carried in her hand.

"I have unfortunate news," she announced, and Olivia felt a surge of nerves, wishing she could grab Marcello's hand under the table. Instead, she twisted her fingers together, waiting to hear what this sharp-eyed detective had uncovered.

"Signor Vernon Carrington did not die from natural causes," she announced. "The first toxicology tests have been done. The initial results show, without a doubt, that the victim was poisoned."

Olivia's eyes widened. Poisoned? How?

Briefly, she met Nadia's eyes. The winemaker looked appalled, quickly dropping her gaze to the wooden table.

"What poison? How could this have happened?" Marcello asked in a low voice.

"Ethylene glycol was detected in his system," the detective said.

The three Vescovis were clearly shocked by this. Marcello clutched his forehead, Antonio gasped sharply, and Nadia shook her head as if refusing to believe this was possible.

"Either commercial antifreeze, or a chemically similar substance," the detective continued inexorably. "The laboratory is unclear as yet."

Antifreeze? Olivia hadn't even known you could kill someone with antifreeze. It was an ordinary household product!

"Could he have ingested it accidentally?" she asked. "I mean, does it occur naturally in anything?"

She wondered if there were something she was missing. Perhaps it was like arsenic, which she knew was present in certain fruit seeds, although not in quantities that could kill people.

"A question I am also interested in."

Now Caputi was looking sharply at Marcello. Although Olivia felt relieved to be out of the beam of her laser-like stare, she was nervous that she was now targeting Marcello. Caputi always seemed to have some sinister motive up her sleeve, and as soon as she started to speak, Olivia realized that her instincts were correct.

"You have used antifreeze in the winery?" she asked him, in a voice that could have cut glass.

Olivia goggled at her. What was the detective implying? She didn't think anything in the thick-walled winemaking room would get frozen up, and certainly not at this time of year. She was hinting at something, but what? Carelessness? Improperly washed vats? Dropping engine parts into the barrels?

Olivia had no idea what nuances she was missing, and wondered if one of the Vescovis knew.

Marcello cleared his throat, and Olivia realized he had picked up on the direction of the detective's questioning.

"In the 1980s, there was an incident where certain European wineries, including some in our country, deliberately added diethylene glycol to their product," he said. "I believe this was done to try and bolster the sweetness of the end product, and make the late harvest wines seem of a higher quality and more full-bodied."

Olivia listened, fascinated. It seemed that winemaking had a checkered history. How could wineries have done such a deadly thing?

"We do not produce late harvest wines," Marcello said firmly. "We are not a participant in the sweet wine market at all."

Now Olivia felt dizzy as she realized where the detective's questioning was heading. Nadia, in particular, was flushed with anger—or, perhaps, Olivia wondered if it was nerves.

"You have never used any banned chemicals in your winemaking?"

"Never!" Nadia snapped at the detective, unable to conceal her anger. Or perhaps, Olivia wondered if her quick retort had been defensive.

The detective made a note on her pad.

Then she continued, and her words made alarm bells ring inside Olivia's head. Caputi's instincts had identified a weak spot, and Olivia felt filled with horror at where this questioning might lead.

"You organized this auction very suddenly, I understand. Why did you feel the need to part with a historic bottle of wine at such short notice?"

She looked from one Vescovi to the other and Olivia held her breath as she realized that nobody was brave enough to meet the detective's eyes.

Eventually, Marcello broke the tense silence. As he spoke, Olivia realized her palms were damp.

"Detective, we had to make up a shortfall in our summer sales urgently."

"Why?" Caputi's voice was like a whip. Clearly, she wasn't letting this one go.

Marcello sighed.

"Several large barrels of Sangiovese were found to be tainted and unusable."

"A-ha!"

Caputi pounced on the confession as if she'd been waiting for it all along. Olivia found her gaze snapping back and forth between the winery owner and the detective as if she were watching a tennis match.

A tennis match, where the winner got to stay out of jail, she acknowledged.

"So you have recently had a problem with tainted wine in this establishment?"

Detective Caputi's comment felt to Olivia as if she'd scored an ace.

"TCA taint. It is common. And harmless," Marcello protested.

The detective shook her head.

"The irregularities with your manufacturing process must be thoroughly investigated. We have to rule out accidental contamination, as well as deliberate sabotage. Therefore, this will now be passed on to the experts to assess."

Out of the corner of her eye, Olivia saw Nadia cover her mouth with her hand.

"The tracker in Signor Vernon Carrington's hired sports car showed that he traveled directly from the winery to his villa last night. He stopped nowhere else along the way," Detective Caputi said. "We found no empty wine bottles, nor used glasses, in his villa. So we must conclude that the last time he ate and drank was at the winery."

She paused, gazing at each one of them in turn. Olivia felt her stomach start to tighten. There was something else coming. She was sure of it.

"Although police searched the villa most thoroughly, the historic wine that you said Signor Carrington took possession of at the auction was nowhere to be found," Caputi announced.

A sense of doom had settled over the table.

Olivia's mind reeled. How was that possible? What had happened to it? How could the prized bottle have disappeared?

Clearly, the inference was that somebody at the winery had been responsible for its disappearance.

"Did you check his car?" Olivia asked, pleased with her sudden brainwave. "Maybe he left it in his car?"

Detective Caputi gave her a withering glance.

"Our highly trained detectives have, naturally, searched all locations where the bottle might have been kept. Including Signor Carrington's rented Porsche Cayenne."

Inexorably, the detective continued, "Your tasting room will remain closed. Your wine manufacturing plant will close. Your tourism and manufacturing operations will be placed on hold until I have organized a team of forensic experts to test everything currently in your winemaking process, as well as random bottles from your recent manufacturing and storage."

Olivia felt appalled. Detective Caputi was basically shutting down the winery. This was a disaster for the Vescovis. She couldn't believe the dreadful consequences of this decision. Nadia had been working fourteen-hour days to meet her winemaking deadlines. Late summer sales had a short window to reach the market.

"How long will we need to remain closed?" Marcello asked, and Olivia had never heard him sound so hopeless.

Detective Caputi shrugged.

"The investigation can take from one to two weeks. Once the team is available, of course, which might take an additional week."

Nadia let out a defeated groan. Unable to stop herself from offering comfort, Olivia reached across and took the winemaker's icy cold hand in her hot, sweaty one.

"Now," Detective Caputi continued, "I must interview you individually. Starting with you, Olivia Glass. I understand from what you said to me earlier today, that you knew the victim previously, from when you worked in America. The rest of you can leave, while Olivia explains her connection with the deceased."

The surprised gazes of the Vescovis swiveled in her direction. Then they got up. Olivia was shocked by the change in their demeanor. Nadia was blinking tears out of her eyes, while Antonio's shoulders bowed, as if carrying a heavy weight. Even Marcello looked somber and tight-lipped after the bombshell that the detective had delivered.

With a twist of her stomach, Olivia realized that the negative implications of this closure could go far beyond the two – or three-week delay that the detective had so casually proposed.

A forced police closure due to suspected contamination would be extremely damaging for the winery. Olivia's advertising background meant she understood the implications loud and clear.

That could do more than just destroy a season's sales; it could permanently affect the winery's reputation. Sales and tourism would suffer and might never recover.

When the word got out, it would have horrific consequences. As a wine enthusiast, she herself would not want to visit a winery that had faced accusations of producing fatally contaminated wines, and she knew other customers would feel the same. As an advertising executive, Olivia realized that this was a potential PR disaster of the same magnitude as the Valley Wines debacle.

Olivia thought fast as the detective turned to her.

All she could do, faced with this terrible scenario, was try and persuade her that La Leggenda's owners, and their wines, were all innocent of any crime.

"Tell me about your relationship with the victim," Detective Caputi said to Olivia, after making more notes and starting a fresh tape recording.

"Well, I used to work in advertising back in the States. I worked for a big firm and Vernon Carrington was one of the firm's clients. We saw each other a few times at meetings."

That was the start and end of it, Olivia decided. She was not going to let Detective Caputi draw her out on this or trick her into making any further confessions. Above all else, she must not disclose her involvement with Valley Wines. Gabriella might be hiding the information to use against her, but she knew Detective Caputi would blast her entire secret out into the open if she discovered it.

To her surprise, the detective seemed content to leave this explanation be. Hooking a stray lock of steel-gray hair behind her ear, she asked, "Did you have any contact with Vernon Carrington on the evening of the auction?"

Olivia gave her a winning smile.

"Well, we recognized each other and said hello. He was interested to learn that I was working here. Beyond that, there wasn't time for much conversation. I was running around, pouring wine, taking food out, looking after the guests. He was focused on the auction and making the winning bid."

"So you were pouring the wine for guests?" the detective asked meaningfully.

Olivia hesitated, worried about where this line of questioning could end up. It seemed that any word coming out of her mouth could be interpreted as a guilty confession.

She decided to reply with nothing more than a calm nod.

"I understand that the winery was very reluctant to part with the bottle and that it had great emotional value to the Vescovis," Detective Caputi said.

Olivia agreed enthusiastically, glad that the detective had changed tangent in her questioning.

"Oh, yes, definitely. They were torn up about having to sell it. They didn't want to lose the history it represented. It was a really tough, sad choice for them to have to make."

Then she realized the implication of her words.

"Well, no, not so much," she added hurriedly. "What I meant is that organizing the auction was tough. It was a lot of work, you see. The wine was just an old bottle, stuck away in a vault. They never even saw it from day to day! They weren't that bothered about selling it. In fact, they couldn't have cared less about it."

Despite her best efforts, she'd put her foot in it and managed to incriminate the Vescovis. And herself, as she realized, listening to the detective's next words.

"Interesting that you are prepared to backtrack, and even lie, to try to protect your employers," the detective observed. "I wonder what other lengths you were prepared to go to in order to help them."

Olivia felt sweat spring out on her forehead.

"They're good people!" she protested. "They would never dream of killing somebody just to get back a valuable bottle of wine that meant a lot to them emotionally!"

"But would you?" Detective Caputi stared at her, narrow-eyed.

With her stomach constricting, Olivia realized that her efforts to clear the Vescovis had made Caputi doubly suspicious of her own motives.

"Would you?" the detective repeated thoughtfully, twisting her pen between her fingers.

CHAPTER SEVENTEEN

O livia was relieved to walk out of the winery after her questioning was over. She felt as if she'd been freed from prison. That was what it felt like to be sequestered for interviewing with Detective Caputi, especially when she made it very clear that actual prison was only a slip of the tongue away.

Olivia hadn't even been able to say a proper goodbye to the Vescovis, because they were still being interviewed.

Striding briskly down the driveway to try to straighten out the confused thoughts boiling in her head, and put some distance between herself and the intimidating detective, Olivia was glad to see Erba leap down from the winemaking room's windowsill. The goat capered over to her, ready to join her on the walk home.

"Erba, today has been a disaster," she told the goat.

Erba gazed up at her intelligently. Olivia was convinced she understood most of what she was told. Not only was she very clever, but also, with her distinctive orange-spotted coat, one of the prettiest goats Olivia had ever seen.

"The detective is closing down the winemaking facility until she can get everything tested. That's an absolute tragedy for the business. Although, I think she might be threatening to do it in the hope that someone confesses to the crime," Olivia mused. Detective Caputi didn't care how long it stayed closed. For her, the waiting game represented a win-win in terms of her investigation strategy.

The longer the winery was closed, the greater the chance that somebody would break under pressure and confess.

As Olivia reached the winery gate, she resolved that there was only one possible solution. She would have to try to investigate this herself.

If she could find out who the killer was, it would allow the winery to reopen.

She had to start as soon as possible.

As she headed down the narrow, cypress-lined road that was one of the prettiest sections of her walk, Olivia reluctantly admitted that the Vescovis were the biggest suspects.

Parting with that bottle had been an emotional wrench for them. None of them had wanted to do it. But would any of them have gone to the lengths of murder to get it back?

If any of the Vescovis had, then the poison could only have been administered once Vernon had won the bottle. Before then, they wouldn't have known who to kill.

Olivia cast her mind back to the confused minutes after the winning bid.

A lot of people had gotten up and left immediately. There had been a sense of anticlimax permeating the room. Vernon's insults, and the way he'd humiliated the other bidders, had destroyed the congenial atmosphere that had built through the auction. Every other winning bid had received generous applause, but not the final one.

Marcello had been very busy afterward. He'd been handling the release forms for the earlier items. Seated at the desk in the hallway, he'd been wishing guests a good evening and ensuring no successful bidder left without the correct paperwork, apart from Vernon Carrington, who had been one of the last people to leave.

Vernon hadn't gone near Marcello, Olivia remembered. He'd been holding court in the tasting room, with the prized bottle in one hand and a glass of wine in the other, drinking and bragging to anyone who would listen, as the winery staff did their best to straighten the place out around him. Not many people had stayed for a final drink, but a few had.

Antonio hadn't been at the auction at all. He'd been overseeing a final harvest of vermentino grapes, which had taken longer than expected to ripen, so he couldn't have done it.

But Nadia had been the one serving wine after the bidding had ended.

And they'd all known, thanks to the incident that had happened in the 1980s, that antifreeze could be added to wine, making it taste sweeter but not unpalatably so.

For a moment Olivia mused over the fact that there was no way Vernon Carrington would have picked up on any unusual flavors. He hadn't even come close to an accurate analysis of the red wine she'd seen him taste. He'd taken a wild, and totally wrong, guess. Added sweetness would probably have made the wine more agreeable to him, Olivia decided. And if anyone had picked up that fact, it would have been the Vescovis, and particularly Nadia.

Olivia thought about that with a pang of worry as she turned down the colorful, flower-lined lane that led to the villa.

Vernon had insulted the Vescovis' guest of honor, Alexander, and had spilled wine down his shirt.

Nadia had rushed to his rescue and whisked him off to save his shirt and his dignity. And she'd been furious. Never mind the fact that Vernon had bid on the winning bottle. Olivia had seen murder in Nadia's eyes over that one single incident before the auction had even started.

Nadia could have brought the poisonous substance back with her after helping Alexander.

In fact, Olivia realized that Alexander could also have committed this crime. He'd suffered public insults and abuse from the victim. Although his anger had seemed to pass quickly, he might have decided to take revenge.

Olivia sighed.

She didn't think that incident would have caused a reasonable person to commit murder as a result. To her, Alexander seemed like a reasonable person. She couldn't take him off her list of suspects, because of the episode that had occurred before the auction, but he wasn't at the top of the list.

In any case, the whole point of her efforts was to exonerate her friends and colleagues, and get things back to normal before the season's sales were lost and the winery's reputation destroyed.

How could she do this? Olivia fretted, as she opened the villa's front door, glad to be safely home. With Detective Caputi involved, the risk of spending the night in a jail cell always seemed uncomfortably possible. It was a relief to hear Charlotte call, "You're back!" as soon as she heard the front door open.

"Wait until you hear what a day I've had!" Olivia shouted back, making a beeline for the kitchen.

Ten minutes later, she and Charlotte sat at the kitchen table with icy cold glasses of pinot grigio in front of them.

"I can't believe it!" Charlotte exclaimed. "Another murder? And you're a suspect?"

Olivia nodded before taking a grateful sip of the delicious, dry wine. She thought she could pick up the hints of lime and apple, and the faint overtones of honey, that the label had described.

"I'm sure that scary detective will try to pin this on you again, especially since you knew Vernon Carrington from your previous job. That's a very unfortunate coincidence. You need to clear your name," Charlotte urged her.

"And the winery's reputation!" Olivia emphasized. "They could be in big trouble as a result of this."

"Where are you going to start?" Charlotte asked. Then, leaping up from the kitchen table, she added, "We have to start with making dinner. Duh! No good sleuthing was ever done on an empty stomach."

"Exactly!" Olivia put her glass down and headed for the fridge. "What about pasta puttanesca?" she said. "We've been wanting to cook that for a while. The sauce doesn't seem too complicated, so I can give it a try."

Olivia had been fascinated by this authentic Italian dish ever since she'd first heard about it. Not only did it contain some of her favorite ingredients—garlic, chilis, anchovies, and capers—but its history was a story all on its own. Legend had it that this dish was created by prostitutes who used the pungent, delicious aromas to lure customers into their lodgings.

"Good idea," Charlotte agreed. "I'll make some garlic butter in the meantime, and turn that ciabatta we bought yesterday into garlic bread."

As she assembled the ingredients for her culinary project, Olivia found her thoughts going back to the mystery of Vernon Carrington's death.

What important details was she missing?

Carefully, she sliced up chilis and anchovies before adding them to the pan, where the garlic was sizzling in olive oil.

She snapped open a can of tomatoes and added the luscious, red plum tomatoes to the pan, crushing them with a wooden spoon, before turning the heat down. While the dish simmered and reduced, she added linguini to the large pot of boiling water.

Over the past few days, what with the auction and the light lunch she'd enjoyed today, Olivia had been made uncomfortably aware of Gabriella's cooking prowess.

Gabriella might have a dislikeable personality—no, Olivia corrected herself, there was no "might" about it. She had an awful personality. But she was an incredible cook. She'd conceptualized all those delicious snacks for the auction, and had also whipped up the light lunch they'd had while waiting for the police to arrive. She seemed to do it so effortlessly, and everything that came out of the kitchen was mouthwateringly perfect.

If Olivia ever dated Marcello, and she knew this was a big "if"—she would have huge shoes to fill in the cooking department.

Relaxing in the evenings after a long day in the winery, Marcello would surely appreciate a home-cooked meal, made with love and skill. Would she be up to the job?

Olivia looked doubtfully at the spattering pan before adding salt and pepper to the dish.

"Practice makes perfect," she said, adding the sliced black olives and capers and turning down the heat, before draining the pasta and adding salt and olive oil.

"It's looking great," Charlotte encouraged her. "And smelling divine. If I was a passing customer, I would be lured in for sure."

Olivia served it up, staring at her handiwork in satisfaction.

"Should we add some cheese?" she asked. "The recipe didn't say so."

"When can you ever go wrong with cheese?" Charlotte asked, taking the foil-wrapped ciabatta out of the oven.

Olivia grated some fresh Parmesan into a bowl while Charlotte refilled their wine.

"Now we can discuss the case," Charlotte decided, as Olivia brought the steaming plates to the table.

"I can't believe that we're facing so many serious problems," Olivia summarized, adding freshly ground black pepper to her food. "We're all under suspicion of murder. The worst-tempered detective in Italy is responsible for handling the case. And the police closure is going to end up destroying the winery's reputation, not to mention putting a massive dent in the end of summer sales."

She took a mouthful of the pasta. Delicious! She was sure if she'd served it to Marcello, he would have thought so too. Charlotte's appreciative murmur confirmed this recipe was a success.

Never mind Marcello's romantic life, Olivia chided herself. She needed to help him save his winery!

"So, are there any other suspects, apart from you and the Vescovis?" Charlotte asked.

"Yes. I can think of a few guests at the auction who might have had motives. Especially since this happened straight after Vernon bid on the sought-after bottle of wine," Olivia said.

Charlotte nodded wisely.

"There was the Frenchman who lost out to Vernon in the bidding. He's the biggest suspect. He wanted that bottle badly, as he had a customer lined up for it, and he seemed like a very organized person, who could have arrived with poison as a back-up plan. Unfortunately I didn't notice where he was after the auction ended, so I have no idea if he had the opportunity to spike Vernon's wine."

Olivia tore off a crust of ciabatta, glistening with garlic butter. The crispy bread was the perfect accompaniment to the pasta.

"There was a bidder at the back of the room who also stayed in the war till near the end, but from where I was standing I couldn't see him. The other main bidder was the blond woman whose husband was smoking cigars at the pizza restaurant. Remember her? Talking about her mansions?" Olivia asked.

"I do remember her. Clearly used to getting what she wants," Charlotte observed.

"Then there was Vernon's friend Patrick. I don't think he's a potential suspect, as he left as soon as the bidding for the wine barrel was over. That was the first item."

They ate in contented silence for a few minutes.

"The Frenchman sounds like the most promising lead to me, although you can't rule out the spoiled blond," Charlotte said. "Don't they say poison is a woman's weapon?"

Uncomfortably, Olivia found herself thinking about Nadia again.

Charlotte continued. "You need to find out who the bidder at the back of the room was, and investigate him, too. Is there a way you can do that?"

Olivia sighed.

The only person she could think of who had been circulating in the tasting room, and who might recall what had happened after the auction ended, was Gabriella.

The last thing Olivia wanted to do was speak to her archrival, who also happened to represent the biggest threat to her future at the winery.

But then, again, after prolonged police closure, there might be no future at all if Olivia weren't brave enough to ask the difficult questions she needed to.

No matter how risky it was, she was going to confront Gabriella as soon as she had the chance.

CHAPTER EIGHTEEN

Olivia woke up at sunrise, feeling nervous about what the day ahead would bring. She'd dreamed the whole night about this mystery. In her dreams, Olivia realized, she had solved the case at least five times, in five different ways.

Now, with morning light streaming through her window, she unfortunately couldn't remember what any of them had been.

Olivia sat up and pushed back the covers. She felt too restless to stay at the villa for the day. There was a mountain of work waiting to be done at her farm, and even though the tasting room was closed, she decided she would go to the winery at the usual time. This would allow her to continue with her investigation, and hopefully also provide moral support and help to the Vescovis.

After giving Erba a quick breakfast of carrots and slipping a packet of cat food into her purse, Olivia was ready to head out.

Seeing she was leaving so early, she decided to detour into town and buy herself a to-go coffee and a breakfast treat from one of the two bakeries, before doing some work on her farm.

At this hour, the bakeries would be the only stores open in town. They were rival establishments, located across the road from each other, and Olivia had seen the owners shouting insults at each other, and shaking their fists in anger, many times.

She'd realized since then that the rivalry was so well documented that the bakeries had started to become a tourist attraction. Curious visitors trickled into town to see the identical layouts and identical prices of the goods on display, and to watch the public shouting matches that frequently broke out between the two owners.

She'd seen numerous tourists filming the fights, and had to admit that the owners got so extravagantly angry with each other that it almost seemed comical at times, and would make captivating YouTube footage.

Olivia took care to alternate between the two establishments, so as not to further inflame this terrible vendetta. This time, she was due to buy from Mazetti's. It was early enough that there would be no traffic in town, so she felt confident to have Erba tagging along.

To Olivia's disappointment, as she headed down the empty main street, she saw the bakeries' shutters were both closed, although the mouthwatering smell of baking bread wafted toward her. Both establishments must already be hard at work, preparing their identical breads and sweet treats for the day ahead.

Mazetti's side door was open and she wondered if it would be possible to sneak in and buy something. She didn't care what. Now that she'd smelled that delicious fragrance, anything that was ready from their ovens would make her happy, whether it was a mini ricotta cheesecake or a slice of chocolaty torta caprese, or even just a freshly baked focaccia bread.

Olivia peeked inside the door—and stopped, staring incredulously.

There were the two owners, sitting together at the bar table with their backs to the door, laughing and talking as they drank espressos.

How was this possible? Her eyes felt ready to pop out of her head with amazement.

The owner of Mazetti's was showing the owner of Forno Collina some photos on his phone. Looking down at them, the other man gave an uproarious guffaw, squeezing his supposed rival's shoulder affectionately.

Olivia spun away from the door, clapping her hand over her mouth to suppress an astonished snort of laughter. This was absolutely surreal!

She'd never dreamed that these two bakery owners were, in fact, the best of friends. Presumably, the rivalry had been started as some sort of a joke, and then continued when they realized how much additional tourist attention it was bringing to both stores.

She couldn't possibly let them know that she'd eavesdropped on their friendly get-together.

It would spoil everything.

Olivia turned and tiptoed away, giggling to herself as she retraced her steps up the main road. What a lucky moment she'd had, and how fortunate she felt to know the real story behind this legendary rivalry.

She wondered how many other people in town knew, and were keeping it a secret for the sake of appearances.

As Olivia peeled off on the road that led to her farm, she thought there was a lesson to be learned from the encounter she'd just had.

She was a trusting person and generally accepted people at face value. She'd been convinced that the bakers were arch-enemies. Now, a chance insight had revealed the truth.

Olivia sighed impatiently. She had to stop being so innocent in her assumptions. The experience she'd just had at the bakery needed to be applied to every area of her life, and especially when she was investigating.

She couldn't afford to take people at face value, when they might be deliberately presenting a different face to the world.

Arriving at her farm, she felt her heart lift with happiness. The farmhouse looked at its most beautiful with its eastern walls bathed in the morning light, causing the warm-cream stone to glow golden.

Erba, too, seemed thrilled to have made this detour. She headed purposefully to the herb garden that Olivia had created and took a mouthful of the newly planted rosemary bush.

"Only one bite, Erba," Olivia warned.

The goat seemed to understand. She wasn't a greedy animal at all, Olivia thought lovingly. Mischievous and full of fun, but not destructive in the least.

Returning to the front of the house, Olivia was pleased to see that the black and white cat had appeared again.

She got down on her hands and knees, just the same way Danilo had done.

"Psspsspss," she called.

To Olivia's delight, the small cat sniffed at her fingers and then gave her hand a friendly rub with its head.

Progress! Olivia was able to stroke the cat all along its back. It arched against her, purring thunderously, as if all this affection was needed to make up for a life that had been lacking in it.

"You are such a lovely cat," Olivia told the ecstatic feline. "I should name you, but I don't know if you're a boy or a girl. Maybe I can give you a gender-neutral name. Like Pirate. Would you like to be Pirate? It's more of a boy's name, actually, but I have a feeling you're a boy."

Olivia tried the name aloud, watching the cat closely. She wasn't sure if the cat liked it. The feline remained inscrutable. Olivia guessed it might never have had a name before. Naming a cat was a big responsibility. It had to suit the animal's personality.

"You're Pirate for now," she decided.

She was sure the young cat was a boy. When it had tamed enough to be put into a carrier for a vet examination and neutering, Olivia was sure that her gut feeling would be confirmed.

Pleased that the adopted cat now had a name, Olivia did a quick walk-through of the house, planning what furniture she needed to buy and where it should go. She'd left a sketch pad in the hallway, and as she progressed through the house, she drew diagrams, setting out exactly what would go where, so that she could estimate the sizes she needed and visualize what the rooms would look like.

This was exciting. It was also going to be expensive. She had money set aside for the purpose, but having that money in her bank account felt like security.

Spending it would be a scary step to take and would represent a final commitment to her new life.

What would happen if the winery's closure meant she no longer had a job? It would be better not to invest in buying new furniture until she had progressed as far as she could with her sleuthing.

Since she was hesitant to go any further with her furniture planning, she decided to make a start on clearing the barn. The mountain of rubble inside would have to be removed at some stage. Although it was a huge job, it could be handled by one person, working with a shovel and wheelbarrow. If she removed one or two barrow loads a day, the barn would be clear in no time at all.

Olivia tied her hair back and quickly changed into her shabby pants.

Then, wheeling her small wheelbarrow with a shovel inside, she thumped and rattled her way down to the barn.

"Hey! I thought I'd walk this way and see if you were here."

Olivia was pleased to see Charlotte heading up the driveway.

"That's a pretty dress," Olivia complimented her, admiring the lime green sundress her friend was wearing.

"Isn't it? I got it in the village. That clothing store is so tiny it's like a hole in the wall, but it's crammed with the most gorgeous stock. There's a blue one that has your name on it."

"You're going to need a bigger suitcase," Olivia warned.

"I've already bought one. Part of my last-week-in-Italy shopping spree, since I leave next Friday. So, are you going to clean out the barn this morning?"

Olivia grimaced. "Every time I look at that pile it seems to get bigger. It'll take me months. I'm tempted to hire someone with a bucket loader. That would move it in no time."

Charlotte nodded in sympathy. "I'd be tempted, too. On the other hand, though, there's the satisfaction of doing it yourself."

"Yes, this is my dilemma. I think I'll make a start, at least. Can you check the barn for spiders?"

Charlotte looked doubtfully at Olivia, and then down at her dress.

"From a distance?" Olivia pleaded.

"All right." Charlotte turned on her phone's flashlight and stepped into the barn.

"It's very dusty!" she called. "I'm only doing this because I'm a true friend. This bright lime color shows up every scuff, and I'm planning to walk to town for breakfast at the bakery."

"Thank you," Olivia called back gratefully.

A minute later, Charlotte reappeared, brushing at her skirt. She sneezed violently.

"No sign of any unwanted wildlife. A few ancient cobwebs, but my guess is that all the spiders moved into the farmhouse long ago. That barn urgently needs a door on it to keep the dirt out."

"Only once it's clean. Until then, a door would only keep the dirt in," Olivia countered.

She wheeled the barrow inside.

Digging the shovel carefully into the base of the pile, she began to clear it. As the spade touched the dirt, Olivia felt a sense of achievement. She was making a start. From here, the job could only get easier.

"You're doing great!" Charlotte called.

Glancing around, Olivia suppressed a snort of laughter. Her friend was standing a safe distance away from the barn door and wasn't even looking in Olivia's direction, but messaging on her phone.

"Stand clear!" she warned. She wheeled the full barrow out, dust spilling from its sides, and wrestled it across the uneven ground to a place where she wanted to level the ground to create a covered parking bay near the house.

Arriving back, her sense of achievement evaporated as she saw the pile looked just as big as before.

In her mind, the timeline was stretching out from months to years. That was how long it might take. Years!

Just one more barrow load, she persuaded herself. Then she was done for the day, and perhaps even the week, she thought, sneezing violently as she returned to the dusty space.

This time, as she dug the spade into the pile, she heard an unexpected and weirdly familiar sound. It was the solid thunk of glass.

Olivia drew back the spade at once. There was glass in this pile. She hadn't expected that, and she didn't want to smash what was probably a discarded windowpane. That would only complicate her clean-up plans.

She knelt down on the dusty floor and, sighing that she was going to get ten times dirtier than she'd planned, started carefully clearing the rubble away with her hands. She worked as delicately as she could, knowing that a sharp glass surface might already be lurking inside this dusty mound.

But to her astonishment, when she finally touched the glass, it wasn't flat or sharp at all.

It was a shape she knew instantly and recognized perfectly.

"Ah!" she exclaimed in surprise. "An empty wine bottle!"

Glad that she hadn't inadvertently smashed it with her spade, Olivia cleared the bricks away carefully. She was curious to know what vintage it was, which might give her an idea of how long it had been lying there, and what type of wine it was.

Olivia grasped the neck of the bottle and drew it out of the pile, small stones scattering around it.

It wasn't an empty bottle at all. It was full, and sealed.

Olivia gasped in amazement. What a discovery!

"Charlotte!" she shouted.

"What?" her friend called, from somewhere out of Olivia's sight. "I'm busy with your goat. She's demanding head scratches."

"Come and see! I've unearthed a unique artifact!"

Olivia carried the bottle outside.

"It's unopened. Look."

"Wow!" After giving Erba a final rub on her head, Charlotte hurried over to admire Olivia's find. "That's incredible. I suppose it could be from the local area. It looks ancient. Do you think there's a date on the label?"

"There must be, but it's so encrusted with grime, I can't tell. I don't want to damage it. It might be too faded to read, but if it isn't, maybe there's a way to clean it up."

"Google is your friend?" Charlotte advised. "Let's put it somewhere safe for the meantime."

Abandoning her rubble removal for the day, Olivia took the bottle to the farmhouse. What could it tell her, she wondered, about who had lived here in the past? Where was this wine from? Had this old barn been used as a cellar at one stage?

Most importantly, if she'd uncovered one bottle already, Olivia was sure that other important historical finds might be buried in this dusty pile.

CHAPTER NINETEEN

Standing in the farmhouse kitchen, Olivia brushed grime off the dark, solid glass shape, marveling at her lucky find. An unused, unopened, intact wine bottle from a previous era. How amazing! She brushed lightly over the dirt-covered label with her fingertip, peering down at the almost-illegible pattern.

"What do you think? Is it a logo?" she asked Charlotte.

"I would say it is, definitely," Charlotte agreed.

It looked like a twined image of three ovals, joined to look like grapes. There was writing, too, but she couldn't make it out. Perhaps the label could be professionally cleaned up, restored the same way paintings were. Then she might be able to trace what wine it was, and its origin.

How had it ended up in this rubble, she wondered, and who had discarded it there, long ago?

Removing the debris with a front-end loader, as she'd been tempted to do, was going to be impossible now. She'd only just missed smashing this bottle, and could not risk damaging other important items hidden in the dump.

"Are you thinking what I'm thinking?" Charlotte asked.

"What are you thinking?"

"I'm remembering that locked storeroom, the one we found by accident, hidden away in the hills. If you've just found an old bottle in the shed, imagine what might be inside that room."

"You're right."

With a flare of excitement, Olivia visualized the secret room, secluded in its hilly hideaway. What if there were other bottles there, cellared in the hidden space?

Who would have thought her new farm would turn into such a treasure trove of exciting and mysterious artifacts?

Perhaps, one day, this bottle could be part of her very own dining room décor—a reminder of the rich winemaking history in her new home country.

Hoping that this amazing find would mean this turned out to be a good day, Olivia set the bottle inside the newly renovated cupboard under the kitchen counter. Then she changed back into her work clothes and headed to La Leggenda.

As she approached the winery, she forgot the delightful find at her farm, and her thoughts returned to the more serious challenge of who could have killed Vernon Carrington.

If she didn't manage to solve this mystery, her job, as well as the winery's future, was in jeopardy. Olivia knew that the pressure was on her, and that because of the police shutting down operations, time was of the essence.

It was disturbing to see the tasting room's tall entrance doors closed, and to have to turn the large bronze handle and push the heavy door open to walk inside. It was surprising how dark the hallway was, Olivia realized, without the light streaming in through the wide, welcoming doorway.

"Ah, Olivia. Good morning. It is kind of you to come to work," Marcello said. "It means a lot to me, personally, that you are here today. More than you know."

He walked over to her and slid his arm around her waist, before kissing her gently on each cheek. He looked deeply stressed, and as if he was short on sleep. Unusually, he looked a few years older than his forty years.

Olivia had a sudden desire to wrap her arms around him and give him a huge, loving, comforting hug, and then straighten the rumpled collar of his shirt and smooth out his dark hair, which was in uncharacteristic disarray.

She didn't, though. Instead, controlling her emotions, she gave him a professional smile.

"I'm here to help and support in any way I can," she emphasized. "You have my absolute loyalty, and I'll do whatever it takes to fix this situation as soon as possible."

From the look of gratitude on Marcello's face, Olivia thought her words might have meant more than any hug could do, however big and loving it was.

Then his phone rang and he answered, looking stressed all over again as he strode back to his office to take the call.

Olivia felt a furious gaze drilling into her from behind. Turning, she saw that she had sensed correctly. Gabriella was standing at the restaurant's entrance, glowering at her. Clearly, she'd seen Marcello greet Olivia and the friendliness in the gesture had triggered her.

Just as well she'd refrained from that warm, loving hug, Olivia thought, hurrying across the empty tasting room to confront her nemesis.

"I want to ask you something quickly, please," Olivia called.

Gabriella looked surprised as she approached. Then Olivia thought she looked guilty, as if she'd been caught out for staring and thinking her evil thoughts.

The expression only lasted a moment before Gabriella recovered her usual poise, and looked down her aquiline nose at Olivia, while flicking a perfectly tonged curl behind her ear.

"I wonder what you want to discuss. Shall we speak about your previous workplace? We could have a very interesting conversation about that, I am sure!" Gabriella's crimson lips curved into a nasty smile. "Perhaps we should bring in Marcello to listen. Or should we keep it between us girls—for now?"

Olivia felt herself writhe inwardly as she realized what a huge disadvantage she was at. Gabriella was enjoying taunting her so much that Olivia began to wonder if she'd ever reveal the awful secret. She seemed thrilled to be the sole owner of this damaging information.

"Please don't mention that," Olivia begged her. "Right now, there might not be a winery at all, if the winemaking operation gets closed down and the word gets out about what happened. Then the restaurant would have to close, too. We'd all be out of a job."

Gabrielle's unpleasant smile vanished. Olivia saw that her words had hit home.

"I wanted to ask you something very important," Olivia said, striking while the iron was hot. She knew she wasn't going to get many opportunities to be in a strong position with Gabriella. She needed to make the most of them.

"What?" Gabriella folded her arms.

"I'm doing some research into Vernon Carrington's death, so that I can help to clear the winery's name," Olivia said.

She was also hoping to clear her own name, but knew Gabriella would have scant sympathy if she learned that. It was best not to mention it at all.

"There were two people at the auction who I think could have poisoned Vernon's wine, and who might have had a motive," Olivia said, lowering her voice. She was pleased that Gabriella leaned forward as she listened, abandoning her defensive demeanor.

"The first one was the Frenchman who bid against him at the end. He was an antiques dealer, I think. The other was the bidder at the back of the room, who dropped out of the bidding just before the end. If they wanted the bottle badly, one of those two might have planned to walk away with it regardless."

"And you are telling me about this, why?"

Olivia smiled, hoping that Gabriella would interpret it as a friendly gesture.

"I was busy after the auction and didn't see either of them. I was wondering if one of the two would have had the opportunity to add the poison to Vernon's wine. You see, I'm looking to help out by investigating. After all, we need to have this awful crime solved."

Olivia hesitated.

Another, horrible idea had just occurred to her. Her thoughts fragmented into panic as the thought hit home.

"Go on?" Gabriella asked, but now her tone was cold.

"I—I wonder if—you might have seen? Them? At all?" Olivia finished, in a small voice.

It had just dawned on her that there was another suspect at that auction. Somebody who had just found out about Olivia's past connection with the victim and who had realized it was the perfect opportunity to frame her for a crime.

Someone who had a strong motive of jealousy, because her ex-boyfriend seemed to have romantic feelings for Olivia.

As Olivia smiled nervously at the other woman, she cringed at her own stupidity.

She could be confessing her suspicions to the real murderer.

CHAPTER TWENTY

Olivia felt as if all the air had been sucked out of the restaurant. Why couldn't she have thought this through before she'd blurted out to her biggest rival, and a newly discovered suspect, that she was investigating the case?

If Gabriella had been the killer, she'd been able to use a lethal poison with skill and without anyone realizing it. She was an expert with flavors, and seemed to know how to stay out of the spotlight of suspicion. She'd even passed under Detective Caputi's oversensitive radar.

Olivia would never be able to enjoy a light lunch in the restaurant again! She'd even feel nervous opening a sealed bottle of mineral water, knowing it had come from Gabriella's storeroom.

She wished she hadn't said a word. In fact, she wished she could rewind time and start afresh, from the moment she'd opened the winery's heavy oak doors.

All she could do was wait, in the lengthening silence, to see how Gabriella would react to her words.

She tore her gaze away from the safety of the desk and risked a glance at the other woman.

Gabriella had a perfectly manicured finger pressed to her temple. She was thinking—or pretending to. Possibly, she was creating an alibi to mislead Olivia deliberately.

Well, Olivia thought, whatever Gabriella said, at this point, she'd better agree with her story! If Gabriella said she'd heard the entire Vescovi family plotting together to add antifreeze to the wine, Olivia resolved she would thank her enthusiastically and then leave the area as fast as she could.

"The Frenchman followed me into the kitchen straight after the auction," Gabriella said. "He was in love with my macarons, and my food in general. He wanted to take a box of sweet treats away with him, which I put together for him, and to ask if I could do catering for his future events." She smiled smugly. "He does a lot of business in Tuscany, mainly antiques sales and historical tourism. So we spoke for about twenty minutes, I gave him my details, and he gave me his card."

She opened the till drawer and produced it with a proud flourish.

Olivia nodded, making sure Gabriella could see how impressed she was.

"The other man was a tourist. From Scotland, I think. He was bidding on the bottle for fun, as he has a big wine collection in his country house. He was there with his wife and son. He was competitive during the auction, but didn't seem overly disappointed to lose, and they left straight afterward. They had a dinner reservation at a restaurant near Florence, so they barely touched any of my snacks. I offered them about six different trays of food, and only his wife ate anything." Gabriella sounded petulant.

Again, her story rang true. Focused on food, Gabriella would definitely have been offended if her snacks were turned down, and would have listened for the reasons why.

Olivia began to think that Gabriella was telling the truth, and why would she do that if she was guilty? She'd want Olivia to run in as many different directions as possible, so that she didn't look in hers. Gabriella could have said she hadn't known anything about either of the men. Instead, she'd given a very clear explanation.

"Thank you," Olivia said.

She hoped that perhaps this might mean Gabriella was willing to set aside her evident loathing of Olivia, but there was no such luck.

"Is that all?" the restaurant manager asked in an unfriendly tone, and Olivia knew that the temporary truce was over.

"Yes, that's all," she said, and hurried away.

Olivia decided that the interview had cleared Gabriella as a suspect, due to the information which she'd willingly shared. However, she wasn't so sure about the Frenchman. He could have slipped poison into his victim's wine, and then deliberately created an alibi for himself in the winery's restaurant.

That was something a good planner might do.

But would somebody have had the foresight to bring poison to an auction in case they didn't win the bottle they wanted, and have been able to create such a seamless alibi straight afterward? If that was the case, the Frenchman seemed to be less of an antiques dealer and more of a criminal genius.

She thought it unlikely that an antiques dealer would possess such a range of nefarious talents. Nonetheless, he would have to remain on the suspects list. If she didn't find anyone with a clearer motive, Olivia would have to contact him and question him herself.

As she left the restaurant, Olivia saw Nadia stomping out of the storeroom. She seemed in a foul mood, and was holding a clipboard and pen. Olivia guessed she was stocktaking, trying to work out the damage and losses that had been caused by the contaminated wines, and which would now be exacerbated by the winemaking operation's closure.

Nadia glowered at Olivia.

Olivia knew her well enough not to take it personally. When Nadia was happy, the world laughed and smiled along with her. When she was angry, everyone at the winery crept around trying to avoid her. Except Olivia, who now had to confront her. Hopefully, she could use subtle questioning techniques to remove her from the suspects list.

"This is such a terrible predicament," she sympathized.

Nadia jabbed her pen into the slot in her board.

"More than terrible. I am stressed out! We have such a small deadline to make these wines and get them to market. The detective does not understand how a supply chain works. Stupid woman. She does not know or care about wine at all."

"I don't think Vernon did, either," Olivia sympathized, hoping that this would encourage Nadia to speak out.

"I could have cried when he won the bottle. I felt like going and snatching it from his grasping, greasy hands," Nadia hissed. "Our wine never deserved to be owned by such a rude, insulting ignoramus. The person who took it from him, I will only say that they saved it from him!"

"Who do you think it could have been?" Olivia asked.

Nadia shrugged expressively. Then she turned on her heel and marched out of the tasting room.

Olivia stared after her, frowning.

This conversation had by no means cleared Nadia, but now Olivia had a bigger worry. She was certain that the outspoken vintner would have shared her sentiments during her interview with Detective Caputi, and that the policewoman would be treating her words as highly suspicious.

Olivia needed to clear Nadia's name, and pinpoint the real perpetrator, before Detective Caputi closed the net around her.

Checking her phone after work, Olivia saw that Danilo had sent her the list of what she needed to feed her soil and nurture the vines.

"Go to the hardware store and they can help you with everything," he ended the message.

Eager to get her seeds off to the best possible start, Olivia drove to the hardware store straight after work.

"*Ciao, ciao.*" The friendly owner smiled. "You have come to buy some compost and soil fertilizer? Danilo said you would be visiting again soon!"

Olivia gave her a forced grin in response. She had the feeling that Danilo might already have regaled his hardware store friend with an eyewitness account of her winegrowing ineptitude.

"Danilo said you had one hundred percent enthusiasm but zero percent knowledge," the clerk continued in a ringing tone, glancing up at Olivia. "Is it true that you chased him off your property?"

Now both the closest shoppers were listening, as they pretended to browse the shelves near the till. Olivia knew with a sinking heart that this drama had probably been the talk of the village.

"Yes," she admitted, her face burning. "He was being annoying so I asked him to leave."

The clerk laughed uproariously. Even the young woman standing by the closest shelf covered her mouth to suppress a giggle.

"You shocked him," the clerk confided in Olivia. "He said you seemed offended by the comments he made in this store, so he drove to the farm to try to help. He could not believe that a pretty *turista* like you would refuse his assistance, and then become angry when he tried to explain your mistakes. He said he was hurt. I told him he should have asked more nicely, and that not everybody wants to know they are doing something wrong."

Touché, Olivia thought. That had been her, all right. Three months later, and she had been served up the portion of humble pie that had been waiting for her.

"I'm grateful he's helping me now," she confessed. Might as well own up to her ignorance. After all, she had an audience listening in. She didn't want the whole town to believe she was an arrogant *turista*.

"Danilo has a big heart!" The clerk placed her hand expressively on her own chest to illustrate her point. "He is always trying to help others."

"I'm glad we sorted out our miscommunication." Olivia smiled.

"Now, tell me," the clerk said, lowering her voice. "You work at La Leggenda, no? I hear there was some trouble after the auction? That the bidder who won the final item was found dead the next day?"

Olivia stared at her in consternation. She wasn't used to small-town life! Did word really travel so fast? How had the clerk even known?

"Um," she said.

She was aware that the closest shopper, a woman, was sidling even closer, feigning a deep interest in the display of shovels under the counter.

"I don't really know anything about it," Olivia mumbled, but the clerk smoothly called her bluff.

"They say the winery has been closed. Is there a problem there? Why did the police close it?"

"There was no problem at all," Olivia said hastily. "They just—the police had to come and check something, and they didn't want tourists going in and out."

Her face was turning crimson. She was a terrible liar, and it only made things worse when she realized that the clerk had probably acquired a fair amount of information already.

She might even know more than Olivia did. Probably, she simply wanted to confirm her version.

One of the shovels clattered to the floor, and the female shopper, looking embarrassed, righted it and retreated to a polite distance.

Olivia paid for the goods and wheeled the cart outside as fast as she could, packing the bags into the Fiat until the trunk and the back seat were full.

Then she scarpered back to her farm. Spreading compost suddenly seemed like a fun and appealing job, compared to dealing with the community's fascination with the crime.

This time around, Olivia had Charlotte to help her. She was bribing her friend to provide an extra pair of hands to finish dressing the seed beds, with the promise of buying her dinner afterward.

Charlotte had willingly accepted this offer and Olivia was glad she thought it was a great deal. Olivia hoped that the extra help would allow them to finish faster. She was eager to be in good time for the restaurant on the other side of town, where she'd booked a table. It was a fancy place so they'd need to spend some time getting ready first.

As they worked, she updated Charlotte on her investigation.

"The problem is that I keep returning to Nadia as my main suspect," she said. "She had the motive, because of losing the family's historic bottle, and she had the opportunity to grab poison when she left the auction. By then, she knew how obnoxious Vernon was. She could have brought the poison back with her as a precaution."

"Sounds like something any thinking woman might have done," Charlotte agreed.

"I had very high hopes for the two other bidders who lost out to Vernon," Olivia said. "But the Frenchman seemed to have an alibi afterward, and the other man seemed to have been bidding for fun. Or maybe he wasn't. Maybe that was a front."

She sighed. Investigation wasn't easy. In fact, once you started to think, rethink, and eventually overthink everybody's possible motives, Olivia realized it made her head spin.

Carefully, she loaded another sack of compost into the wheelbarrow.

"What about that man who was speaking to Vernon before the auction?" Charlotte asked. "The one we overheard at the restaurant, bragging about his cellar?"

Olivia nodded. "Patrick? He left straight after the bidding for the first item. That means he couldn't have been a suspect."

"Even so, it would be worth speaking to him," Charlotte insisted. "They knew each other through business, and you know how shady Valley Wines was. Vernon could have shared important information with him."

"You're right," Olivia agreed. "It would be worth following that up."

From behind them, there was a loud throat-clearing.

Olivia dropped her spade and spun.

Danilo stood a few yards away, looking sharp in a trendy pair of ripped jeans and a blue checked shirt. His hair was parted to the side this time, and slicked down with gel, giving him a 1920s look.

How long had he been standing there? Olivia was horrified by the fact he might have overheard her sharing her suspicions about Nadia. She didn't want anyone to think that Nadia might be guilty.

Staring at Danilo in consternation, Olivia realized that her innocent conversation with Charlotte might have been a huge mistake.

CHAPTER TWENTY ONE

"*Buon giorno*. I came to see if you needed any help," Danilo said. "I was driving past when I saw you wheeling a barrow to your vineyard."

Olivia smiled nervously at him, wishing she could replay the last few minutes and take back what she had said.

"*Buon giorno*," she replied, finally remembering her manners. "We're almost done. This is the last bag we need to spread, and then we're heading out to dinner."

"Allow me to wheel this one for you, please?"

"Well, what a kind offer," Charlotte enthused, before Olivia could say anything at all. Clearly, she'd reached her threshold of grapevine nurturing for the day.

Olivia had to admit it was a relief when Danilo grasped the barrow's handles. Even though she and Charlotte had alternated trips, her back was starting to ache.

As he wheeled the barrow to the seed bed, Danilo said conversationally, "So I understand that the winning bidder died after the auction at your winery? Although I was not trying to overhear anything, I could not help picking up that you two were discussing whether other bidders were involved in his death."

Olivia tensed.

She was sure he hadn't come to help, and that this was an information-gathering trip.

She felt fearful all over again that Danilo had heard too much, and that his knowledge might compromise the Vescovis. There was a delicate investigation under way. The winery's reputation was hanging in the balance and as Olivia knew only too well, the community was already starting to gossip.

"Well, yes, it was very unfortunate. After he won the historic bottle, the bidder, Vernon Carrington, was—er—was—er—"

Olivia fumbled with the words.

"Poisoned?" Danilo offered helpfully, and Olivia tripped over a rock and almost fell flat on her face.

Quickly, Danilo grabbed her arm.

"Sorry," she said, feeling her face start to glow red—and not just from all the hard work moving the compost. "I didn't look where I was going."

"There is talk in the village," Danilo explained. "Nobody thinks anyone from the winery could be responsible," he added, hurriedly. "Or that there is any problem with the winemaking facilities at La Leggenda. Everyone is very clear about it. The Vescovis are innocent, without a doubt, and their wines are free from any contamination. Our community will support each other. I think you need to know that."

He stared at her, his dark gaze earnest and wide-eyed.

Olivia was relieved to hear this, even though she knew it wouldn't take long for the bad news to filter out to the wider world, which wouldn't be so forgiving.

"I'm trying to help," she confessed.

"You are?" Danilo regarded her with admiration. "That is wonderful! So you are becoming—how do you call it—a sleuth? Like Veronica Mars?"

"No, no." Hastily, Olivia downgraded his expectations. "I'm really just trying to find more information, that's all. The problem is that I'm almost out of suspects, apart from one, who sort of has an alibi."

Charlotte nodded loyally.

Neither of them mentioned Nadia's name. Not at all. Olivia tried to stop herself from so much as thinking about the winemaker, in case she inadvertently let something slip.

"Vernon was an unpleasant man," she added.

"I believe his behavior at the auction was appalling," Danilo agreed. Clearly, he had a good informant.

Danilo carefully tipped and swung the barrow.

The last load landed in its assigned place. Olivia was pleased to see how rich and fertile the soil was looking. At last, there was a layer of nourishment for the young vines when they sprouted.

"You know, perhaps it was somebody else," Danilo suggested. "It might have been nothing to do with the auction at all. Perhaps he had other visitors who came by the villa. Don't they say, the leopard does not change his stripes? He would have treated others badly, too. It was not as if he took a pill before the auction, to make himself become nasty."

Olivia nodded.

Danilo's words made sense. In fact, the more she thought about this, the more she realized that he might be right.

Vernon Carrington probably had hundreds of enemies.

One of them might have caught up with him in Tuscany and come to the villa to make sure justice was done.

"That's a good idea," she said. "I'm going to investigate it right away. As in, immediately."

"Just be careful," Danilo warned.

Olivia nodded reassuringly. "All I'll do is ask a few innocent questions," she promised.

"Have a good evening, Olivia and Charlotte," Danilo said with a smile, after parking the barrow on the porch. He stopped to greet the cat, who had appeared as soon as it heard his voice.

"I've named him Pirate, for now," Olivia said. "I'm sure he's a boy."

"Pirate, a good name. Come here, little one!" Danilo's face lit up as he scratched the cat at the base of its tail.

Olivia suddenly felt bad.

Danilo had helped her three times so far. He'd gifted her grapevine seeds, he'd helped move rubble, and most importantly, he'd proved to be a pivotal influence in taming her cat. It struck her that the relationship, so far, was unequal. She needed to do her part. She was living in a village now, and should extend the hand of friendship wherever she could.

"You've been so kind. Would you like to come around next Thursday evening?" she asked. "By then I will have moved in and bought some furniture, and will be more organized. I'd love to offer you a glass of wine and a thank-you gift."

Danilo looked delighted.

"Thank you. I look forward to it."

He headed back to his truck with a spring in his step.

Charlotte took off her gloves and brushed the dust off them.

"That went well," she commented, looking admiringly at the results of their efforts. "Are we going to head back to the villa, and then go straight out to dinner? We might be a little early."

Olivia shook her head.

"We won't be early, and might even be a little late, because I have to make an important stop-off along the way. Thanks to Danilo, I have an idea for a new line of investigation that might just reap results."

The row of ostentatious villas frequented by the wealthiest tourists was a quick drive from the place where Olivia and Charlotte were staying. It took just a couple of minutes for them to circle over the hill and arrive at the top end of the street.

Although these villas sat well back from the road, they were within view of each other. Olivia hoped one of the neighbors had seen something.

Charlotte was driving while Olivia was acting as lookout.

"Go slowly here," Olivia said, as they approached the villa. It felt weird to be outside it again, and she couldn't help flashing back to that spooky moment when she'd walked into the quiet villa. All her hair had stood on end, she remembered. It was as if she'd sensed from the moment she had walked in that something was wrong.

If only her instincts for investigation were as finely tuned! She'd have everything solved by now.

"There it is! You can just see it from the road. That big yellow house behind the trees? That's where Vernon Carrington was staying."

Charlotte slowed the car and peered over, staring in fascination at the distant building.

"If you look here, the next-door driveway on the left is close to this one. And if you drive a few yards further, you can see that the villa on the other side would have a view of its front door from their front door."

Charlotte nodded.

"So are we going to knock on the neighbors' doors?"

"Yes, we are. They may have observed the murderer," Olivia explained.

She had the highest hopes for the villa whose driveway was close. The two homes had a partial view of each other. Plus, Vernon Carrington would have headed home from the auction at about the time when people would be coming back from a day's sightseeing, or going out for an early dinner. There was every chance that someone could have observed a crucial interaction as they passed.

Charlotte drove in between the tall, elegant gateposts.

"Villa Splendido," she said, reading aloud the crystal-studded sign on the right-hand gatepost.

"They all have swanky names," Olivia explained. "And equally over-the-top interiors."

They parked the tiny Fiat next to an oversized black Maserati SUV.

Then, taking a deep breath, she walked up to the enormous front door, painted a brilliant white. Charlotte was close behind her and she felt grateful for her friend's reassuring presence. Never mind the next-door villa, just being on this road was making her come out in goose bumps all over again.

The knocker was bright gold, in the shape of a champagne bottle.

Olivia heard quick footsteps approaching. She took a deep breath.

Then the door opened and she found herself staring into the surprised, heavily made-up eyes of the blonde who'd attended the auction.

CHAPTER TWENTY TWO

Olivia stared at the blonde in shock.

Faintly, she picked up the inevitable whiff of cigar smoke floating toward her from somewhere deep in the swanky villa.

"Well, look who's here," the blonde said, sounding incensed. "It's the lady from the winery. Have you come to offer us an apology, or a bottle of free wine?"

"Um," Olivia said. She felt totally taken aback. She hadn't expected to see the blonde here at all. And what did she mean by an apology?

"Harold, the winery has come to apologize," the blonde called.

Over the cigar smoke, Olivia caught a hint of her perfume. It smelled very expensive.

The blonde turned to her again.

"That winning bidder was very rude and insulting. We felt offended by him and had a negative experience at your winery as a result. We've been planning to put a poor review of La Linguine on Trip Advisor."

"La Leggenda," Olivia corrected her automatically. "I'm so sorry about that. Please don't. We also thought he was rude."

"I said to Harold, if I see him around in town, I'm going to go speak to him and tell him he was out of line. Harold doesn't approve of confronting people in public, but I feel in this instance, it's justified."

"Yes, dear," Harold called from the depths of the villa.

"Anyway, be that as it may, I feel that your winery, La Lasagne, should have done more to stop him."

Olivia was starting to suspect that the blonde had no idea what had happened to Vernon Carrington, or that he had in fact been their neighbor.

For a terrible moment, she wondered what the woman would say if Olivia informed her that Vernon Carrington was dead, probably due to his own atrocious behavior.

Firmly, Olivia told the devil on her shoulder to be quiet. Now was not the time to say such a thing, and she was appalled at herself for having even thought it.

"It was most unfortunate that he was so obnoxious during the bidding. We were also very shocked, and definitely didn't act in time," Olivia soothed.

The woman sighed, raking a red-nailed hand through her perfect hair.

"It's been the only blot on an otherwise enjoyable holiday. This villa has been superb. Very quiet. Not that we've spent much time here, but it's been extremely peaceful. And the restaurants in town are charming. Rustic, but charming."

"We're heading to Gianni's now," Olivia agreed enthusiastically. "It's been one of our favorite places in the area so far."

"Yes, we were there yesterday and enjoyed it. I can recommend the gnocchi and salmon. You'll have a good time, I'm sure."

She seemed to be warming to Olivia.

"Anyway, we're going to a brilliant seafood place tonight, on the beach. It's right on the beach, isn't it, Harold, with a sea view table?" she called.

"Yes, dear."

"So I'd better go and finish getting ready. But thanks for dropping by. I appreciate the apology. Sometimes a personal visit makes all the difference. I won't leave a bad review of La Lambrusco."

"I appreciate that," Olivia said. "Enjoy your seafood dinner."

She turned away, her mind racing as the bright, white front door clicked shut.

"That was unexpected, but interesting," Charlotte said, as they climbed back into the car.

"She didn't seem to know a thing about the murder," Olivia said. "Or that Vernon was staying next door. Could she really have been so unaware?"

The blonde had seemed convincing at the time. Her blue eyes had been wide and unblinking as she'd stared at Olivia. Privately, Olivia thought the blonde didn't seem like the cleverest person she'd ever met.

She warned herself to stop taking people at face value. Had her chance encounter at the bakery taught her nothing?

The blonde could be hiding sharp intelligence and murderous motives behind her vacuous façade.

Charlotte nodded. "The police were there most of the day, you said. Did she and Harold really not notice anything unusual during that time? Or were they coincidentally away from home for the entire duration?"

"If it was her, she was playing innocent. But we're forgetting Harold could also have been aiding and abetting her," Olivia decided.

Charlotte snapped her fingers as they climbed into the Fiat.

"Exactly! Those 'yes, dear' comments sounded suspicious to me. It's the quiet ones you always have to watch out for."

"I wonder if the police have questioned them," Olivia said. "Detective Caputi is very thorough. Yet she didn't mention anything about that, either. Perhaps they were hiding the information."

"I think Harold and his wife must remain as suspects," Charlotte agreed. "Your next step could be to find out more about them and research their background. That might uncover a link to Vernon, which could provide an additional motive, over and above wanting the bottle for themselves."

"Good idea," Olivia said. "Now, we'd better go and investigate the house on the other side of Villa Diamante quickly. If Mrs. 'Yes, dear' is innocent, it would be better for her to keep thinking we came to apologize, and not let her see us again."

"Agreed," Charlotte said.

"What's this one called? Villa Ultima?" Charlotte snorted as she read the sign.

They drove up the immaculately paved drive.

Ahead, Olivia saw the large garage was open and empty.

"Looks like they're not home," she said, disappointed.

Charlotte stopped the car and Olivia climbed out and ran up the marble stairs to the arched, highly polished front door.

She rang the doorbell and waited, but there was no reply from inside.

"Definitely out." Olivia hurried back to the car. "I don't think we should waste any more time here, or else Harold and his wife really will leave a bad review of La Lasagne!"

"It might be worth coming back," Charlotte said. "You get a clear view of the next-door villa's front door from this vantage point. They could easily have seen someone coming or going, if they'd been outside at the right time."

"Yes. I agree. Every avenue must be pursued," Olivia said. "But now, our restaurant reservation is waiting."

"If every avenue is being pursued, you mustn't forget about calling Patrick, Vernon's friend," Charlotte said. "I have a strong feeling he might remember something, or be able to provide some background."

Olivia nodded. "I promise I will. The winery will have his details, as he made a successful bid on the antique barrel, so I can look up his number tomorrow."

She would have to think of a good reason for calling him, she decided. Patrick would probably have heard that Vernon had died, but if Olivia told him it was murder, he might not feel comfortable to reveal too many details, especially given the underhanded nature of Vernon's new planned venture into winemaking.

Perhaps she could call him on the pretext of finding out whether he had been satisfied with the service and food at the auction.

After all, even if she didn't get the information she was seeking, it might lead to another positive review on Trip Advisor.

In the face of a prolonged closure, with whispers about contamination and poison leaking beyond the local area, the winery would need all the rave reviews it would get.

She felt relieved when they reached the main road and turned in the direction of the luxurious trattoria on the hillside overlooking the castle, where they'd decided to treat themselves to dinner. For the next while, she could focus on the pure enjoyment of food and friendship, and allow herself to forget the complexity of the investigation she'd become embroiled in.

At any rate, for a few short hours.

CHAPTER TWENTY THREE

O livia stared at Detective Caputi through the thick, steel bars that separated them.

She was in jail. How had this happened? Would the detective explain? Why couldn't she remember having been arrested?

"Here is your charge sheet! You had better get yourself a good lawyer!" the detective snapped.

She shoved a long piece of paper through the grille.

Olivia's handcuffs clanked together as she picked up the page and began reading.

It was filled with one-star Trip Advisor reviews for the winery. There were hundreds of them! Thousands! Each one was terrible!

"Aaargh," Olivia screamed.

She erupted from her dream to find herself sitting bolt upright in her bed, with a beam of morning sunshine slanting over the floor and Erba peering in at her through a gap in the curtains.

Olivia was still hyperventilating after the dream. Detective Caputi was now invading her sleep. That was out of bounds. The bad-tempered detective shouldn't be allowed to do that!

Her heart was still thudding, and after the adrenaline charge of that disturbing nightmare, there was no way she was going to get to sleep again.

As a wine-farmer-to-be, she might as well get used to early mornings, and perhaps now was the chance to change her schedule, Olivia decided.

Of course, even farmers probably slept in after late nights at wonderful restaurants, which included lots of excellent wine. But she'd have to catch up on sleep some other time. After all, there were urgent matters she needed to focus on today.

Number one on the list: saving the winery and tracking down the killer.

Feeling motivated by the thought that her investigation might make progress today, Olivia jumped out of bed. Early though it was, she intended to make a strong start.

Half an hour later, showered, dressed, and caffeinated, she headed out of the villa, with Erba trotting alongside.

Olivia calculated by the time she reached the row of wealthy villas, it would be eight-thirty a.m. Perhaps at that hour, the occupants of Villa Ultima might be home. They could even be heading out on a healthful run, Olivia thought optimistically. At any rate, she was going to walk past, and see if there was any sign of them.

Erba seemed excited by the new route. Olivia had to turn back and fetch her a few times after she made unscheduled detours down people's driveways. Clearly, the carefully manicured hedges and landscaped flower beds represented an irresistible temptation to an adventurous goat.

"Come, Erba," Olivia urged, herding the goat away from a colorful hillock of flowers that, to Erba, clearly represented the most beautiful breakfast buffet she had ever seen.

She'd thought that Erba was well trained, but Olivia now realized that she'd been growing complacent and neglecting the goat's further educa-tion. Walking the same route every day, Erba had no idea how to behave in a civilized manner when exposed to a broader world.

The blame lay squarely with Olivia. Erba was not the one at fault here, she was.

"You can't get into a comfort zone with goats," Olivia told herself sternly. If she ever wrote a goat training manual, she would be sure to put that warning in Chapter One.

Her heart jumped as she saw a sleek silver sports car parked under the covered bay in Villa Ultima. Her early start had reaped results, and the occupants were home.

Of course, that didn't mean they'd seen anything. Olivia did her best to manage her expectations as she strode up the driveway. Investigation was all about following promising trails that petered out into overgrown dead ends or quicksand traps.

She rang the doorbell and waited, trying to remain calm and positive but not unduly hopeful.

Footsteps approached and Olivia stood straighter.

The door opened and she found herself staring at a tall, blond-haired, blue-eyed man who looked to be in his late thirties. He was wearing a bright green baseball cap that read "FlavaWorld" across the front. From his appearance, Olivia guessed he might speak with a Swedish, or perhaps a German flair, and she was surprised when he addressed her in a distinctly American accent.

"Hello! How can I help you?"

Glancing past him into the hallway, which was so large it could have doubled as a tennis court, Olivia saw a small leather valise. Did that mean he'd just arrived, or was he getting ready to leave?

She hoped he hadn't just arrived, because that would mean he hadn't seen anything at all.

Olivia realized that her spur-of-the-moment decision to arrive on this man's wide, spotless, marble front doorstep meant that she didn't have any plausible story ready for why she was there.

She couldn't exactly blurt out that a dead body had been discovered next door, and ask if he had seen anything.

Olivia decided that tact would be of the essence. Even though he was over six feet tall and solidly built, she didn't want to startle him with unexpected information that might cause him to clam up.

"How lovely to meet a fellow countryman." She smiled. "I hope you don't mind me interrupting you so early? I wanted to ask you something."

The man's broad forehead creased into a slight frown.

"What's it about? It will have to be quick, as I'm packing up this morning and heading to Pisa to catch my plane. Sadly, my vacation here ends today."

"What a pity," Olivia sympathized.

Inwardly, she was panicking that he might be preoccupied with getting to the airport and be unwilling to open up to her in such a short time. What could she say that would be persuasive enough?

Her mind raced as she tried to come up with a convincing yet innocent reason for being on his doorstep, and one that would allow her to
spend some time speaking to him.

"I'm writing a book," Olivia said, grateful that the idea had popped
into her head. Back in her advertising career, she'd known a few cre-
atives who were aspiring authors, and they'd done all sorts of crazy
research.

"You are?" The man looked mildly interested.

"It's a romantic novel," Olivia said, deciding to steer away from any
mention of a murder mystery. "My hero is a chef who lives in a villa very
similar to this one, and I was wondering if I could have a look at your
kitchen? It won't take me long but it would be a great help with writing
those scenes. Imagination can only get you so far!"

She smiled at him winningly.

"Of course," he agreed. "Come on in. By the way, my name's Sven
Miller. And you are?"

"Olivia Glass," she said.

So she'd been right about guessing at his heritage. An American
Swede.

She followed him inside, relieved that her hastily thought up excuse
had managed to get her past the front door. She couldn't help rubbernecking at the vaulted ceiling, the silver-painted hall table, and the modern art
on the far wall—a massive painting consisting of a bright pink square on
a white background.

"Wonderful, isn't it?" Sven said, following Olivia's gaze.

"Incredible. It—it's very meaningful," Olivia said.

She was sure it was. Just not to her.

This villa's kitchen had gone for the pastel effect. The myriad of
cupboards, shelves, islands, bar stools, and surfaces were decorated in
sky blue and bright white, with a few accents of pale orange.

"Coffee?" Sven asked.

"Thank you. May I take a few shots of this interior on my phone?"

Olivia paced around the kitchen, photographing the enormous stove
from every angle she could think of, as well as the chef's knives in a
massive block of wood, and the array of gleaming pots and pans in the

cupboards. She took snapshots of the kitchen's wall art, and the white granite counters, and the silver-and-white chandelier. Then she sat on a pale orange bar stool while Sven operated the coffee machine.

"What a pleasure this villa is," he commented. "All the gadgets one could need. I've enjoyed my week's vacation, I must say."

"I've loved my stay in the area, too. It's been more of a creative retreat," Olivia said, embellishing her story. "I'm glad I got to see this kitchen. I tried asking next door the day before yesterday, but there were police everywhere, and they told me there had been a suspicious death."

Sven nodded.

"There were people coming and going throughout the day. When I saw the coroner's van arrive, I guessed something was up, and then the police knocked on my door in the afternoon."

"Did they question you?" she asked.

"I had just started an important conference call with the States. The detective left her business card and I called her back in the evening. I said I hadn't noticed anything untoward, but even so, she said she would like to interview me in person before I left, so I am sure she will be here any minute."

Olivia glanced nervously over her shoulder. She hadn't expected Detective Caputi to be making a return visit to the villa. She needed to finish her questioning as soon as possible.

"If it was murder—" she began, before stopping herself. Sven hadn't said anything about that.

"As a highly experienced and hopefully soon-to-be-published author, the police presence indicates to me that the suspicious death was due to murder," she amended. "In which case, the perpetrator might have done the deed the night before. Perhaps he or she arrived at the villa, pretending to be an innocent visitor."

"That's true." Sven cupped his chin in his hand, thinking. "Now that you mention it, I do recall seeing someone arriving the previous night. I remember assuming that I'd seen my neighbor. But now I'm thinking perhaps it wasn't the neighbor. I should have told the police about it. I wish I had, now."

"About what time was that?" The time might prove the deciding factor.

"Shortly after eight p.m."

That made Olivia hopeful. Everyone had left the winery by seven-thirty p.m. So this late visitor might just have been the suspect.

"Can you describe this person?" Olivia asked, mentally crossing fingers that this would prove to be a breakthrough.

Sven considered for a minute.

"He was an older man. Gray-haired. A commanding looking character. He had a hook nose and bushy eyebrows."

Olivia stared at him, confused. This wasn't the description she'd expected at all.

"What was he wearing?" she asked.

"A top quality black jacket and a lilac dress shirt. I particularly noticed the shirt. It had ruffles on the front. I'm glad you reminded me about this. I'll be sure to tell the detectives about him when they arrive."

Olivia's heart stopped.

Up until now, she'd thought that Sven might have been describing somebody else and that the resemblance she was picking up had been coincidental. But now she knew it was not. There was no way it could be.

Sven was describing Alexander—up to and including the borrowed lilac dress shirt he'd put on after Vernon Carrington had deliberately insulted him by splashing wine down the front of his outfit.

"Goodness. How fascinating. You have a great eye for detail."

She probably looked as if she'd seen a ghost. Olivia wasn't great at hiding her emotions. Her mother always said she wore her heart on her sleeve. Sven must have noticed how startled she appeared.

"I'd better get back to work now, while this ambience is fresh in my mind. Sitting here, I've had a breakthrough regarding my plot. I need to write it down before I forget it," Olivia gabbled.

She wanted to run out of the house, sprint to the winery, and confront Alexander immediately. Every nanosecond counted. It took all her self-control to finish her coffee in one quick gulp and calmly replace the cup on the saucer.

"Good to meet you," Sven said politely.

Olivia hustled out of the enormous kitchen and power walked her way through the enormous hall. Sven closed the front door behind her, and she let out a tense sigh.

Alexander? It didn't seem possible! Surely it couldn't be? He was so polite, so suave. Never mind that, he was a famous, world-renowned expert.

Why would he go to all the trouble of putting poison in somebody's wine?

But, with a chill, Olivia remembered how viciously rude Vernon had been. Alexander was probably accustomed to respect. Approachable as he was, an expert of his standing must have an ego.

Vernon had disrespected him in public and who knew how deep a gesture like that had cut? Olivia knew how egotistical people could be. She'd worked in advertising for more than ten years, and the creative world was full of prima donnas. Some of the nicest seeming people could turn vicious in a heartbeat if they didn't get what they wanted at the right time.

She'd witnessed their atrocious behavior often enough to consider herself unshockable.

Olivia sighed. Why, then, was she battling to put Alexander in the same category?

She needed to speak to him urgently.

Olivia hustled down the driveway. She was out of the gate and charging down the road when the nagging suspicion that something was wrong crystallized into certainty.

Olivia stopped so suddenly she kicked up a stone, clapping her hand over her mouth in horror that during all the excitement, this crucial fact had slipped her mind.

She was short a goat.

Where on earth had Erba gone?

Chapter Twenty Four

Olivia ran back to Villa Ultima, relieved to see that the front door was still closed. That meant Sven would be going about his business, unaware that a rogue goat had invaded his property.

"Erba?" she called.

She felt flustered. The goat had been uncontrollable this morning. She'd been way out of line. During the time that Olivia had spent having coffee and questioning Sven, Erba could have roamed anywhere. Anywhere!

The villa's front garden was neat and tidy; an expanse of verdant grass with the occasional well-trimmed shrub. There didn't seem to be anything that would have attracted Erba. Olivia knew her goat too well. The orange and white animal loved herbs and flowers.

Olivia bit her lip.

Perhaps the goat had retraced her steps down the road. She'd seemed obsessed by the gardens farther back.

She was about to go and investigate when she heard a metallic clang from around the corner.

Olivia rushed around the side of the house.

She squeaked in horror as she saw the scene of devastation that met her eyes.

A metal trash can was hidden out of sight in a neatly paved area behind a wall. Erba had found the can and overturned it!

The can was on its side and the goat—her goat, her adopted animal—was rooting through it as if she'd never had a square meal in her life.

As if Olivia hadn't lovingly fed Erba her breakfast carrots less than an hour ago.

This goat had become a delinquent!

"Erba," Olivia hissed. She couldn't risk shouting. She didn't want Sven to hear. This was downright embarrassing.

The goat looked up and Olivia thought she saw a flash of rebellion in her eyes.

"You know you are not supposed to do that!" Olivia snapped, hoping she could quell this unwanted show of defiance immediately. "You've been horrendously behaved this whole morning. This is not how we do things! You're a better goat than this, Erba, and you know it!"

Now, she thought the goat looked abashed, as if she'd reconsidered her behavior and seen the error of her ways.

Erba abandoned the trash can and sidled back to Olivia.

"Now I've got to pick it up!"

She couldn't leave it overturned. She'd just have to do it quietly.

Luckily, there was a tap on the wall nearby so she could rinse her hands afterward.

Olivia walked over to the steel can. There were only two items inside—or rather, lying on the paving.

One was a box from Forno Collina, one of the two bakeries in the village. From the label, it had contained a takeout breakfast panini. The other was an empty wine bottle.

Olivia stared in surprise at the bottle.

"Valley Red?" she said incredulously. "What's that doing there?"

Was she dreaming this? Nope, she knew that bottle and label all too well. After all, she had helped to design it.

Olivia remembered, with regret, how much back-and-forth it had taken to create the pretty label that was classy, wholesome, tasteful, and appealing—everything the wine inside was not!

This explained Erba's obsession, she realized. The goat seemed to love unpalatable wine. When Olivia's first winemaking experiment had resulted in an explosion of fetid grape juice, Erba had been first on the scene, lapping up the rotting liquid with great enjoyment.

Olivia feared that had been the gateway incident that had led the goat down the road of an unhealthy addiction to inferior wine.

"Erba, you have no palate," Olivia sighed.

She righted the can as quietly as possible.

Then she glanced at the house in puzzled amusement. It was clear that Sven didn't have any palate, either! How could he have brought this dreadful wine the whole way from the States, to what was probably one of the finest winemaking areas in the world?

Holding the bottle carefully, as if just touching it might contaminate her all over again with the memories of that campaign, Olivia placed it in the can and put the lid back.

Then she scrubbed her hands clean under the tap.

"Come, Erba," she whispered sternly.

This time, as if realizing she'd pushed the boundaries too far, the goat scampered obediently up the driveway and followed Olivia, remaining a goat's length behind her with an innocent expression, as if she would never dream of straying.

As Olivia reached the end of the road where the fancy villas were located, she saw a passing car slow down.

Out of the corner of her eye, Olivia recognized the gray Fiat that Detective Caputi drove. Glancing up, she thought she saw the detective's disapproving gaze drilling into her before the car turned in the direction of the villas.

"Damn," Olivia muttered.

The detective was hot on the trail.

When she spoke to the friendly Sven, he would undoubtedly share the fact that Olivia had just been visiting him. That would lead to awkward questions about why Olivia had been there, and why she'd given such a fake and patchy story. Writing a book! She could imagine how Detective Caputi would squint at Sven in her trademark incredulous fashion, when he told her that Olivia had said she was researching a romantic novel.

As she headed briskly to work, Olivia wondered what it would take to outpace the dislikeable detective. Of course, Caputi had gone off on the wrong tangent by suspecting Olivia and Nadia. That was deflecting her from pursuing the right direction.

At any rate, Olivia hoped so.

She wasn't as methodical as the detective, nor did she have her talent for scary questioning. So Olivia guessed she had to use her strengths.

She was an easy person to get along with, most times. And she was very detail-oriented. Olivia thought about that in-depth, as she headed down the quiet lane to the winery. That was why she'd excelled in her previous field. Advertising was partly creative, but it was also focusing on the smaller details, the important nuances.

How did things look, how did they make people feel? Was a campaign's message consistent? Was anything out of place?

Proofreading press releases that had to be perfect to the last period had given her a big advantage in that regard.

So, what details had she gleaned from her questioning so far, and what seemed out of place?

That occupied Olivia's thoughts to such an extent that the rest of her walk passed in a flash.

For once, Olivia didn't feel her heart lift as she headed into La Leggenda. Instead, she felt a cold tension in her stomach. She was dreading her confrontation with Alexander, but the sooner she got it over with, the better.

She headed past the winery and followed the paved drive as it wound between the trees. This was where the Vescovi residences were. Marcello's house was first in the row—a simple, square, double-story cottage.

She guessed that the kitchen and living room were downstairs and the bedrooms upstairs. Wondering if she might, one day, visit that upstairs area made Olivia feel dizzy. It was better not to think about it at all.

At any rate, Alexander wasn't staying there, nor was he staying in Antonio's tiny cottage, sequestered in a gorgeous garden farther down the hill.

He was staying with Nadia, who lived in the original farmhouse. It was a simple, yet elegant family home, covered in climbing creepers whose green leaves contrasted with the golden stone, and surrounded by well-established trees.

Olivia felt breathless as she reached the house, and not just from the brisk walk. She was terrified of having to ask Alexander these difficult questions. He was one of her icons, someone who had helped and taught and encouraged her.

Now she would have to think of him as a possible murder suspect.

Her stomach twisted as she saw him seated on the porch.

He was leafing through a wine magazine. On a tray in front of him stood a coffee plunger, a jug of cream, and a plate of almond and cherry biscotti. The sweet treats were chunky, generously studded with cherries, and clearly homemade.

"Ah, Olivia!" Alexander's face lit up when he saw her. "How nice to have some company. Nadia is busy doing yoga in her home gym. Can I offer you some coffee?"

Olivia couldn't have choked a sip down if someone had paid her good money to do so.

"I just had some, thanks. May I sit down and speak to you for a moment?"

"Of course." Alexander looked at her curiously. "You seem flustered."

There it was again. Her heart on her sleeve! Better just to be honest, especially since Alexander had become a friend.

Olivia perched on the faded but plush green cushion on the wrought-iron chair opposite his.

"I happened to pass by the villa where Vernon Carrington stayed, and I saw one of the neighbors," Olivia said.

She glanced at Alexander nervously. He regarded her with mild curiosity.

"Who was that?" he asked.

"A tall blond man. Sven was his name."

Alexander frowned, clearly puzzled.

"What is the relevance of this?" he asked.

Olivia took a deep breath.

"Sven said he saw you arriving at Vernon's villa after eight p.m. on the night of his death," she blurted out, feeling a rush of butterflies accompany her words.

Alexander drew in a sharp breath.

"I did not see the neighbor," he replied. He shook his head, frowning deeply. "I had no idea anyone had noticed me there."

Alexander seemed disconcerted that he'd been found out. Although his presence at the villa was suspicious, Olivia was relieved that he hadn't tried to lie his way out of his predicament. He had immediately admitted it—to her, at any rate, but perhaps not to the police.

"Why were you there?" she asked.

For a while, the only sound was the clinking of the teaspoon as Alexander stirred cream into his coffee, and the cheeping of an Italian sparrow in a nearby tree.

Alexander sighed.

"My quest was fruitless. The outcome I hoped for was not achieved. That is why I have not told anyone that I visited Vernon after the auction."

"I'm surprised you wanted to speak to him, after what he did to you," Olivia said, hoping her empathy would hold the door open for Alexander to share his true feelings.

"I did not. But although I am a proud person, and he did indeed offend me, I decided I would swallow my pride for the sake of the Vescovis, whom I like and admire immensely."

"Go on?" Olivia encouraged.

"I thought I would plead with him to return the bottle to the winery."

"Really?" Olivia was astounded. In terms of fruitless quests, she guessed Alexander's might win a prize for Most Fruitless of the Year. But then, he didn't know the back story that she did, or why Vernon wanted that wine so badly.

"I planned to ask him if he would donate the bottle back to the winery. I had an idea that they could even display a plaque to him on the wall, thanking him for his contribution."

"Good idea! I'm guessing it was met with a no, though."

Alexander sipped his coffee before nodding.

"Vernon was friendlier than I expected. He apologized for his earlier rudeness. He seemed magnanimous in victory. He invited me in, and said he had just been gifted an excellent vintage of wine. The bottle was open, and he fetched a second glass and invited me to share."

"Really?"

Olivia frowned. Alexander's description didn't match with what she had seen when she'd walked in the following morning. There had been a single unused glass, and an unopened bottle of wine on the counter. What had happened to the open bottle? she wondered.

"I refused the offer, and said I had only come to plead on behalf of the Vescovis. But he laughed at my words. He said nothing and nobody could make him part with his new acquisition, and that in any case, I didn't have the money to make him a counter-offer."

Olivia snorted angrily. "Insulting!"

Alexander shrugged. "I do not think he meant it so. A man like him, all he understands is to judge his fellow humans by what he thinks they are worth. That is his failing, not mine."

Alexander's wisdom impressed Olivia.

Surely someone who was offering this reasoned perspective wouldn't have suddenly decided to commit a murder? Or was she wrong?

She waited, hardly daring to breathe, as he continued.

"I realized that he was not open to my pleas. And I did not care to spend time with him further. So I wished him a pleasant evening and said my goodbyes. As I left, he was pouring the wine and toasting to his victory."

Alexander drained his coffee.

"And that, my dear Olivia, is the explanation of why I was there, and what happened."

"You didn't tell the police?" Olivia asked.

Alexander shrugged.

"You are right. I did not. I felt that the information I had was not useful, and I was reluctant to divulge it, especially since I was not questioned about my activities after the auction. The detective simply asked me if I had interacted with the victim while at the winery. So I answered her questions directly. She did not ask me for further information, and in fact, I found her to be accusatory and aggressive. Under such circumstances, I felt that volunteering information would be unwise." He rubbed his forehead. "Unfortunately, that could land me in a lot of trouble now."

"Not if we can find who the killer really is," Olivia insisted.

She couldn't suppress a flare of satisfaction that her approach was working better. Alexander had just revealed important information to her. It was all about the approach. One had to empathize. Instinctively, she felt that Detective Caputi had low empathy levels. She was not a sympathetic individual. And Olivia was, naturally.

Of course, Detective Caputi had not spent more than ten years of her life sitting in advertising pitches and strategy meetings where one wrong word, or even an eyebrow raised at an inappropriate time, would see the client storming out and taking his business elsewhere. If she had the benefit of Olivia's experience in this regard, she might have more tools to use in her approach than her default mode of blunt aggression.

"Thank you so much for explaining this to me. I'd better go now. I have a phone call to make," Olivia said.

"I will see you at the winery later," Alexander said, but he was still frowning uneasily.

Olivia walked away, feeling encouraged that she was making solid progress and that the loose ends of her investigation were coming together.

However, there was something about Alexander's story that was nagging at her mind. While he was speaking to her, even though she'd welcomed his story with relieved acceptance, there had been a point where she wondered if it was all true.

Olivia sighed.

The moment of suspicion had been nothing more than a brief flash, and now she wasn't sure when she'd felt it, or which of his words had triggered it.

As she headed back to the winery, Olivia reminded herself not to be too trusting. There was still a chance that Alexander had committed this crime, and was pulling the wool over Olivia's eyes with ease.

After all, he was worldly and experienced enough to be able to read people accurately, and his impeccable reputation would make it difficult for anyone to suspect him of a nefarious crime.

She needed to keep an open mind and look out for any other evidence that might come to light.

Now, it was time for her to follow up on her final lead.

She was going to call Patrick, Vernon's friend, who'd bid on the wine barrel at the auction.

After that, Olivia would have to stretch her budding detective skills to the utmost as she pieced the fragments of puzzle pieces together, hoping she would see a pattern emerging which would lead her in the suspect's direction.

CHAPTER TWENTY FIVE

O livia pulled open the winery door and stepped inside. It was starting to weigh heavy on her seeing it closed. Every hour that passed without tourist business was affecting sales, and ultimately this would start to erode the winery's reputation.

Marcello had updated the closure on the winery's website and social media and had put a printed notice on the door saying "Tasting Room Temporarily Shut for Renovations! Please Join Us at Our Renowned Restaurant for Lunch or Dinner, and We Will Be Pleased to Offer You a Free Tasting of Five Fine Wines!"

This loophole still allowed him to offer tasting and sales, and since he'd published it, the restaurant had been fully booked. Gabriella was rushed off her feet, which suited Olivia just fine. The less time Gabriella had to work on her wicked revenge plans, the happier everyone would be.

Paolo was organizing the wine tasting for all the guests taking advantage of this offer. So far, he reported that very few guests had left without ordering a few additional bottles.

Since it was a breezy day, Olivia had thought that after obtaining Patrick's phone number from the copy of the auction list behind the counter, she'd make her call in the quietness of the tasting room. But once inside, she realized how her voice would carry in the unusual, echoing silence of this room. Any conversation she had might be overheard, either by Gabriella in the restaurant, or by Marcello in his office.

The ladies' restroom it was, then.

Olivia tiptoed up the corridor and into the quiet privacy of the sparkling clean and fragrant restroom.

She stood at the far end of the room, with her back to the white table which had a large flower arrangement on it, watching the entrance door in case anyone else—namely Gabriella—walked in.

On her left were the four cubicle doors. On her right were the pristine sinks, with fragrant hand gels and skin creams and mini towels waiting for use. The restroom was quiet and empty.

She dialed the number, hoping Patrick was still in Europe. He'd said he was traveling to London in his private jet. With any luck he would still be there, because it would be the small hours of the morning back in the States.

He answered after three rings. He didn't sound sleepy so she guessed he was still in London, going about his morning.

"Hello, Patrick!" Olivia was aware she sounded breathless. "I'm calling you from La Leggenda. I was the person you spoke to before the auction."

Patrick paused.

"Oh, you were the friendly blonde?"

"That's me." Olivia smiled as she spoke, hoping the friendliness would come across over the phone line.

"Well, I thoroughly enjoyed the evening," Patrick said. "And I'm very pleased with my wine barrel. Do you know, I had to spend nearly three hundred thousand dollars enlarging my cellar, as it's underground? They had to blast into solid rock. We had three teams of engineers involved."

"How incredible," Olivia enthused, remembering what Alexander had said about people who only judged each other in monetary terms. "Such a rare and expensive barrel will be the perfect enhancement to such a valuable space. How lucky you were able to crush the competition and make the winning bid."

Patrick laughed. "It wasn't really competition. Just a bunch of small-time locals."

"Exactly!" Olivia giggled sneeringly. "What a great opportunity to win a valuable antique at a knockdown price!"

"You are so right." Patrick sniggered.

Olivia glanced at the hand gel. She already felt like she needed to wash her mouth out with it. This wasn't like her at all. Saying these words was awful!

"I hear that Vernon died afterward," Patrick said. "Someone told me he died that night, in fact. Is that correct?"

"Yes, unfortunately he passed away. I don't know the details," Olivia said. "Was he stressed at all? Perhaps the auction caused a medical condition to flare up."

"He didn't seem stressed," Patrick said. "He was very busy, that I do know. You see, he was starting afresh with his new venture. Sourcing a whole bunch of different suppliers for his wines—new, cheaper flavorants, additives, that sort of thing. Canceling old contracts, which he said required some legal shenanigans because people squeal when they don't get their money, but it's the way things go. Business is business."

"I can imagine," Olivia said.

Was it wrong of her to feel deeply relieved that this wine would never reach the market? It would have made Valley Wines look like an award-winning health beverage!

"He went through a divorce recently," Patrick said thoughtfully. "I don't think that stressed him, though. His wife left him for somebody of higher net worth, so it was amicably done and not too costly for him."

"Goodness!" Olivia said. "What a relief!"

She felt out of her depth here, not sure what to say. The only thing she was sure of was that she was glad she didn't move in these circles all the time. Just having a brief conversation with Patrick was making her temples throb most unpleasantly.

"I appreciate your time," she concluded. "Enjoy your wonderful wine barrel."

"Thank you for the call," Patrick said.

Olivia disconnected. She scrubbed her hands hard with the gel, which smelled of bergamot and rose, and then washed out her mouth vigorously with water.

Even though the conversation had not provided any obvious clues, Patrick's words stuck in her mind as if they were glued there. She wished she could get some of the bergamot gel into her head, to clean them out.

As Olivia walked to the restroom door, she heard Gabriella's piercing voice outside. The restaurant manager had obviously just arrived, and from the sounds of it, she was heading to Marcello's office. Probably, she was collecting a print run of menus for the day.

Olivia didn't want to bump into her. It would be better to wait in here, out of sight, until Gabriella had taken the print run through to the restaurant and occupied herself with setting up for lunch service.

It was all about the timing, Olivia thought.

At that moment, in a blinding flash of insight, Olivia realized exactly what part of the conversation with Alexander had triggered her suspicions.

The realization felt like a splash of cold water down her back. She drew in a quick breath, feeling shivers cascade down her spine.

It had been one word that he had used. One little word.

The word "just."

What Patrick had said to her had pointed Olivia's suspicions in the right direction, and remembering that one word had allowed her to deduce who the criminal was.

Was there a way to confirm what she now guessed to be true?

There was a way, she realized. She remembered the information that she needed, and she had the Internet at her fingertips.

Opening her phone, she quickly navigated to Google and looked it up.

As Olivia stared down at her phone, it was as if Gabriella's sharp voice faded away.

The information staring back up at her from the small, bright screen was shocking. More than that, it was enlightening.

Reading and rereading the words, Olivia felt the puzzle pieces fall into place, and the gaps between them were suddenly small enough for her to see the pattern.

She knew who had done this, and how—and why—Vernon Carrington had been killed.

Now, all she had to do was find the proof she needed.

Olivia froze as another familiar voice rang through the tasting room.

"Signor Vescovi, I need you to call a meeting urgently."

The voice was Detective Caputi's.

With her ear pressed against the door and her heart accelerating, Olivia listened to the detective's sharply worded orders.

"I returned to the crime scene to interview the neighboring residents," the detective snapped. "The occupants of Villa Splendido, who were finally home, said they had gone to dinner after the auction and had seen nothing. However, the resident in Villa Ultima revealed important new information." Clearly, she was speaking to Marcello, and Olivia could imagine his expression as Caputi continued. "Thanks to his input, you will call Nadia Vescovi, Olivia Glass, and Alexander Schwarz in here immediately. Our strategy regarding this case has changed."

Olivia's eyes widened even more as she heard the main door to the tasting room open, and footsteps click inside.

"*Ciao*, Marcello," Nadia said. Then, in surprised tones, "Good morning, Detective."

"Signorina Vescovi, you will proceed to the car immediately, escorted by one of my officers," Detective Caputi ordered Nadia, without as much as a *good morning*. "We are taking the three of you into custody. You, Glass, and Schwarz. All of you are under suspicion and we will interrogate you at the station until one of you confesses to this crime." She paused. "If nobody does, then all three of you will be arrested on suspicion."

Olivia's eyes were so wide they felt ready to pop out of her head.

Taken into custody? Arrested?

She heard Nadia shriek and then, listening carefully, the distinctive clinking of handcuffs.

Olivia clutched at the door handle, clinging to it for dear life because her legs felt suddenly weak.

"Take her to the car," Caputi snapped, clearly ordering one of her officers. "Lock her in the back. Where are the other two?"

"I—I'll call them immediately," Marcello stammered.

"Quick! We do not have time to waste."

Now Olivia's heart felt as if it were going to jump right out of her mouth. She cowered back from the door. She was about to be arrested! If she walked out of the ladies' restroom, there would be a pair of handcuffs waiting as soon as Caputi saw her.

This was unthinkable! Just as she'd solved the crime!

The stumbling block was that Caputi wouldn't listen to her. The steel-haired detective had a nasty habit of talking right over Olivia's ideas—steamrollering them, in fact. It had been a problem last time they had met, and Olivia was sure it would be an issue again.

She had to obtain the evidence that would prove to Caputi that her suspicions were correct—and she had to do it without being taken into custody first!

Quickly, she snapped her phone onto silent. Loud ringing emanating from the ladies' restroom when Marcello called her would alert Detective Caputi in a flash as to her whereabouts.

However, she didn't intend to stay in the restroom for much longer.

Olivia eyed the window.

It was a small window, set high in the wall, but she thought she'd fit through it—just. And if she clambered onto the counter, she could reach it.

It would be a race against time. She might get into a lot of trouble.

Olivia corrected that thought. She was already in a lot of trouble, and this was her only way out. She knelt on the counter and stretched up to push the window wide.

She could feel her muted phone buzzing in her purse and knew Marcello was calling.

She'd better let him know that she had solved the crime, and would be unable to comply with the detective's invitation at this time, because she was on her way to corner the suspect.

Olivia took out her phone and quickly swiped the answer button.

"Hello, Marcello," she said softly.

There was a surprised silence.

"Olivia? Olivia, who were you expecting to call? Did you say Marcello? Do you have a new boyfriend?"

Olivia gritted her teeth as she heard her mother's voice.

There had never been a more inopportune time for Mrs. Glass to call. Why, oh why, had she not checked the caller ID before answering?

"Uh, Mom, no. Marcello is my boss at the winery. Also, I'm a little busy right now," she began, but as she'd expected, her mother forged ahead.

Crouched on the counter, Olivia could only listen, as she tried to push the window wider.

"You sent me the diagrams of the furnishings you have planned for your new home. I must say, I'm impressed. You have certainly inherited a little of my flair for interior design. However, my angel, I have one important comment to make."

"What is it?" Olivia asked.

"As you know, Laurel Islington, who has been a friend of mine for more than twenty years now, specializes in feng shui. I'm not sure if you know what that is, but it's a Japanese art of laying out your living area to create the best possible energy."

"I think it's Chinese," Olivia muttered.

"What was that? I didn't catch what you said."

"Nothing," Olivia whispered.

She got her head and shoulders through the window, feeling the breeze tug her hair. It seemed like an awfully long way down.

"Anyway, she had a look at your plans. She said you should position the hallway table on the left instead of the right. But you should hang pictures on both sides of the walls, to channel the energy into the house," her mother continued.

"Channel it in," Olivia agreed. She threaded an arm through the window, tensing as she heard Detective Caputi's imperious voice from the tasting room, barking out orders.

"And you must ensure good lighting! She was very concerned about the lighting. A dark hallway is a terrible place for energy. It can affect the happiness of your entire home!"

"I will," Olivia breathed.

"She can do you a full home consultation at the special friends-and-family rate of seventy-five dollars. Think about it! You don't want any bad energy right now!"

"No, I don't! I'll make sure the hall is well lit."

"Promise me, Olivia! No bad energy! Will you install a chandelier? We will pay for it if needed."

"I will install one. I promise! I don't want any bad energy now. If you want to pay, that would be a wonderful gift. I have to go now, Mom. Thanks for the call."

Olivia disconnected the phone and put it back in her purse.

Could you bargain in advance with karma? she wondered. If her plan succeeded, she decided she would install the biggest hallway chandelier she could afford, as a thank-you to the energetic forces.

"Good energy, please," Olivia begged any deity who might be listening.

Threading her other arm through the window, Olivia squeezed through and wriggled out, feeling uncomfortably like toothpaste coming out of a tube. The gap was narrow, and the drop to the ground below seemed dizzyingly far. There didn't seem to be an opportunity for her to turn herself around or grab onto anything. This was just a case of wriggling forward until tipping point was reached and gravity had its way with her.

"Aaargh," Olivia whimpered, as she reached the point of no return and felt herself somersault down.

She landed with a thud on her backside, in the flower bed below. It was a soft landing, as the bed had recently been dug and mulched.

That was both a good and a bad thing, Olivia realized, scrambling to her feet and wrinkling her nose as she brushed herself off. Small lavender bushes had been planted at intervals, and there was now an Olivia-sized dent in the neat row.

Well, the first part of her plan had been successful. She was out of the winery itself.

Olivia stared at the paved pathway which joined the road leading up to the Vescovis' residence. Now it was time for the second part of her plan, which was to reach her suspect and prove he was the guilty one.

"Alexander," she said firmly. "I'm coming for you!"

Then she set off at a run in the direction of Nadia's house.

Chapter Twenty Six

Olivia sprinted up the paved road that led to Nadia's house. She was puffing for air as she ascended the steep hill, but she knew she was racing against time and didn't dare slow down. Not when Detective Caputi would be prowling impatiently around the tasting room, already checking her watch and wondering why Marcello's efforts had not yet resulted in the appearance of her two remaining suspects.

"Alexander," Olivia gasped again.

The expert was the only one who could help her now, and she hoped she could reach him in time.

There he was! He was heading down the hill toward her, at a brisk walk, with a light, white jacket slung over his shoulder.

"Ah, Olivia. Marcello just called, sounding stressed, and said he needed me in the tasting room urgently. Are the police there? Should I bring anything? I have my phone with me."

He slowed and glanced back at the house, as if worrying he was not well enough prepared.

Olivia wished she had more air available to explain. A brisk uphill run was the enemy of coherence, she decided.

"You...mustn't...go to the...winery now," she gasped out. "You...and I...will be arrested!"

Alexander's bushy eyebrows shot up.

"Indeed?" he asked, frowning in concern.

"I've worked out...who killed Vernon Carrington...thanks to what you told me!" Olivia told him. "But I need to prove it. The detective...wants to arrest both of us. She's already...locked Nadia into her van. So we have to hurry."

Olivia was relieved that Alexander picked up on the urgency of the situation.

"I am guessing we must escape the winery?" he asked.

"Yes! Do you have a car available?"

"I do. Come with me."

Grasping her hand, Alexander strode back the way he had come, leading Olivia around the house to the garage at the back.

There, a sleek, black Mercedes coupe was parked next to Nadia's Fiat Spider.

Alexander ran through a doorway at the back of the garage and returned a moment later with the keys. The doors snapped open, and Olivia scrambled into the passenger seat.

"I'll show you where the service road is," she said. "We can't risk leaving by the main entrance. The police will be watching out for us."

Reaching into the cubbyhole, Alexander removed a pair of gold-framed Silhouette Atelier sunglasses and put them on.

He glanced in his rearview mirror as the car's reverse sensors started beeping.

"There appears to be an object blocking our way," he said. Then he added, in surprise, "It's a goat!"

Looking behind her, Olivia felt herself go crimson with embarrassment.

"It's my adopted goat, Erba," she said. "She follows me everywhere."

She climbed out of the Mercedes and hurried around to the back, waving her arms.

"Erba! Go back to the dairy!"

With a mischievous glance, Erba ducked past her and jumped into the passenger seat.

"Out, Erba! I'm so sorry, Alexander. She's usually very well trained."

Olivia was horrified by the goat's wayward actions. Why was she behaving this way? Was this the start of Erba's adolescent rebellion?

Erba stared at her impassively and then climbed nimbly behind the seat, wedging herself into the plush, leather-lined space.

Olivia felt like tearing her hair out in mortification, but luckily Alexander had the situation under control.

"Jump in," he told Olivia. "The goat can come with us."

Relieved, Olivia scrambled inside again.

"Direct me to the service road," he commanded, tires screaming as he reversed out of the garage.

Quickly, Olivia fastened her seatbelt.

"Turn left here," she directed Alexander. "Now you'll see a road to the right. Take it, and then veer right again just after the goat dairy. That's the service road. It joins up with the main road a half mile farther on."

Once through the service gateway, Olivia was flattened against her seat by the brute force of acceleration as the Mercedes's wheels bit into the tar road.

She felt breathless with amazement and relief. They had escaped the winery and, for now, were ahead of Detective Caputi. They might have avoided her clutches, but she hoped they would still be in time for what she needed to do next.

There was a chance her suspect might already have made his getaway.

Two minutes later, the Mercedes screeched to a halt outside Villa Ultima.

"This is it!" Olivia said, her heart still racing from the breakneck journey. It seemed that Austrians were even more ferocious on the road than Italians. Who would have guessed?

They climbed out. After cranking the window down a few inches, Olivia closed her door. In the shade of the spreading oak tree, Erba would be comfortable in the car and couldn't get up to any more mischief.

She leaned on the doorbell, feeling uneasy as the seconds passed by.

Then she tried the door.

It was locked.

"Damn, damn, damn," Olivia said under her breath.

Of course the door was locked. You didn't leave an expensive villa wide open when you left. What if someone walked in and stole all the armless Greek statues, or the Swarovski-encrusted vases, or the huge, meaningless framed squares on the walls?

"We need to get in here? Shall I look for a way?" Alexander asked.

"Yes, and yes. Perhaps he left a window open," Olivia said.

Sven, her prime suspect, must already have left for the airport. Now, they needed to search the house to see if the evidence Olivia expected to find was there.

"There's a kitchen door at the back," Olivia told Alexander. "Maybe it's open."

Alexander headed off to the left, and Olivia ran around the house in the other direction.

Clearly, Sven's thorough and detail-oriented Swedish heritage had meant he'd shut the villa thoroughly before leaving. Or perhaps it wasn't his Swedish heritage, but rather that he didn't want any amateur investigators snooping around the house before it was cleaned and ready for the next occupants. At any rate, she couldn't see as much as an open window.

She and Alexander met at the back of the house, exchanged hopeless shrugs, and then each continued on their route until they met again at the front door.

"There seems to be no way in," Alexander observed calmly, patting his wavy hair back into place. "We could break a window?"

He gazed around the garden confidently, as if looking to identify a suitable rock for the purpose.

Olivia's eyes widened. Alexander was a lot more gung-ho than she was. She'd be terrified to break a window. That was a criminal act! She could imagine how Detective Caputi's eyes would light up as she realized Olivia had done something which would result in actual, concrete charges being pressed.

"We'd better not," she said. "Or at any rate, only as a last resort. There has to be another way in, or something we're not thinking of."

"Where would the keys to the villa have been dropped off?" Alexander asked. "Is there an office in the village, perhaps?"

That was a good question, and Olivia gave it serious thought.

Wealthy people's time was precious. They didn't want to waste it driving into town to find a rental office, denting their massive SUVs and sports cars while negotiating the narrow roads and struggling to find parking in the shoebox-sized gaps.

Such inconvenience would most definitely result in negative Trip Advisor reviews.

What would she do if she was a rental agent? Olivia wondered.

The answer came to her in a flash.

She would tell them to leave the keys safely on the premises, in a prearranged hiding place.

"They're here somewhere! They must be!" she decided.

Stepping back, Olivia lifted the edge of the doormat. It was rubberized and brand new, with a bright gold border.

The key was not under there and she felt a thud of disappointment. She'd had high hopes for that location.

Alexander walked over to the statue near the front door. It was of a stone eagle, its wings outstretched and its beak open.

Its beak?

Alexander reached inside the eagle's gaping maw and took out a set of keys on a Swarovski-studded key ring. The sun flashed off the crystals, almost burning a hole in Olivia's retinas.

The front door unlocked smoothly, and Olivia walked into the empty hallway, with Alexander close behind. The small leather valise was no longer there. Sven had indeed left for the airport.

"We must search the house," she explained. "That wine bottle Vernon offered to share with you when you went to plead with him—do you remember what it looked like? Would you know it if you saw it again?"

Alexander nodded gravely. "Of course," he said. "I can recall the exact name and vintage of the bottle he offered for me to share. I am not personally familiar with the year of that particular wine, but I have tasted the same varietal in other years and it is superb. The wine farm, in northern Italy, is a small but excellent one. I have visited it twice."

Olivia felt encouraged by Alexander's expert knowledge.

"We must search the villa as fast as we can," she said. "Oh, and we mustn't forget to check the outside trash can. Erba knocked it over last time I was here, looking for wine. We could see if he threw that bottle away in there."

As Olivia headed to the kitchen, surely the most logical place and therefore her first port of call, she knew they were running out of time, and fast. She had seen how much patience Detective Caputi had. Her patience could be measured in individual grains. Not even in quarter-teaspoons.

To her dismay, the kitchen was devoid of empty bottles. There was nothing in the trash can under the continent-sized kitchen island, and after checking every one of the approximately three hundred spacious cupboards, Olivia drew a blank there, too.

"The outside garbage can contains only one bottle of Valley Wine, and an empty bakery box," Alexander announced, meeting up with Olivia as she searched the dining room.

"Damn. That's what Erba discovered earlier, but not what we need. We have to keep looking."

"I will check the bedrooms," Alexander said.

"I'll look in the lounges," Olivia decided.

She raced through the spacious rooms, looking on every solid oak shelf, and in every gilt-covered ottoman and ivory-handled cupboard. Nothing. A total absence of the evidence she needed.

She returned to the hallway as Alexander hurried down the stairs.

"I could not find anything," he said.

At that moment, the answer came to Olivia.

She understood why the bottle was nowhere to be found in the villa, and she knew what her next step would need to be.

"I have a plan, Alexander," she said. "We need to go—"

Her words were interrupted by the ringing of her phone.

This time, it *was* Marcello.

She had a vision of him standing in his office, with Detective Caputi breathing down his neck. Should she answer or not? Answering might give away her whereabouts if Detective Caputi was able to trace the call, but then again, Marcello might have important information for her.

Putting a finger over her lips to warn Alexander to be quiet, Olivia answered the call, but didn't speak.

"Hello?" she heard Marcello say. "Hello, Olivia, are you there? If you can hear me, please can you come to the winery urgently? Detective Caputi wants to question you."

He put a lot of meaning into the words. Olivia got the sense he was trying hard to tell her that there was trouble ahead.

The detective was definitely with him. Perhaps the phone was even on speaker.

Olivia thought fast.

She could use this to her advantage. After all, there was only one way to get the police where she needed them to be, and that was to make sure they were chasing her.

"Marcello," she said loudly. "I'm very scared. I'm innocent and I know it, but I don't think Detective Caputi will ever believe it!"

There was a horrified silence on the other end of the line. Olivia could imagine Marcello, feeling as if his world were crumbling around him as she confessed her trusting words, while Detective Caputi's eyes narrowed in malevolent glee.

"So I have decided I'm going to get on a plane and go somewhere else for a few days," Olivia continued, making sure to speak as clearly as she could.

"I'm heading to Pisa International Airport as fast as I can! Marcello, if only you could come with me! I wish there were a way you could manage to meet me at Pisa Airport. We could elope together!"

Olivia clapped her hand over her mouth in horror. In the stress of the moment, the wrong word had slipped out. How Freudian! She felt her face flood crimson with embarrassment.

"I meant abscond. We could abscond together by airplane from Pisa. Not elope. Sorry, my bad."

She paused. There was no need for overkill. By now, Detective Caputi would have gotten the gist of where she planned to go.

"Alexander is giving me a ride to the airport, in his black Mercedes sports car, the one that has the custom number plate with the word 'Wine' in it," Olivia said. "We've been discussing this at a secret location close to La Leggenda. I guess we'll head to the airport right now. So I'd better go. Remember, if you can get away, I'll see you there!"

She disconnected.

Breathing hard, she stared down at the phone triumphantly. Having successfully thought on her feet, she had laid the foundation for the plans she needed.

Olivia realized she felt exactly the same way she used to after having done a successful pitch to an advertising agency client. She'd created a scenario that the client—in this case, Detective Caputi—had bought into.

Alexander was staring at her, frowning in confusion. Clearly, he'd bought into her story too.

"So, we are going to the airport? Where are you flying to?"

"No, no, I'm not flying anywhere!"

Olivia realized that she was all out of time to brief Alexander on the finer details of her cunning plan. Even now, Caputi and her team would be leaping into their cars. Okay, so the basic Fiat models they drove definitely didn't have the brutal acceleration of the Mercedes, but even so, for all she knew, Caputi could be an expert on cornering. That could make up a lot of time, especially since Olivia wasn't great at it. She always drove slowly around bends.

"We need to go!" Olivia said.

Then, as they collided in the front doorway, she suddenly rethought her plans.

Both of them didn't need to go. Alexander, in fact, should stay here, just in case.

"Wait! Can I drive your car?" she asked.

"Of course!" Alexander handed her the keys with a flourish.

"Please could you search this villa high and low for anything else that might be helpful. Anything. I think after the police arrived at his villa, Sven left in a hurry, and that means he may have forgotten other incriminating evidence. Will you call me if you find something? And will you look after the goat?"

"I will do," Alexander reassured her. "Leave Erba with me. I'll take care of her."

Olivia sprinted out of the villa and opened the Mercedes's door.

"Out!" she commanded.

Erba jumped out of the car and headed for the closest flower bed. Olivia guessed being locked inside had been boring for her.

She scrambled in and spent a precious few seconds adjusting the seat so she could easily reach the accelerator.

She was going to have to drive like Gerhard Berger, because she would have the entire Tuscan detective force hot on her tail.

Chapter Twenty Seven

"Wow!" Olivia gasped. This Mercedes had serious acceleration. Coupled with the sensitivity of its power steering, she narrowly missed annihilating one of Villa Diamante's marble gateposts on her way out.

She hoped she would be able to negotiate the steep learning curve of driving what was clearly a supercar. She couldn't risk a collision, or even the smallest fender bender, when there was so much at stake.

Gripping the steering wheel and easing off on the gas pedal, Olivia roared onto the main road.

"Wheee!" she squeaked, trying to pretend she was enjoying this experience and that her palms weren't damp with fright. She'd always thought of herself as more of a conservative driver. Now, she knew she was.

Still, if there was ever a time to channel her inner Grand Prix champion, it was now.

Buzzing the window down, Olivia waved her fist out of it, leaning on the horn as she approached a slower-moving car.

Quickly, it buried itself in the hedge, allowing her to zoom past.

It was all about attitude, Olivia realized. She just had to bristle with the right attitude, and everything should go according to plan.

She headed onto the highway and bit her lip as the car leaped forward, the speedometer needle curving all the way to the right. Olivia didn't dare look at how fast she was going. This really wasn't her! She was such a law-abiding person at heart that it was almost embarrassing. She'd have to offer to pay any speeding fines that the Mercedes incurred. It wouldn't be fair if Alexander ended up with them.

Even though she was flying down the highway, Olivia was still worried that she could hear the blare of sirens behind her. She was certain the police were in hot pursuit. They might already have alerted a team at the airport, to be waiting for her.

Olivia would just have to hope that at such short notice, there had been no additional officers available to set a trap.

Clutching the wheel more tightly than ever, Olivia swerved to overtake another car. Was that a Ferrari? As she mashed her foot onto the accelerator, she risked a glance at the sleek, low-slung red vehicle. Yes, it was, and the driver, wearing trendy shades and designer stubble, was gawping at her in amazement, clearly unable to believe that a blond madwoman in a German car was outpacing him.

She was overtaking Ferraris? Well, if that were the case, she didn't need to worry about the police catching up. Hopefully, her crazy drive had bought her the time she needed.

She breathed a sigh of relief as she drove into the airport parking lot and screeched to a halt in the first available bay.

Quickly, she jumped out, impressed by the expensive *thunk* as she closed the car door. So different from the tinny bang of her rented Fiat.

Now she really did hear sirens. The police were arriving at last, and before they caught her, she had to find Sven.

Grabbing her phone, Olivia ran into the airport.

She'd only been here once before, and that had been when she'd first landed in Italy. She remembered how she'd felt. She'd been sleep-deprived and excited and overwhelmed. She'd been looking forward to a two-week holiday, with no clue that a new and exciting future lay ahead.

The last time she'd walked out of this pretty airport building, draped in greenery, she'd expected that the next time she returned would be to take her flight back home.

She'd never imagined that her second visit to this modern and eco-friendly terminal would be to lead the Italian police force to a murder suspect.

What a surreal situation she'd landed herself in!

Olivia had absolutely no memory of the airport's layout. She'd been far too excited about being in Italy.

She stopped inside the entrance, looking from left to right, frantically getting her bearings, because if she headed the wrong way, it would mean disaster.

She forced herself to look calmly at the airport's layout and signage, even though her brain was imploring her to run, just run!

There were the international check-in counters. And that way, the domestic check-ins. They were in different directions, which meant Olivia had an important decision to make. Where would Sven be heading? A domestic flight, or international?

International was more likely, Olivia decided. He would be planning to get out of the country as soon as he could, and not linger around after his "vacation," which she now believed had been two nights at the most, and not the week he'd so convincingly told her. Most probably, he was flying straight back to the States.

Olivia raced toward the international check-in counters.

Where was he? Surely she couldn't be wrong—or could she?

She couldn't see any tall blond men at the check-in.

Olivia hurried down the line, feeling tense inside at the thought she'd made a huge mistake and led the police all the way here for nothing.

Nothing except, of course, to arrest her. She didn't want to think about how many felonies might be listed on the charge sheet if she weren't able to prove her case.

She had to be right—she had to! She knew she had solved this crime.

There he was!

Olivia hadn't noticed him the first time because he'd been bending down, taking something out of the small valise before he checked it in.

Already, the bag was getting weighed. That would be a quick process because it was so small. Sven wouldn't be paying any excess baggage charges, but Olivia had to get to him before that bag left the scale and went onto the conveyor belt.

There was a line of eight or nine other tourists, snaking around the cordoned-off barriers. In the front was an officious-looking airline worker, who was controlling the flow of passengers and sending them to the next available counter.

A shout echoed through the airport.

Olivia spun around.

There were the police. Two uniformed officers, led by Detective Caputi in plainclothes, looking classy and severe in a beautifully cut navy blue jacket. They had arrived, and they had seen her.

Olivia ducked under the barrier tape. She was heading for Sven, but had reckoned without the attendant at the front of the line.

"*Non autorizzato!*" the hefty woman exclaimed, grasping Olivia's arm in a swift, practiced gesture. Clearly, she was used to having desperate tourists try to jump the line, and assumed Olivia was one of them.

She pointed sternly to the back of the line.

At that moment, with a clatter of footsteps, the police arrived.

Detective Caputi spoke rapidly to the attendant, who let go of Olivia's arm. That wasn't much comfort, seeing one of the uniformed officers immediately grabbed it instead.

The detective glared at Olivia.

"You are under arrest. We are taking you into custody on suspicion of murder, and for attempting to flee the country."

Despite the high-speed car chase, and the swift pursuit through the airport, Detective Caputi's shiny, steel-gray bob was immaculate, with not a hair out of place. Olivia distrusted people like that. In fact, she didn't feel that the policewoman was human at all. Olivia knew she showed all the signs of how her morning had gone. Her clothes were rumpled, her lipstick and mascara were undoubtedly smudged, and as she turned to glance at the counter again, a large flake of mulch dropped from her hair onto the officer's sleeve.

He let go of her arm to brush it away and Olivia seized her chance.

"It's not me you need to arrest," she told Caputi. "It's him!"

Leaping away, she dodged past the airline official and ran up to Sven.

Thank goodness, he hadn't yet checked in his bag. He was still busy discussing a free seat upgrade with the man behind the counter.

"I'd really appreciate it if there's a place in business class," Olivia heard him say in earnest tones as she rushed up. "I'm a doctor, and have been working nonstop after volunteering at an accident scene."

"You're a murderer!" Olivia said, placing her hands on her hips as she faced him. "And you're not a doctor. I looked up the logo on your baseball cap. You are the CEO of a supplement and additive company and most of your products have been banned!"

Sven stared at her, and she saw a flash of raw horror in his eyes, before he concealed it with a polite, puzzled smile.

"You're the girl I met at the villa this morning," he said. "You told me you were writing a romantic novel. It looks to me as if you might be in a whole different kind of trouble, seeing as how you are being pursued by police officers. Were you telling me the truth?"

Humph, Olivia thought. She hadn't expected him to point the finger right back at her.

"Open your bag," she demanded.

She leaned over and dragged it off the scale—just in time, because the conveyor belt was already whirring. The valise thumped down on the floor and Olivia felt a surge of relief. She'd managed to secure the evidence.

"Sven Miller, you poisoned Vernon Carrington. And, in that bag, you have stashed the empty wine bottle you used to do it," Olivia said.

She pointed triumphantly down at the small leather valise.

Then she looked at Sven, and at Detective Caputi.

Both were staring at her with the same expression of incredulity.

Olivia turned to the detective, giving her an appealing smile.

"I know I've given you the run-around today," she said. "But it was for a very good reason. You see, now you're here, with the suspect. He's still on Italian soil, so it will be easy for you to arrest him, and the evidence is in his bag."

"You are saying there is an empty wine bottle in his suitcase? Why would he be carrying that with him, and what is its significance?" Detective Caputi asked in a slow and surprisingly calm voice, as if she thought Olivia was suffering from heatstroke.

"Well, you see, he put the poison in the wine," Olivia explained. She was beginning to worry that the detective's focus was elsewhere. Why was she not picking up on the gist of the conversation?

"The bottle was nowhere to be found in his villa. So he must have packed it," she explained.

"Search his bag," the detective snapped. Now she sounded as if her patience had reached a breaking point.

Sven stepped back politely as the third officer stepped forward.

The uniformed man carefully unzipped the bag and opened it.

Inside was a small leather toiletry bag which looked as if it had been part of a set with the valise, as well as two shirts, a pair of socks, the base-ball cap she remembered him wearing, and a pair of green boxer shorts.

"What bottle are you talking about?" Caputi hissed.

Olivia peered down at the suitcase, frowning in concern.

There was a FlavaWorld logo on the boxer shorts. That fact momen-tarily distracted her. Right there, right then, was the proof Caputi needed. Only psychopaths wore their company logo on their underpants!

That was the good news. The bad news, however, was there was no other proof in sight. No wine bottle at all was present in the compact valise.

Apart from the clothing and toiletries, the suitcase was empty.

CHAPTER TWENTY EIGHT

"Signor Miller, I apologize most sincerely for the inconvenience and delay," Caputi said to Sven.

Olivia bristled. It was the first time she'd heard the detective sound even remotely polite, and she was turning on the charm for a criminal? Why wasn't she investigating this further, after Olivia had practically served Sven up on a plate for her?

"No problem," Sven said courteously.

He flashed a smug, secretive glance at Olivia before zipping up his bag and putting it back on the scale.

The conveyor belt whirred, and it was gone.

"Wait!" Olivia shouted, because the third policeman had turned to her now, with handcuffs in his hand.

He was going to arrest her. In public! In front of a grinning Sven, a shocked-looking airline official, and a growing crowd of at least a dozen fascinated tourists. This situation had spiraled totally out of control, and it couldn't be more frustrating. She was standing in front of the guilty party, but couldn't prove it.

She was going to watch him walk free, board a plane, and return to his life, having gotten away with murder.

"Handcuff her!" Caputi ordered, as Sven turned away to resume his check-in.

"Wait, wait," Olivia continued, with urgency in her tone. She'd felt her phone buzzing in her pocket. "I have to take this call. Don't you get one phone call, if you're arrested?"

Caputi frowned, looking confused by Olivia's question, and she took the opportunity to grab the phone. Perhaps, somehow, this call would prove to be her salvation.

She put it onto speakerphone, hoping that it would distract the police. The caller was Alexander.

"Olivia, come back to the villa! We have uncovered crucial evidence!"

"You have, Alexander?" Suddenly, the airport felt lighter and brighter. She'd believed she had reached rock-bottom. Now, Alexander was providing a lifeline.

"What evidence?" she asked.

"Your goat found the wine bottle we were looking for, buried in a flower bed."

"You found the bottle?" Olivia's voice was squeaky with excitement. This was the critical item they needed. How fortunate that Erba had jumped into the Mercedes. Olivia was reminded all over again of her goat's uncanny intelligence.

"It was buried under a shallow layer of soil in a flower bed, but she pushed the soil aside with her hoof," Alexander continued. "There was also a small plastic container buried there. I did not let Erba touch anything. We are standing guard over them until the police arrive. I found something else important there as well."

"Oh, my word!" Olivia exclaimed. "Thank you! The police will be on their way now, won't they, Detective Caputi? We just have to arrest the suspect before he gets his boarding pass!"

Olivia's voice rose to a shout as she saw the counter attendant hand Sven his pass.

He turned to look at her again, and this time she saw doubt in his eyes.

"Arrest him, now!" Olivia pleaded. "We've found the wine bottle you used, Sven, buried in a flower bed at Villa Ultima. And the plastic container which I'm sure is also yours. The police can test that bottle, and the container. Glass holds fingerprints beautifully. I bet you didn't wipe down the bottle, not if you buried it. I can guarantee you, Sven, that anyone who has their company logo printed on their underwear thinks they're too important to be found out by a simple thing like fingerprints!"

Olivia was glad she'd been able to make mention of the boxer shorts. It was unacceptable, in her opinion.

To her delight, she saw her words had struck home. Sven looked stunned. In fact, he was panicking. As Caputi's gaze snapped between the two of them—probably trying to work out if there was a way she could arrest them both, Olivia thought—Sven broke and ran.

He ducked away from the counter, vaulted clumsily over the barrier tape, and charged headlong through the airport, heading for the exit.

Caputi made her decision.

"Chase him down!" she shouted, barking commands into her walkie-talkie.

The officers sprinted away in pursuit, hurdling the barrier with significantly more ease than Sven had done. Olivia guessed they would catch him before he reached the exit.

Even if he did, there was nowhere for him to go.

Olivia felt deeply relieved that thanks to Alexander's quick thinking and Erba's incredible talent for sniffing out bad wine, Sven's bag, and his branded underwear, would be heading home without him.

But as she glanced at the detective, she saw to her consternation that Caputi was not yet convinced.

"We will all return to the villa for further questioning," she declared, taking Olivia's arm in an iron grip. "After all, Signor Schwarz could have planted the bottle in the flower bed himself."

Olivia marched alongside the detective, filled with trepidation all over again. How was she going to manage to pin the crime on Sven, when he'd already shown himself to be an accomplished liar?

Half an hour later, they were gathered in Villa Ultima's enormous kitchen.

This time, they weren't using the pale yellow stools, but were seated around the sky blue table in the corner. Olivia perched uneasily on her ice-blue steel chair, glancing up in anxiety as she heard footsteps approach.

Nadia had arrived.

She no longer had handcuffs on, and was stomping two paces in front of the detective who'd been put in charge of her.

Olivia thought the detective appeared browbeaten and demoralized. After having to deal with Nadia's fiery temper for nearly two hours, she wasn't surprised. You didn't want to get on the wrong side of Nadia, ever. Handcuffing her, or trying to, had been his first big mistake. Clearly, he was regretting many of his life choices, starting with arriving at work that morning.

Behind them, Marcello followed, looking anxious.

Seated on Olivia's right-hand side, Alexander was betraying his nerves by fidgeting with the blue strap of his Montre Exacte wristwatch.

Even Erba, peering in through the kitchen window, looked concerned.

The only one of the party who was completely calm was Sven. He was lounging in his chair, tipping it back, glancing from face to face as he took in the others' anxiety.

Olivia knew she'd have to be on top of her game to outwit him. The problem was that she didn't feel that way. Rather, she felt panicked. If Alexander, or Nadia, or herself ended up being accused of this crime and going to prison, it would be her fault and her failure.

"I apologize for my speedy retreat from the airport," Sven said, giving Detective Caputi a deprecating smile. "I realized I had forgotten my house keys in the hired car. Or rather, I thought I had. It was only as I sprinted back to the drop-off area that I remembered they were in my jacket pocket."

Detective Caputi seemed to have developed some immunity to Sven's charm, Olivia was glad to see. She glowered in response, and then turned to Olivia.

"Explain yourself," she snapped. "Why did you publicly accuse this man of the murder?"

Olivia swallowed, glancing down at the tape recorder in front of the detective. She couldn't afford to say the wrong thing when every word would go onto the police records.

"I first started to suspect Sven when I saw the size of his luggage," Olivia said.

"What?" Sven burst out laughing. "My what?"

Olivia glared at him, feeling defensive.

"You said you'd been on a week's vacation, but that was an overnight case—there was no way you could fit a week's worth of clothing inside."

"And that means I committed a murder?" Sven rolled his eyes, spreading his hands wide. "Please, Detective, if I hurry I can get the next plane. I've missed out on a free business-class upgrade on this flight already. If you must know, I have to go straight from the airport into a long meeting, so I sent the bulk of my luggage home yesterday with one of the courier firms that provide door-to-door customized transport."

Olivia was convinced this was another lie, but yet, it sounded plausible. His confidence was rattling her and she worried it was making her look foolish.

"While I was speaking to Sven, Erba rooted through his garbage can and knocked it over. I noticed an empty bottle of Valley Wine there, and thought it was very odd. The presence of that bottle was suspicious, and it also provided a link to Vernon, and made me wonder if there was a connection between the two," Olivia said.

She was reassured to see Marcello nodding supportively as she spoke.

He believed her. Now all she had to do was convince the detective.

"I apologize. My taste in wine is pedestrian, to say the least," Sven said.

Olivia thought that he looked less confident than he had. Sven wasn't happy she'd found that empty bottle in the flower bed, which was being guarded by a police officer until the forensic team arrived.

Detective Caputi sighed. "Can we move on to the point of your conversation, Signorina Glass? We have a busy morning."

"I soon realized that Sven was a liar," Olivia said. "He told me that he didn't know who his neighbor was, which was untrue. Of course he did. That's why he hired the villa at short notice—so he could get close to Vernon. It was Alexander's words that finally crystallized my suspicions about Sven. You see, when Alexander arrived at Vernon's villa to try and plead with him to return the wine bottle, Vernon offered him a glass of an excellent wine that he had 'just' received."

Now it was Olivia's turn to spread her hands wide.

"Just received it? He had gone straight home from the auction, and had just received a fine bottle of wine? How was that possible? It had to have come from somewhere. And since Sven told me he had noticed Alexander as he arrived, that made me think Sven could have been the one delivering it."

"I could not have been!" Sven countered.

Olivia sensed he was losing his temper and decided to push it. She needed to force him out of his cool complacency.

"Oh, yes, you could have been!" she shot back.

"Could not!"

"Could too!"

"No way!" Sven retorted angrily.

Detective Caputi slammed her hands down on the table, causing the recorder to jolt sideways.

"Continue!" she thundered.

Hurriedly, Olivia resumed.

"If Sven had been guilty of delivering poisoned wine to Vernon, which he was perfectly positioned to do, there must have been a motive. So I did some research to find out who Sven really was."

"And who was I?" Sven jeered. Olivia thought he was going to say something else, but Detective Caputi glanced in his direction and he shut his mouth hurriedly.

Silence fell around the room as everyone waited for her to speak again.

"I found out that Sven is the CEO of a supplements and additives company called FlavaWorld. I remembered the logo on his baseball cap, from when I questioned him. I looked them up, and discovered they provided all the flavorants which were used in Valley Wines, including a few formulations that had actually been banned for health reasons. But clearly, Sven still sold them to Vernon, and Vernon still used them."

Olivia touched her fingers to her temple. Even now, thinking of sipping the odd-tasting Valley Red made her head start to throb in sympathy.

"Valley Wines was FlavaWorld's biggest customer. From a quick search online, I found that, after the deal was done, the company doubled in size and acquired new premises. Sven's social media told me that he became a member of the 'International Yachting Vacations' Group and the 'Luxury Homes Around the World' Group earlier in the year. Then, of course, the FDA raid happened and Valley Wines closed down."

More nods from around the table. Everyone except Sven seemed to be following her story easily, and without any confusion.

Sven's face was brick red. He hadn't met Olivia's gaze since she'd mentioned the luxury homes. He was frowning deeply, tapping his fingers on the table. Olivia wondered if that meant he was thinking fast, wondering how he could explain away her accusations.

"Worse still for Sven, when Vernon started again, he planned on moving his operation out of the States, and sourcing cheaper suppliers for his additives. That's what his friend Patrick told me when I called him. He said that Vernon had canceled all his existing supplier contracts, because business was business."

She paused, summoning up her courage before continuing, because she sensed that Sven was seething with anger.

"That was a death-blow to Sven's company, and to his aspirations to become mega-wealthy. So he followed Vernon out here. I'm sure he planned all along to murder him, but knowing Sven, he probably made a final pitch for a new contract first."

"That would seem in character," Alexander agreed.

Sven let out a sharp, angry snort.

"Vernon, no doubt, turned it down in his usual rude and uncaring style, just the same way he turned down Alexander's plea to return the wine to La Leggenda," Olivia continued. "But Sven anticipated this and had a plan ready. When Vernon refused, he gifted him the poisoned wine as a token of goodwill. Vernon had such an ego that he wouldn't have suspected anything. He would have considered it his due."

Olivia wondered again how people could run their lives that way—as Alexander had pointed out, judging each transaction solely by the dollars and cents it produced.

"Being the owner of a supplements and additives company, Sven would know exactly what the effects of ethylene glycol were, and would have been able to obtain it easily. Perhaps he even brought a more concentrated version with him in that plastic container that he buried next to the wine bottle."

Sven was shaking his head vigorously.

"No, no, no," he muttered under his breath. "What a fake story, you little liar."

"Where did the bottle of Valley Wine come in?" Alexander asked.

That was where Olivia's detective work had reached a blind alley, because she had no idea. There must have been a reason for Sven having brought that bottle along. She theorized that he might have taken it over to Vernon's villa to prove his loyalty, but that didn't sound very convincing.

Olivia opened her mouth to say, "I don't know."

Before she could announce this uncomfortable truth, Sven lost his temper.

He leaped to his feet, the steel chair clattering onto the tiles.

"I decanted that pig swill wine into the good bottle and gave it to that rat-faced Carrington, because I wanted his last drink to be the wine that put me out of business!"

He stared around the table and Olivia saw his triumph dissolve into horror as he realized what his words had revealed.

Chapter Twenty Nine

Half an hour later, Olivia arrived back at La Leggenda. She climbed out of the Mercedes's passenger seat feeling weak-kneed with relief.

Sven had confessed and been taken into custody. She, Nadia, and Alexander had been cleared of the crime.

Marcello parked alongside her, and Nadia held the SUV 's back door open for Erba to leap out. The goat looked satisfied, as if she'd enjoyed the excitement of the day.

Marcello walked up to the winery's tall oak doors and flung them wide open.

"We are back in business," he announced. "As of this afternoon, we may trade to the public again, and since we have been cleared, our wine-making may continue."

Alexander applauded.

"Bravo, bravo," he shouted, putting his arm around Nadia and giving her a friendly hug. "I believe we should enjoy a glass of wine together, before you get to work."

"Olivia, this was all due to you," Marcello said, and she saw he was looking at her without the usual guarded professionalism. His blue eyes blazed with emotion. "Thank you for your help and courage in solving this!"

His arms wrapped around her, holding her tight, and Olivia felt his lips tickle her ear.

She couldn't help herself. Olivia hugged him back, giving that full-body hug she'd been wanting to do ... well, ever since she'd first met him.

She pressed herself against him and heard him whisper, "Olivia, it feels so good to hold you this way," and felt a shiver that tingled through every cell of her body.

This entire ordeal had been worthwhile, just for the incredible moment that she and Marcello were sharing. Their unspoken romance had taken another invisible step toward becoming reality.

What a thrill!

It seemed like long minutes before they finally let go of each other, and Marcello smoothed back one of her stray blond locks before he stepped away.

Or perhaps, Olivia thought worriedly, he was removing more of the mulch from her hair.

Even so, she felt as if she was floating on a happy cloud, right up until she glanced in the direction of the restaurant and saw Gabriella there.

Then her stomach crash-landed.

Gabriella's stare skewered her, spearing all the way through her body and into the stone-clad wall some distance behind her.

Clearly, the restaurateur was furious about what was happening.

Olivia had no doubt that she would seize the right moment to take her revenge, and that the moment would be coming soon.

She felt apprehensive all over again as she headed into the tasting room.

Marcello uncorked a bottle and poured it out.

"*Salute*," he said.

They clinked glasses and Olivia sipped the red blend. It was incredible. Robust, earthy, fruity. To her, this vintage embodied Tuscany, and reminded her how grateful she was to have made this dramatic life change.

"Alexander, you mentioned on the phone that you had found something else important in the flower bed," she said. "The police took you outside after Sven's confession. Now that you've been questioned, and shown them what was there, I was wondering if you could tell us what that item was?"

Her throat felt dry from all the talking she'd done at the villa. After the day's stresses, the magnificent Sangiovese Special Blend was certainly hitting the right spot.

Alexander nodded.

"The final piece of the puzzle, and the final nail in Sven's coffin, if you will. While Erba was digging, she also uncovered the auctioned bottle of wine, half-buried in the back of the same flower bed. It was empty."

Olivia gasped, seeing her own shock reflected in the others' eyes.

Alexander continued calmly. "As soon as Sven confessed, I took Detective Caputi to the flower bed and showed her this additional proof." He glanced at Olivia with a knowing expression in his eyes. "I did not mention it beforehand. I thought it wise to keep this card up my sleeve while you were speaking, in case the police believed Sven's lies."

"What do you think happened to the bottle?" Nadia asked in a small voice. "How did it end up there?"

After a pause, Olivia replied.

"Sven would have returned to Vernon's villa later to wash the glass and remove the contaminated bottle, covering his tracks so that there was no evidence left behind. Perhaps he noticed the prized auction wine then and took it with him. He wasn't at the event, so he would have had no idea how Vernon had obtained it. I think he drank it afterward, as a celebration for having gotten away with murder, and without any idea of the value it held."

"*Mio Dio!*" Marcello exclaimed in dismay. Nadia looked crestfallen.

Alexander, however, gave them an encouraging smile.

"The wine is finished, yes. But the bottle itself remains, and the cork, too, was there, so you have not lost this piece of history. In fact, with the wine gone, there is no need for the magnificent bottle to be kept under lock and key in the vault. Instead, it could be proudly displayed in the tasting room, as an example of the vineyard's heritage. The bottle itself can then be admired and enjoyed by all."

He cleared his throat. "I, for one, believe that wine should always be consumed. I will tell you a guilty secret. No bottle stays in my collection for longer than five years. When it reaches that time, I drink it. After all, a gap in the wine cellar is the best reason in the world to buy new stock to fill it."

Olivia stared at Alexander in admiration. Words to live by, she thought.

"I am sure the detectives will need to fingerprint the auction bottle," Alexander said. "It may form part of the evidence for trial. However, after that, your winery should be able to have it back."

Marcello raised his glass again.

"We will get the original bottle back. Never mind the wine. More than ever now, the item itself has become part of our story. Olivia, you have saved us. I cannot thank you enough for what you have done. Thanks to your investigation, we can open our doors again and can benefit fully from the late summer tourist sales."

Nadia nodded. "If it were not for you, we would be sunk! I will soon catch up with my winemaking and will be back on track if I work a few twelve-hour days," she said, rolling her eyes.

Alexander smiled. "What an unexpected pleasure to have been part of such an unforgettable episode in La Leggenda's history," he said. "Olivia, I, too, am at your service. You have cleared my name. It was a frightening experience to be wanted by the police. Up until now, my only brushes with the law have been in the form of speeding fines."

"Thank you, Olivia," Marcello said again.

He stared at her, and for a moment it was as if they were the only two people in the room. That look was back on his face again. Olivia felt the room grow fuzzy around her. The only thing—or things—that seemed in sharp, clear focus were Marcello's deep blue eyes.

And then the moment was shattered by Gabriella's furious, piercing voice.

"Perhaps you wouldn't all be such fans of Olivia if you knew who she really is, and what she has done!"

The restaurateur had arrived at their table. She stood, glaring triumphantly down at Olivia.

Her heart plummeted. The moment she'd dreaded had finally arrived. For Gabriella, this was payback time.

Olivia wondered if there was any chance that the tasting room's sparkling clean, granite-tiled floor might open and swallow her up. It was her only hope for avoiding the disastrous consequences that she knew would follow Gabriella's bombshell.

The floor remained stubbornly solid. Even it was not on her side at this crucial moment.

"What do you mean?" Marcello asked Gabriella, sounding confused and doubtful. "What are you saying Olivia has done?"

"Olivia used to work for Valley Wines," Gabriella spat the words out. "She did all the advertising and marketing for that brand in her previous career in the United States. She is the reason those wines achieved such prominence and made so many other good wineries go broke. She is the reason so many people ended up drinking that—that cleaning fluid! I bet she did not tell you that?" Gabriella paused.

Marcello gave a tiny shake of his head. Olivia couldn't read his expression.

"See? It was her dirty little secret until I overheard Vernon Carrington on the night of the auction, asking if she had been fired after the wine-making facility was raided and they found the rats!"

Olivia couldn't look at Gabriella as she triumphantly uttered the words. She stared down at the table, taking in the fine, polished grain of the wood. Strong, solid wood. It had been there before she arrived at the winery, and it would be there after Marcello dismissed her. The table would endure. Olivia's job? Not so much.

"Now you know. You know who she is. And you know what she has done, the things she never chose to tell you. She is not fit to be even a guest at the winery, never mind to work for our prestigious establishment!"

Gabriella took a deep breath, clearly intending to drive a few more nails into the coffin of Olivia's sommelier career at La Leggenda, but at that moment, there was a shout from the restaurant, even as a sweet, charred smell wafted out.

"Gabriella, come quick! The *schiacchiata alla fiorentina* is burning!"

With a muffled curse, Gabriella turned on her stiletto heel and ran back into the restaurant.

Olivia fixed her gaze on the table, waiting in despair for the hammer blow to fall.

CHAPTER THIRTY

It seemed like hours before the tense silence was broken, and then it was Nadia who spoke.

"I don't understand," she said, sounding confused.

"What do you not understand, Nadia?" Marcello asked.

Olivia glanced at him appealingly, hoping for a final reprieve.

"I thought we only made the *schiacchiata alla fiorentina* cake during carnival, in February," Nadia explained.

Marcello shook his head. "We started presenting small slices to the restaurant guests as a sweet treat, with their coffee. The variety made with orange zest. They loved it so much that it has become a permanent fixture."

Nadia nodded. "Well, I guess Gabriella will have to remake it. Serves her right for being so moody. Marcello, you should have a talk with her. It is not acceptable to shout at co-workers in public the way she just did."

Marcello rolled his eyes. "I know, I know. Do you think I have not tried to reason with her in the past? I will try again, as soon as the new *schiacchiata* is in the oven."

Olivia couldn't stand the suspense any longer. This entire conversation felt surreal. They were talking about cake. Cake! What about firing her? When would that happen? Or was she meant to just get up and leave?

Nadia glanced sympathetically at her.

"I am sorry you have had to listen to her being so nasty, Olivia," she sympathized.

Olivia's hands were shaking and she buried them in her lap so nobody would see.

"But what she said …?" she began in a small voice.

Marcello frowned. "About Valley Wines?" He looked perplexed, as if this insight into the subtleties of womankind was too complex for him to fathom. "Why would she think that was a problem? I do not understand."

He tilted his glass, as if the remaining sip of ruby-red wine might provide some insight.

"Blaming you for that was bizarre," Nadia consoled her. "As if you can be criticized for doing your job well. I think it is rather funny, actually. You were not dealt a good hand of playing cards there! Imagine having to promote such terrible wine, as a wine lover! That is making me want to laugh. Not shout. Like I said, Marcello, you need to speak to Gabriella about how she behaves toward others."

"I will," he promised. "For the time being, Olivia, will you walk outside with me? There is something that I want to ask you in private."

Olivia got up. She felt wrung out, as if she'd lived through ten lifetimes while sitting there in the comfortable wooden chair, expecting the hammer to fall.

All her fears had been for nothing, and her job was safe. In fact, the Vescovis seemed mildly amused by the secret that Gabriella had revealed.

It was as if the massive bomb explosion she'd anticipated had fizzled out, without so much as a tiny spark.

The thought of a private conversation with Marcello soon restored the spring to her step. As she followed him outside into the bright, warm sunshine, it occurred to her that everything might, just possibly, turn out for the best.

They walked into the shade of the big olive tree and Marcello cleared his throat. To Olivia's surprise, he now seemed nervous.

"I must make it clear, this is just a question. Just a question," he emphasized. "You must please not agree to it, or even consider it, unless you are sure."

"What is it?" Now Olivia was just about jumping up and down with curiosity. What could Marcello be going to say?

Marcello picked a leaf off the tree and twirled its deep green oval form between his fingers.

"I have been looking for someone who could handle our marketing," he confessed at last. "La Leggenda is sorely in need of it. It has not been given enough attention. And, with the acquisition of Franco's winery, we are in desperate need of somebody who can put together a proper campaign for these wines, to promote them properly, so that they appeal to the consumer and get the sales they deserve."

Olivia stared at him with the beginnings of hope in her heart. Was this conversation really going the way she thought it was?

"I knew you were in marketing, but I had no idea you had handled such big, relevant campaigns. You would be the perfect person to lead us in this venture, if you want. Obviously, not if you hated it and never want to do it again. We would increase your salary accordingly. And you could continue working at the tasting room as our head sommelier for part of the time also, as I know your passion is there."

Olivia finally found the breath to speak.

"I accept," she said breathlessly. "I adore marketing! To be honest, although I never thought I would, I've missed doing it, and I'd love to use my experience in helping to promote your amazing wines. And if I was able to do it in addition to my tasting room work—well, that's the perfect career for me. Right there! Custom made! I couldn't ask for anything more satisfying."

Her mind was already buzzing with ideas on where to position these wines, and how the taglines of the La Leggenda premium wines would need to differ from the affordable, easy-drinking ones.

All her experience and enthusiasm was bubbling up, ready to spill over into a brand new direction.

What a beautiful day it was, she thought, suddenly feeling as if Marcello had picked her up and placed her on top of the world, on a fluffy cloud of happiness.

Their day trip to Pisa seemed so long ago. Olivia recalled how she'd felt on that day—as if life couldn't possibly get any better—and she'd immediately feared that it never would.

Now, standing under the magnificent olive tree and looking forward to an exciting future, she was sure it could.

Olivia stepped into the hallway of her farmhouse.

It looked so different from the first day she'd pushed open the door. Now, it was light and bright, with the windows cleaned, the floors polished, and an elegant, medium-sized chandelier installed, which her mother had chosen from a catalog and paid for.

She breathed in the rich, delicious aroma of the Italian beef stew that was simmering in the slow cooker, with the flavors of garlic and wine permeating the house. After a full day in the pot, she knew that this stew would have reached a state of tender perfection.

Olivia headed into the kitchen and gave the stew a final stir. She opened a bottle of the special Miracolo red and took out three glasses in preparation for when her guests would arrive.

At that moment, she heard a knock on the front door and rushed to answer it.

It was Danilo.

He was holding a large box of chocolates in his hand, and he had a brown leather jacket slung over his shoulder. Although the days were hot, the evenings were cooling down, and Olivia hoped that tonight would be an opportunity to light the fire in her living room for the very first time.

His hair—she hesitated, the welcoming smile and friendly greeting freezing on her lips.

The top of his hair was bright blue.

"Good evening," Danilo said, kissing her on her cheeks. "Congratulations on your new home. And I hear the winery is open again. Does that mean your investigation was successful? I cannot wait to know the full story!"

Olivia was only half-listening to him. She was fascinated by his hair.

"I'll tell you everything. It's quite a saga. The goat helped, and there was a lot of luck involved. But I need to know something, too." She pointed. "What happened?"

I apologize for my hair." Danilo shook his head, looking frustrated. "It is all the fault of the daughter of my sister—how do you say the English word?"

"Niece?" Olivia asked.

Danilo nodded. "The niece of my sister. It is all her fault! She is studying to be a hairdresser. As my sister lives down the road from me, I am the closest victim. So, every week or two, she does something different. This time, I had to bargain with all my power to stop her from coloring it pink. It is very difficult for me," he sighed. "Left to myself, I would have the same hairstyle all the time. I wouldn't change it for twenty years. It is what I prefer!"

Olivia laughed.

"I've been wondering about that. Well, it's one mystery solved. Thank you for the chocolates. Come through to the kitchen and let's pour some wine. I bought a gift bottle for you as a thank-you."

As Olivia headed through to the kitchen, she spotted something shadow-like on the gleaming floor.

Looking closer, she screeched in alarm and jumped back.

She thought she'd gotten rid of all the spiders. She really did! But here was one last, massive, long-legged outlier, crouched in the shade of the skirting board.

With a terrified squawk, Olivia amended that. It wasn't crouched in the shade. It was scuttling out of the shadows, in their direction.

She sprinted into the kitchen.

"Spider!" she shrieked, and pointed with a shaking finger in its direction. "Danilo, can you help? Take it out! Make it go away!"

To Olivia's astonishment, Danilo didn't even attempt to save her from the spider. Instead, in one giant leap, he joined her in the safety of the kitchen. He wrapped his arm around her protectively before slamming the door with a yelp of horror.

CHAPTER THIRTY ONE

"I have a confession, Olivia," Danilo stammered. "I, too, am terrified of spiders. That last small one you wanted me to remove—it took all my courage. I had nightmares for days! I could not wear that shirt again afterward, and gave it to my nephew. But this spider is too big. It is beyond my powers to help."

Olivia's mind reeled at this shocking revelation. She felt as if the entire foundations of her reality had been undermined.

Arrogant, muscular, laughing Danilo, reduced to a quivering wreck in the presence of arachnids?

"What if it comes under the door?" Olivia asked, wrenching her attention back to the crisis at hand.

Danilo glanced toward the courtyard.

"We may have to retreat farther, into your beautiful herb garden, and there will be no shame in doing so. We cannot kill it. It is a beautiful being of nature, who deserves to survive. But so do we. So we must hide away."

"We could put dish towels under the gap in the door and wait till Charlotte gets here. She's not afraid of spiders, and will be able to take it safely outside," Olivia suggested.

"I think that is a brave plan. How many do you have?"

A minute later, three carefully folded dish towels filled every micron of space in the small gap under the door.

"Have some wine," Olivia said, letting out a deep breath of relief. "It's the Miracolo. I splashed out and bought a bottle for us tonight, and another bottle for you as a thank-you."

Olivia was pleased to see how delighted Danilo looked.

She poured the wine, and they drank, savoring the magnificent red blend, with its complexity of flavors and amazing smoothness.

"What is that?" Danilo asked, looking at the other bottle set out on the counter.

"Oh, that's an old bottle I found while clearing out the barn. The label's not really legible. I was thinking of keeping the bottle as a memento, because it must be part of the history of this place, with its strange, worn label, which I could get cleaned up. Then again, this afternoon I started to wonder if the wine inside was still drinkable. It might be fun to try it. What do you think?"

Danilo had picked up the bottle and was examining it, fascinated.

"Olivia, this is a rare find. Please, do not open it. Keep it somewhere safe and let us try to find an expert who could give you more information on it. A lot of the area's winemaking history has been lost. This could be an important part of it."

"Really?" Olivia felt thrilled that her dusty old bottle might end up playing a role in the area's heritage. She was delighted all over again by the luckiness of the find, and the fact the glass hadn't broken under her spade.

"It might even be a bottle from this farm itself," Danilo added casually.

Olivia stared at him in amazement.

"This was a wine farm?" she asked.

Danilo nodded.

"Liora, who owns the hardware store, told me last week that her grandfather knew it well. It was one of the most famous and successful in the area, but nobody knows why it went out of business, or what happened to make the owners move away. It is a mystery."

Olivia felt astounded by his words.

She felt shivers tingle all the way down her spine at the thought that the property had now come full circle, and might, if she were lucky, produce wine again.

"I won't drink the bottle, but I'm fascinated to know more about it, especially if it might be from this farm. Can you find out who might be able to help?"

Danilo nodded.

"I will do some research as soon as possible."

At that moment, the front door latch rattled and they heard the sound of footsteps outside.

"Charlotte!" they screamed in unison. "Spider!"

It was almost dark by the time they headed outside into the breezy evening, Olivia leading the way as they walked down to the old barn.

"That stew was magnifico. A masterpiece," Danilo said.

Charlotte nodded. "It was delicious. Stew, ciabatta bread, chocolates, and great wine. The Italians know how to enjoy life, that's for sure. I'm so glad I was here for your first-ever dinner party, in your first-ever farmhouse!"

"I couldn't have asked for better company," Olivia said, smiling at the others.

"So you found the bottle in this barn?" Danilo asked.

"Yes." Heading toward the gap where the door should be, Olivia trod carefully along the curved pathway that seemed to have been naturally created as a result of all her trips between the house and the barn.

They peered inside the murky building and Charlotte shone her phone's flashlight onto the pile of rubble which, Olivia was concerned to see, looked as if it had grown again.

"It is a beautiful space," Danilo said admiringly. "I can see now that this was custom-built as a winemaking room. That makes your job easier. You will soon renovate it." He peered closer at the mountain of trash. "Once it has been cleaned out," he added, sounding more doubtful.

"It's going to be a big job," Olivia agreed. "I'll have to tackle it carefully, bit by bit, to avoid breaking or losing anything else important."

While she was wondering what artifacts might be hidden in the barn, Olivia's thoughts went back to the locked storeroom, high on the hill. She'd all but forgotten about that mysterious place, with everything else that had been occupying her time. Perhaps, during winter, she would have a chance to hunt again for the key, or even hire a locksmith to try and open it.

"Thank you for a wonderful evening." Danilo kissed her cheek. "Are you sure I cannot give you a ride back to the villa, ladies?"

"It's a ten-minute walk, and all downhill. We need it after the food." Charlotte smiled.

They watched Danilo head to his truck. The taillights gleamed as he drove away.

Charlotte sighed.

"This time tomorrow, I'll be on an airplane heading home. I feel sad, Olivia. I wish I could stay longer. I can't believe this is the last night we'll spend in our rented villa, and from tomorrow night, you'll be living here. I envy you your new life. It's something everyone dreams of, but so few people actually do."

Olivia shook her head.

"Every time I walk through the farm gate, I pinch myself and wonder when I'll wake up and find myself back in Chicago. I still think it's a mad decision, and I might be going back home in a year's time, but at least I've tried."

"You won't be home in a year," Charlotte insisted. "Next summer, I promise, I'll join you here again."

"There's a space for you whenever you want it. My farm is your farm."

Olivia felt tears prickle her eyes. It was terrible to think of life without Charlotte. She didn't know how she'd manage in Italy without her. How she wished Charlotte could stay here forever.

She remembered, though, that her best friend always kept her promises. If she said she'd visit again, she'd pack her bags and arrive on Olivia's doorstep on the first day of summer.

As they left the barn, Charlotte grabbed her arm.

"Look! Olivia, look over there!"

In the darkening twilight, Olivia stared in the direction she was pointing. She forgot her sadness as she caught her breath in amazement.

Her grapevines were beginning to sprout. The first signs of green were emerging from the ground—tiny shoots were making their appearance in the beds she'd so carefully laid out.

Her farm was budding into life. There was hope for her future here.

Now Available for Pre-Order!

AGED FOR MAYHEM
(A Tuscan Vineyard Cozy Mystery—Book 3)

"Very entertaining. I highly recommend this book to the permanent library of any reader that appreciates a very well written mystery, with some twists and an intelligent plot. You will not be disappointed. Excellent way to spend a cold weekend!"

—Books and Movie Reviews, Roberto Mattos
(regarding *Murder in the Manor*)

AGED FOR MAYHEM (A TUSCAN VINEYARD COZY MYSTERY) is book #3 in a charming new cozy mystery series by #1 bestselling author Fiona Grace, author of Murder in the Manor (Book #1), a #1 Bestseller with over 100 five-star reviews—and a free download!

Olivia Glass, 34, turns her back on her life as a high-powered executive in Chicago and relocates to Tuscany, determined to start a new, simpler life—and to grow her own vineyard.

Olivia is thrilled to take her first trip to Florence, and that her love life is heating up. She is even more ecstatic that her small vineyard produces its first bottle of wine. Yet when a famous wine critic trashes her wine—and then ends up dead himself—Olivia finds herself in the crosshairs of a murder that she is pinned for—and that she must urgently solve herself.

Is the Tuscan life really for Olivia? Or was it all just a fantasy?

Hilarious, packed with travel, food, wine, twists and turns, romance and her newfound animal friend—and centering around a baffling small-town murder that Olivia must solve—AGED FOR MAYHEM is an un-putdownable cozy that will keep you laughing late into the night

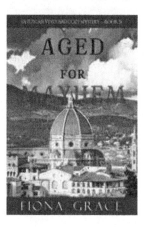

AGED FOR MAYHEM
(A Tuscan Vineyard Cozy Mystery—Book 3)

ALSO NOW AVAILABLE FOR PRE-ORDER!
A NEW SERIES!

BEACHFRONT BAKERY: A KILLER CUPCAKE
(A Beachfront Bakery Cozy Mystery—Book 1)

"Very entertaining. I highly recommend this book to the permanent library of any reader that appreciates a very well written mystery, with some twists and an intelligent plot. You will not be disappointed. Excellent way to spend a cold weekend!"

—Books and Movie Reviews, Roberto Mattos
(regarding Murder in the Manor)

BEACHFRONT BAKERY: A KILLER CUPCAKE is the debut novel in a charming and hilarious new cozy mystery series by #1 bestselling author Fiona Grace, whose bestselling Murder in the Manor (A Lacey Doyle Cozy Mystery) has nearly 200 five star reviews.

Allison Sweet, 34, a sous chef in Los Angeles, has had it up to here with demeaning customers, her demanding boss, and her failed love life. After a shocking incident, she realizes the time has come to start life fresh and follow her lifelong dream of moving to a small town and opening a bakery of her own.

When Allison spots a charming, vacant storefront on the boardwalk near Venice, she wonders if she could really start life anew. Feeling like it's a sign, and a time to take a chance in life, she goes for it.

Yet Allison did not anticipate the wild ride ahead of her: the boardwalk, filled with fun and outrageous characters, is pulsing with life, from the Italian pizzeria owners on either side of her who vie for her affection, to the fortune tellers and scheming rival bakery owner nearby. Allison yearns to just focus on her delicious new pastry recipes and keep her struggling bakery afloat—but when a murder occurs right near her shop, everything changes.

Implicated, her entire future at stake, Allison has no choice but to investigate to clear her name. As an orphaned dog wanders into her life, a devoted new sidekick with a knack for solving mysteries, she starts her search.

Will they find the killer? And can her struggling bakery survive?

A hilarious cozy mystery series, packed with twists, turns, romance, travel, food and unexpected adventure, the BEACHFRONT BAKERY series will keep you laughing and turning pages late into the night as you fall in love with an endearing new character who will capture your heart.

Book #2 in the series—A MURDEROUS MACARON—is also available!

BEACHFRONT BAKERY: A KILLER CUPCAKE
(A Beachfront Bakery Cozy Mystery—Book 1)

ALSO NOW AVAILABLE FOR PRE-ORDER! A NEW SERIES!

SKEPTIC IN SALEM: AN EPISODE OF MURDER
(A Dubious Witch Cozy Mystery—Book 1)

"Very entertaining. Highly recommended for the permanent library of any reader who appreciates a well-written mystery with twists and an intelligent plot. You will not be disappointed. Excellent way to spend a cold weekend!"

—Books and Movie Reviews (regarding Murder in the Manor)

SKEPTIC IN SALEM: AN EPISODE OF MURDER is the debut novel in a charming new cozy mystery series by bestselling author Fiona Grace, author of Murder in the Manor, a #1 Bestseller with over 100 five-star reviews (and a free download)!

When Mia Bold, 30, learns that the pharmaceutical company she works for only cares about money, she quits on the spot, walking away from a high-powered career. Worse, her long-time boyfriend, instead of proposing as she expected, decides to break up with her.

Mia's true passion lies in her own podcast, devoted to debunking the occult and shining light on the truth. The daughter of a con-man father, Mia feels a moral responsibility to the truth, and to spare others from being conned.

When Mia, at a crossroads, receives an invitation from a famous supernatural podcast inviting her to move to Salem and join their podcast as the skeptic-in-residence, Mia sees a chance to start her life over again and to pursue her life's mission.

But things in Salem do not go as planned. When an unexpected death happens—in the midst of Mia trying to debunk a haunted inn—she realizes she may be in over her head. With her own future now at stake, can she really prove that witches and ghosts do not exist?

A mesmerizing page-turner, packed with intrigue, mystery, romance, pets, food—and most of all, the supernatural—SKEPTIC IN SALEM is a cozy with a twist, one you will cherish as it has you fall in love with its main character and as it keeps you glued (and laughing) throughout the night.

Book #2 in the series—AN EPISODE OF CRIME—is also available!

"The book had heart and the entire story worked together seamlessly that didn't sacrifice either intrigue or personality. I loved the characters – so many great characters! I can't wait to read whatever Fiona Grace writes next!"

—Amazon reviewer (regarding Murder in the Manor)

"Wow, this book takes off & never stops! I couldn't put it down! Highly recommended for those who love a great mystery with twists, turns, romance, and a long lost family member! I am reading the next book right now!"

—Amazon reviewer (regarding Murder in the Manor)

"This book is rather fast paced. It has the right blend of characters, place, and emotions. It was hard to put down and I hope to read the next book in the series."

SKEPTIC IN SALEM: AN EPISODE OF MURDER
(A Dubious Witch Cozy Mystery—Book 1)